THE
SHAMAN
SINGS

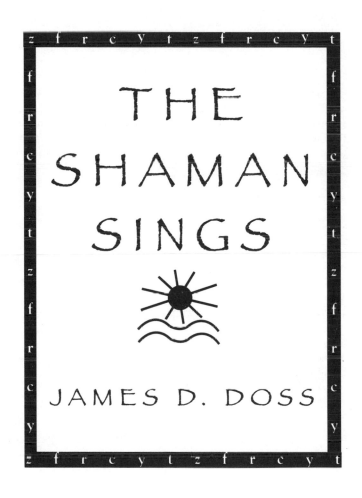

THE
SHAMAN
SINGS

JAMES D. DOSS

ST. MARTIN'S PRESS
NEW YORK

Design by Basha Zapatka

Library of Congress Cataloging-in-Publication Data

Doss, James D.
    The shaman sings / James D. Doss.
        p.   cm.
    "A Thomas Dunne book."
    ISBN 0-312-10547-9 : $20.95
    1. Indians of North America—Colorado—Fiction.   2. Women journalists—Colorado—Fiction. 3. Physicists—Colorado—Fiction. 4. Police—Colorado—Fiction.   5. Ute Indians—Fiction.   I. Title.
    PS3554.075S48   1994
    813'.54—dc20   93-43524
                                                                CIP

10 9 8 7 6 5 4 3 2

For
Annabelle Eagle
and
Bob Newell

"But, of all sources of power, the greatest was the /pituku = pɨ/ . . ."
—Anne M. Smith,
Ethnography of the Northern Utes

THE
SHAMAN
SINGS

1

Yesterday, the Ute woman had only *felt* the creature's approach, the same way she divined the threat of a thunderstorm long before it danced across the mesas on spider legs of lightning. Today, she could smell the musky odors of his lean body. As she watched the sun fall toward its nightly repose in the bosom of the blue mists, the shaman could distinctly hear the beast's panting breaths, the soft padding of his paws.

Darkness was the preferred companion of the beast, and darkness already wrapped its arms around the pleated skirt of Three Sisters Mesa. The unrelenting creature moved ever closer. *Yogovuch* trotted up the dusty arroyo at the base of the sprawling mesa, then through the fragrant thickets of sage and into the forest of gnarled piñon. The woman hadn't actually seen the dwarf's messenger, but his presence was palpable. The limber beast, with scarlet tongue draped over black lips, was approaching her trailer house in brazen fashion, and she was offended by this display of arrogance. Daisy Perika steeled herself and pulled the worn cotton blanket around her stooped shoulders. She stood on the unpainted porch and gripped the pine railing. Daisy waited expectantly for Coyote, servant of *pitukupf*, to speak to her of his elfin master's business. When it came, the eerie sound startled the woman.

"Yiiiooouuuwww . . . aaaooouuu . . . iiieeeooo" the beast

yodeled to the shaman. The somber summons fell on ears that refused to listen.

Daisy clapped her hands together, the sound pierced the twilight like muffled pistol shots. "Leave me in peace, *Yogovuch*," she shouted to the intruder, who covered himself with shadows. "I am full of years and my bones hurt. Know this"—she boldly shook her finger in his direction to emphasize her determination—"I will no longer hear the drum or travel to Lowerworld." It was, she thought, high time for the dwarf to find a younger woman to take over this arduous work. She went inside and threw the bolt on the flimsy door.

She waited somewhat uneasily for Coyote's reply. All she could hear was the rhythmic chirping of the fat black crickets. "That is good," she muttered, "the mangy servant of *pitukupf* has turned tail. Tonight I will sleep without dreams. . . . My spirit will stay in my body." Even as she was consoled by this naïve hope, a puffing gust of wind shook her frail home, rattling the kitchen windows. She shuddered; was this Coyote's answer? "I hope," she whispered, "ticks big as plums suck out all your blood!"

Determined to push the encounter from her mind, Daisy eased her frame into a cane-bottom chair and squinted at the snowy picture on her television screen. Millions of black and white dots attempted to coalesce into figures of human beings and helicopters with pods of rockets. She could not get a good picture when the rain fell between the distant city and her home at the mouth of Cañon del Espiritu. "Aunt Daisy," her nephew had cajoled, "you're too far away from your family; you ought to move into one of those new tribal houses at Ignacio. They got cable TV, running water, everything. You live like a hermit out there, and," he added ominously, "you could have a stroke and die and we wouldn't know until they smelled your body all the way down at the Piedra."

"When I die," she had responded with a poker face, "you're gonna know right away. I make you a promise." The young man had been at a loss for words as he imagined Aunt Daisy's spirit visiting his bedside on some still night. He considered asking her to keep her ghost away from his home, but thought it prudent to drop the subject.

Daisy was considering whether to start supper when her ears picked up the distinctive sound of chugging engine and creaking frame as a vehicle left the gravel road and heaved its weight over the rutted surface of her dirt lane. The identity of the pickup truck became unmistakable when the driver shifted to low gear. The old Dodge had a bad muffler and the shepherd had never learned to use a clutch properly. Daisy got to her feet and pushed the aluminum door open. She shaded her eyes from the setting sun as she watched Nahum Yaciiti climb down from the pickup, his bowed legs challenged by the operation. He was leaning heavily on his shepherd's staff as he shuffled toward the porch.

"You're too little for that big Dodge, Nahum," she teased. "You should buy one of them little Jap trucks." She knew Nahum could afford a new truck; the old sheepherder had a reputation for being uncommonly thrifty. There were delicious rumors, whispered in Ignacio bars, that Nahum buried rolls of greenbacks in wax-sealed canning jars under his grape arbor. Holes made by hopeful treasure hunters sometimes appeared under the arbor when Nahum was away from his home for more than a few days.

When he did not reply, she was tenacious in pressing her point. "You're going to fall out of that big truck someday and break your hip, and then who'll look after you?" Nahum's wife, who had been two decades younger than her husband, had been taken by influenza during last February's cold rains. Now, the old man lived alone in an adobe house north of Bondad on the rocky banks of the Animas. Only a few sheep remained from his large flock; Nahum treated them more like pets than livestock.

The shepherd smiled, displaying an uneven set of pegged teeth. He leaned his oak staff in the corner, hung his hat on it, and dropped his heavy coat on the floor before he sat down at the kitchen table with a deep sigh. Nahum looked hopefully toward the coffeepot and the woman took the hint.

In his youth, Nahum Yaciiti had spent most of his days and nights under a cloud of alcoholic fog. His body still showed the ravages of this addiction, but Nahum had been off the bottle for many years now and his mind showed no signs of the former sickness. Only last week, at an AA meeting at the Peaceful Spirit Center, Nahum had stood up and proudly told the group that for sixteen years he had drunk nothing stronger than Daisy Perika's coffee. This brought an appreciative chuckle from the audience; the old shaman's coffee was widely believed to be strong enough to melt spoons and some whispered that Daisy added "special ingredients" from her store of herbal medicines. A respected member of the tribal council swore that months of impotence had been cured by a single cup of the acrid brew.

Nahum Yaciiti remained silent while Daisy poured a massive heap of grounds into the paper filter and started the coffee maker with only three cups of water. He looked toward the television with eyes that seemed to pierce through the phosphor-coated screen, his gaze fixed on some distant scene. The old woman glanced at him over her shoulder, enviously wondering what far landscape Nahum could see. There were persistent rumors about the bowlegged shepherd. Some of the pious Chicano women who lit candles at St. Ignatius Catholic Church whispered that Nahum was sometimes visited by angels as he tended his flock. Armilda Esquibel, Nahum's neighbor, told the Jesuit priest that she had actually seen the shining visitors from heaven watching over Nahum's sheep while the elderly man slept under a cottonwood. There was an incredible report that, on Easter Sunday of 1990, the old shepherd had suffered from bleeding wounds like those the square Roman nails had made in the hands of the blessed Carpenter. Daisy, who had never seen an angel and shuddered at the brutal savagery of the Crucifixion, considered these reports to be superstitious Mexican prattle.

She placed the cup of coffee on the wooden table her second

husband had assembled from an assortment of knotty pine lumber. That particular husband had many practical skills, but the building of furniture was not to be counted among them. Nahum leaned one elbow on the rickety table, which tilted under even this slight weight as a leg wobbled. The woman scowled at the much-used piece of furniture; "That old table's legs are like mine. Barely manage to hold up the load. I'll send a letter to my nephew in Durango, tell him to come over and fix it."

The shepherd uttered his first words. "Leave the table as it is." His sober expression emphasized this curious instruction. She nodded her assent but felt uneasy. The old man did not waste words, so this must be important. The shepherd had a sip of coffee and grimaced at its bitterness. She stirred another teaspoon of sugar into the dark liquid and watched to see if this would suit him. He squinted at the cup and had another taste.

"What," she asked, "brings you out here to my place?" Nahum did not drop by for casual conversation.

Nahum turned his gaze to Daisy. The old woman saw a deep sadness in his eyes. "Darkness comes."

She tilted her head and regarded her visitor quizzically. Was he predicting his death? Or hers? "What have you seen, old man?"

He considered his arthritic hands, slowly flexing the swollen joints of deformed fingers. "Last night, in my pasture. Balls of fire came. They danced."

Nahum did not have to explain. Every Ute knew that the *bruja* traveled in this manner. She didn't respond; Nahum, like most Utes, didn't care to speak directly of witches. She looked away toward the blackness gathering outside her window. Coyote, who tarried nearby, spoke again. "Ooooeeeee . . . yooouuuwww . . . aaahhhoooo . . ."

"Damn you, Coyote," she muttered viciously, "I hope you choke on your tongue!" Daisy poured herself a half cup of the brackish liquid and sat down across the table from her visitor.

"I feel something bad, too—here in my bones." The woman lowered her voice barely above a whisper, as if someone might be listening at a window. "Last week I found a soft place in the path to the creek. Someone had been digging. I scratched around with my walking stick and found a raven's egg . . . and a plume of owl feathers . . . right there where I walk almost every day!"

Nahum nodded as if he had expected such mischief. To step on an egg or a plume of owl feathers buried by a malicious *bruja* was certain to cause illness . . . perhaps even death.

Daisy continued, her tone becoming even more con-spiratorial. "For three days now, Coyote has been skulking around my house, saying, 'Come along, Daisy, come along with me to see *pitukupf*,' but I don't go. I'm tired of this work. Let someone else go, that's what I say."

Nahum Yaciiti drained the cup and pushed it across the wooden table, which swayed slightly and creaked. He raised his bushy brows and appraised Daisy with his soft brown eyes; it was a frank gaze that she found hard to return. "You," he said gently, "will hear the voice of the dwarf."

Daisy tugged nervously at her blanket shawl. "I am tired of hearing the voice of the *pitukupf*, old man. And I will pay no attention to his servant, *Yogovuch*. Since the day when the world was made, that worthless animal has been lazy. Coyote will grow weary of bothering me; he will go back to his little master."

Daisy's tight lips betrayed her determination. Nahum gazed intently at the cup of coffee as if he could divine secrets from the jet reflections vibrating off its surface. "Many spirits come and go over the earth." He looked up, but Daisy avoided eye contact. "Two spirits we cannot ignore. The Spirit of Truth, who whis-pers softly, here." Nahum tapped on his chest with two fingers. The old man hesitated before he continued. "The Spirit of Lies"—Nahum scowled as he tapped his temple—"he speaks here, spreading sweet poison."

Daisy pretended to be savoring her coffee, but she was concen-trating on every word from the shepherd. Unconsciously, the woman pulled her blanket shawl partially over her face as if to hide from the dark spirits. "Don't preach me a sermon, old man, tell me what is happening. Which of these spirits is working now?"

Nahum Yaciiti used his finger to draw a cross on his wrinkled forehead. "The Spirit of Truth always works. But now the Spirit of Lies comes near to help his servant. I can," the old man added with sudden vehemence, "smell his foul breath when he passes!"

Daisy shuddered, clenching her shawl with brittle fingers. She sniffed tentatively but could smell nothing unusual. Her voice was barely above a whisper. "Who is his servant? What work does the Dark One plan?"

Nahum closed his eyes and remained silent; Daisy could hear her windup alarm clock ticking in unison with the black crickets' rhythmic chirp. Before Nahum replied, he opened his eyes and studied Daisy thoughtfully. "The Liar speaks to his servant, in a village of the *matukach*."

Daisy eagerly grasped at this straw. "If this Dark One works among the white people, that is a bad thing, but it is not our responsibility." Aware of his disapproval, she continued even more forcefully. "Some of my best friends are whites, but I say"—she thumped her knuckles on the table top for empha-sis—"leave it to the *matukach* to deal with their own problems."

He ignored this minor outburst. "You will touch this Dark-ness. Do what is right—"

"How will I know?" she interrupted.

"What is right is written on your heart."

Nahum slid his heavy shepherd's staff under the edge of Daisy's propane stove, placed his foot by one of the stove's legs, and pried until the leg popped loose from the linoleum. Daisy watched in amazement but held her tongue as he moved to the second stove leg to repeat the procedure. Nahum was behaving strangely. Was the old man losing his mind? When his task was completed, he grunted his approval and bent over to pick up his heavy wool coat. He attempted to fasten the carved antler buttons; his arthritic hands trembled with the effort.

Daisy impatiently brushed his hands aside and deftly buttoned his coat. She patted his shoulder in motherly fashion. "You're getting old and creaky, Nahum. You should spend the winter with your relatives down in El Paso, where it doesn't snow so much."

"Before the first snowflake of winter falls," he said, "I will go to be with my family." The shepherd waved a feeble farewell and departed without looking back.

Daisy leaned against the porch railing and listened until the chugging sound of the Dodge pickup was lost in the winds that moaned softly through the mouth of the canyon. First snow would come soon, with the Moon of Dead Leaves Falling. Tonight, the sky was as clear as the water in the Piedra. Her pulse quickened when she realized that the waning moon was not far away from the earth; he was just there . . . sitting on Three Sisters Mesa, resting for a moment on the stout shoulders of the stone women. The shaman could count all the round pockmarks on his silver face. Even *Akwuch* seemed very near, as if Nighthawk might fly to him and perch on his handle. Her grandmother had told her, "*Akwuch* is the dipper that pours out the stars. When the morning comes, all the stars have been spilled into the darkness."

"That is fine for the stars," Daisy muttered. "*Akwuch* will gather them up again before the twilight comes. When I am poured out into darkness, Grandmother, who will gather up my soul?"

2

GRANITE CREEK, COLORADO

While drifting through idyllic dreams of his departed wife and soft, fragrant breezes of spring days, Scott Parris was suddenly jolted awake. It was an odor that had disturbed his slumber, a foul stench. What was it . . . rotten eggs? He rolled over to switch on the lamp on the nightstand and was blinded by the penetrating glare of the sixty-watt bulb. The groggy man rubbed his eyes and sniffed, but the putrid odor had vanished along with sleep. He blinked and focused his eyes on the face of the alarm clock. Two minutes past three. Not a good time to wake up with the shivers. If he started exercising his mind, any chance of sleep's welcome return would fade away.

But it was there, the sour sensation, settling uneasily into his abdomen: the Dread. Unmistakable. Something was definitely wrong. He remembered his father, haunted by recurring bouts of melancholy. "Bad News is coming to town, Scotty," the old man would say as he shook his head mournfully, "and Bad is bringing all his nasty friends."

Parris pushed the covers aside and swung his legs over the side of the Hide-A-Bed. He had not experienced one of the gut-wrenching premonitions since he had accepted the position of chief of police at Granite Creek. He remembered the first time as if it were yesterday. He had been a green rookie on Chicago's South Side. It had been a balmy June afternoon, baseball weather—one of those fine days when trouble could not be imagined. It had visited him unexpectedly as he turned the corner of Halstead onto Sixty-ninth. The sensation was a sudden rush of sick, unreasoning fear that rippled in peristaltic fashion along his entrails. The young policeman had stoically ignored the disagreeable sensation, blaming a hurried lunch of Polish sausage and sauerkraut. He had dismounted from his three-wheeler, a picture of youthful confidence as he proceeded to write a ticket for a sleek Oldsmobile convertible parked beside a fire hydrant on the corner of Sixty-ninth and Union. As he folded the yellow form and tucked it under the Old's windshield wiper, he saw the woman in the second-story window. She calmly pushed the yellowed lace curtains aside and took careful aim at a passing panel truck. He could still remember the sign on the blue van: MARIO'S FINE FLOWERS, FREE DELIVERY ANYWHERE IN GREATER CHICAGO. She pulled one of the dual triggers on a double-barreled shotgun. The truck's rear window exploded under the impact of the lead pellets; the terrified driver swerved into the oncoming lane and sideswiped a Metro bus. After admiring her work, she directed her beatific smile in his direction, closed one blue eye, and aimed the antique shotgun at Officer Trainee Parris.

A bystander might have thought the policeman was watching someone else caught in harm's way, detached and curious about the outcome. In fact, Parris was immobilized, his feet frozen to the pavement as she squinted down the knurled ridge between the blue barrels and calmly launched a wad of bird shot in his direction. The young officer was a few yards farther from the muzzle of the Remington than the flower van, and this had made all the difference.

When they took her away, barefoot in her dirty print dress with her hands cuffed behind her, the satisfied smile had not left her smooth pale face. The troubled woman, a recent arrival from the hills of Tennessee, eventually confided to the court-appointed psychologist that the Darkness had whispered to her ever since her baby daughter had choked on a piece of bread. Parris had listened in the dark room behind the one-way glass while the woman explained. She had been at home with the child while her husband tried to find work in the steel mills. She called for help, but no one came. She ran down the street with her unconscious baby under one arm and beat on doors until her knuckles bled, but her frightened neighbors thought she was drunk or insane and ignored her pitiful pleas. The tiny child had turned cornflower blue, the woman told the psychologist, ". . . and slipped off to that good place where Almighty God wipes every tear away." But the mother remained in the hard world; her tears fell like a warm spring rain and no one wiped them away. On this fine summer day, the Darkness had told her to load the shotgun. "Tell me," the psychologist asked gently, "about this . . . ahh . . . darkness."

The pale woman turned and smiled at her reflection in the mirrored surface of the one-way glass. Parris felt her eyes meet his and shuddered in the darkness. "Ask him," she said as she pointed through the mirror. "He knows."

Now, years later, he ran his fingertips over his face, then his neck. He could feel the tiny scars where the stinging bird shot had penetrated his skin. Sometimes, he could feel the woman's blue eyes staring through the mirror into his own darkness.

The Dread had visited him several times after that. The last time had been barely more than a year earlier at O'Hare International. He had waved good-bye to Helen as she boarded the 737 for Montreal. It was to be an ordinary trip, her annual visit to spend two weeks with her aged mother. The premonition came like a punch to his groin as the aircraft lifted off with a roar that was barely audible through the double-paned plate glass on Concourse C. The flight had been uneventful, but Helen's taxi ride in Montreal had not. The left front tire had blown immediately before the cabbie plowed head-on into a Mack truck loaded with six tons of green plywood.

Scott had numbly accepted the sorrowful condolences, buried his wife, taken a hard look at the dirty snow, and made up his mind. Enough was, damn it, *enough.* The detective had taken early retirement as soon as he found what promised to be an undemanding job. What, he had asked himself, could possibly go wrong in a quiet university town in the Rocky Mountains? There would be the occasional knifing, family quarrels, automobile accidents, a little dope here and there. A normal American burg, but nothing like the city with a heart of dirty ice.

The policeman stumbled, only half-awake, into the kitchen. He searched the nearly empty refrigerator, made a thick Swiss cheese sandwich, poured a pint of milk into an oversized beer mug, and sat down to wait it out. Shoulders tensed, he stared out the window into the darkness, munched on his near-tasteless sandwich, and watched for the cold white rays of morning to spill over the western slopes of the San Cristobal range. The moon, he thought, seemed to be so very close . . . as if you could reach out and touch it.

He peered through the windshield and blinked nervously at the faint yellow light filtering through the third-story window of the Physics Building. What mischief was she up to, this clever girl? He expected the Voice to tell him, but his adviser was silent. He had gradually grown accustomed to this presence and was no longer alarmed by its intrusions into his thought processes. The diminishing part of his mind that was rational suggested that he was suffering from some peculiar schizophrenic delusion. The Voice vehemently denied this assertion.

The presence had been weak when it first addressed him months earlier. The whirring sound in his head was like many voices, muffled by the wind. Their name was legion. But his patience had been rewarded. As he had listened carefully, trying to understand each word and phrase, the multitude had gained in strength and merged into a single personality. For weeks now, he had been able to hear its exhortations quite clearly. He eventually decided the visitor was a gift, a source of power.

As he watched the window, a sinister possibility occupied his thoughts. What if Priscilla was not alone? Could she be meeting someone in the university laboratory? He clenched his hands on the steering wheel until his fingers ached.

He was intimately familiar with Priscilla's activities; he often watched when she thought she was alone. He smiled with satisfaction at his secret; how surprised she would be at what he knew about her habits, the smallest details of her daily schedule!

He rubbed his moist forehead to drive away the throbbing. His neck ached from watching the third-story window; his toes were numb from the cold. He sighed impatiently and squinted at the luminous dial on his wristwatch. The long wait would surely be over soon; the first light of dawn was only minutes away. He lit a cigarette, then took a sip of Jim Beam from a half-pint silver flask. The light dimmed slightly in the third-floor window. That would be one of the small lamps being switched off. He immediately stubbed his cigarette out in the ashtray and waited. Ah . . . there. The window went pitch-black as Priscilla shut off the ceiling lights. Moments later, the graduate student was leaving the side entrance of the building. She must have been tired, but the *click-click* of her high heels revealed a pent-up excitement. This was no longer the shy, insecure transfer from Arizona State. Priscilla Song's gait exuded confidence.

Her car was under the lone street lamp in the center of the parking lot; he watched the pretty young woman toss her long black hair to one side as she slid into the antique Volkswagen bug. He observed, not for the first time, that she had rather attractive legs. He waited impatiently as she cranked the engine to life and chugged out of the parking lot trailing small puffs of blue smoke. Once in the third-floor laboratory, he closed the half dozen venetian blinds. There was no point in alerting anyone to his presence in the building at this strange hour.

The rectangular room was arranged for utility rather than with any concern for aesthetic sensibilities. The walls were lined with olive green benches, dreary relics of the room's earlier service as a sophomore chem lab. The bench on the north wall was divided in the center by a large stainless-steel sink and this was covered by a fume hood with a pair of fans that could exhaust six hundred cubic feet of air every minute. The sink was flanked on the right by a vacuum oven, an electron-beam evaporator, and a surplus helium-neon laser donated by the U.S. Air Force. On the left, there was a variety of equipment, including microbalances, a small lathe, and a miniature drill press. Hand tools were scattered over the bench.

The man peered under the fume hood and sniffed for any pungent odor that might suggest drug preparations. Nothing. He opened the safelike door on the vacuum furnace, taking care not to touch the oven wall; the bimetallic thermometer was still registering eighty-five degrees Celsius. He studied the black interior of the oven carefully but found not a trace of any experimental material. "What sort of muffin," he asked aloud, "is my little Priscilla baking?"

The bench on the south wall was normally kept clear for short-term experiments, but it was currently occupied by a variety of electrical instruments and an assortment of connecting cables. There was an ancient Hewlett-Packard dual-beam oscilloscope, a relic of good funding during the 1960s, and a modern digital voltmeter. There was also an expensive eight-pen chart recorder that the graduate student had borrowed from the Electrical Engineering Department.

He placed his hand on the oscilloscope. Cold. He repeated this simple test on the voltmeter and then the chart recorder. The voltmeter was tepid; it might have been used during the past hour. The recorder was pleasantly warm to his fingertips. So, she was making electrical measurements. Perhaps these were required as she monitored the chemical processes to produce . . . to produce what? Perhaps, just perhaps, a new designer drug to satisfy the appetites of the expanding population of middle-class junkies. He checked the paper-output tray under the recorder. Empty. He suspected that the perforated sheets from the recorder were now neatly taped into her logbook.

The center of the room was furnished with a row of battered

file cabinets, a refrigerator, and a gray metal desk that supported a desktop computer and a selection of catalogs and textbooks. There was a small oak table with a terminal that conversed with the VAX mainframe in the basement. He inspected the terminal, which was never turned off. The screen was blank except for the READY indicator followed by a green cursor. He went through the file cabinets with considerable care, but there was nothing more than the usual folders filled with data from various projects over the past decade.

He sat down at the desk and leaned back in the chair. Had she been alone? If someone had been with her, he must have left by another exit. As he pushed the chair away from the desk, his shin bumped the metal wastebasket. He pulled the can into view and leaned over to inspect the contents. Several wadded paper tissues, one with a lipstick smudge. A half dozen of the free throwaway technical magazines and catalogs on subjects ranging from laboratory glassware to chemicals. Comics from yesterday's *Denver Post*. Chewing-gum wrappers. In the bottom of the can, he spotted a tightly wadded paper. He unfolded the paper with mild apprehension, expecting to find a pink glob of spent chewing gum.

It was a discarded photocopy of a graph made on the paper in the eight-pen plotter. The photocopy machine had malfunctioned. The upper-right-hand section of the page was hopelessly smudged with inky black toner. The rest of the reproduction was blurred and indistinct in some areas, crystal clear in others. A useless copy that Priscilla had carelessly tossed aside. The vertical axis was labeled "R, Norm." The horizontal axis had a penciled scale of zero to one hundred and was labeled with a capital T. Time? Temperature? The plotted line of data ran along the bottom of the sheet, barely above the horizontal axis. It started at 22, was flat until it reached 60, then took a steep rise toward the top of the page, disappearing into the sooty splash of toner. He squinted at the horizontal ordinate again. What was this? Sixty seconds, the time required for some critical reaction?

Or sixty degrees? Something that happened at a particular temperature? There was something familiar about this plot, but he couldn't quite remember where he had seen a similar graph. He studied the enigmatic tracing with a feeling of frustration, sensing that he had found something of importance. He did not understand what he held in his hand until he heard the spoken words inside his head. The Voice explained the significance of the crumpled piece of paper, and the revelation was absolutely stunning. It was difficult to believe such an incredible assertion, even from this unassailable source, but the Voice had *never* been mistaken.

His fingertips began to tingle. In his excitement, he was only barely aware of the warm liquid streaming down his leg as the sphincter on his bladder relaxed. He wiped at bloodshot eyes with his shirt sleeve. "It's not fair," he muttered, "but I know how the bitch's mind works. She won't need me . . . or anyone now." He blew his nose into a wrinkled handkerchief. "I've been good to her . . . but she won't remember. Not now. I'll be yesterday's news."

The Voice asked whether he wanted *everything*.

"Damn right . . . this is my chance for . . ."

He was informed, forcefully, that he should take what he wanted.

"I don't know," he answered uncertainly. "How could I . . ."

The Voice explained how—with two words.

3

Priscilla Song pulled the lavender blanket up to her chin and stared at the spider web pattern of cracks and brown watermarks in the plaster ceiling. Within a year, she promised herself (cross my heart, hope to die!), she would be living in better quarters. Much better. To begin with, a first-class condo in Aspen. In the tall pines, where the crisp mountain breeze refreshed the Beautiful People. Then, a horse farm near Gunnison. Arabians for her, quarter-horse stock for her wild cowboy.

The venerable Bug, of course, would be relegated to the junkyard. She would buy a new car, or maybe a classic. A restored 'Vette for herself, but something quite different for him. A twelve-cylinder XJ-S Jag convertible? Yes, yes! Priscilla closed her eyes tightly and strained to visualize it. Metallic blue, burl walnut dashboard, leather seats soft as a baby's behind. Two hundred and sixty-three horses under its long, sleek hood. She had watched his hazel eyes sparkle with secret desire as her sunburned cowboy gently drew his fingertips along the mirror-surfaced fender of the display model in the Denver showroom. The gesture had been so sensuous that she had (absurdly?) felt a pang of jealousy. An impossible dream at the time, but within a year she would be able to plunk down hard cash for it. Soon, very soon, she would make her move. The young woman rolled over, raised herself on one elbow, and blinked at the red LED numbers on the face of the oversized digital alarm clock. She had been trying to reach him for a week. If he wasn't rounding up strays in the dusty canyons that jutted like skinny fingers off the Rio Chama, her man was off to a rodeo or hauling cattle to the rail head in Denver. He had been behaving oddly of late; she prayed that he wasn't drinking again. Or worse. Their last argument had been stupid, a result of his juvenile jealousies. It was high time, as he would have said, "time to mend some fences." She could not wait to tell him that she . . . no, *they* were going to be shamefully wealthy. Priscilla punched in the area code for New Mexico and then carefully pressed the buttons for the Thorpe Hereford Ranch. The line buzzed four times before she heard his father's drawl.

"Hello, Mr. Thorpe, this is Priscilla. May I speak to . . ."

"Sorry, young lady. Buster headed up to Fort Collins couple of days ago, deliverin' a polled Hereford bull." She hated the "Buster" nickname. "Should of been back by now. Expect he's had some trouble with the truck." That meant he was on another wild drunk. Or something. "He'll be passin' close by Granite Creek. I expect he'll stop to see you." Fat chance, she thought. As always, it would be up to her to make the first move.

"I understand." She didn't. "Tell him I called. I mailed his birthday present today. It's a ring."

"I'm sure he'll be right proud to wear it." The cowboy was not partial to ornaments.

"Please ask him to call."

"I'll tell 'im." He would forget. "That all?"

"Yes," she said. "That's all."

The night air was razor sharp with hints of a hard frost, but then it always was in the Moon of Dead Leaves Falling. Nahum Yaciiti, deeply preoccupied with his thoughts, barely noticed the plaintive bleating of the few sheep milling around in the soft moonlight. The bottom of the night always brought worries with it, and now he sat, hunched forward on a flat outcropping of limestone, troubled about his old friend. Daisy Perika had been sprinkled with the holy water of the Christians, but she was deeply immersed in the spirit world of her ancestors. Always at Easter and Christmas, and occasionally on feast days of the saints she revered, the old woman would set out for St. Ignatius to joyfully revive her spirit with the sacred bread and wine.

But after she had been nourished by the body and blood of the Lamb, Daisy would slip back into the world of her grandmothers. When the white-hot fingers of summer lightning snapped branches off enchanted pines . . . when Coyote barked his urgent summons . . . when the old spirits whispered their rhythmic hymns in the wind . . . she would hear their voices. The medicine woman, carried by the hollow thumping of the Lakota drum, would fly away to dark realms where the daughters and sons of Adam were never meant to visit.

Whatever would become of this creature of two worlds after the first snow blanketed his pasture? Would the aged shaman take her council from the angels or from the voices of her ancestors? Nahum shook his head and sighed. Life was a great war between the spirit forces, and he was weary from many battles.

Willing his worries away, Nahum wrapped his arms around his staff and let his chin drop to his chest for a brief nap. Presently, he felt the warm breath of the ewe as she pressed her head against his knee. He gently caressed her thin neck. "What's wrong, old fuzzball," he asked with pretended gruffness, "you afraid of the dark? Hush, hush. Lie down now, and sleep. Dream dreams of green pastures, still waters." The lamb stubbornly ignored this gentle entreaty, and the others were also gathering close to the tired shepherd.

Nahum arose from his seat on the limestone, leaned on his stout staff, and peered into the stark landscape of moonlight and shadows. The waters of the river were churning tonight, as if they were attempting to speak to him . . . to warn him! The shepherd listened intently to the many voices of the river. Its full name was Rio de Los Animas Perditas, the River of Lost Souls.

The souls of the rippling waters spoke incoherently, but he sensed that his flock was in danger. There was no sign or sound of coyotes, and the black bears would stay in the high country until the snows were deep. Perhaps a hungry cougar watched from the black shadows along brushy banks of the Animas. Nahum remembered his old Winchester, hidden behind the seat in the pickup, and wondered whether it would be wise to leave the sheep alone long enough to get the rifle.

The shepherd was considering his options when he heard a fluttering whistle from the north; this was followed by the sound of laughter. It was a wild, malicious laughter, without a trace of humor. Nahum understood what manner of creature was arriving; it was not the first time. But now there were so many! A dozen balls of fire appeared, dropping from the sky, caroming off the limestone outcropping, bouncing on the dry sage without setting it afire. The fireballs rolled along the ground toward the shepherd and his little flock; some of the sheep scattered in panic; a few animals milled closely around the old Ute, pushing against his legs as they bleated pitifully.

He waved his staff at the flaming spheres. "Go away from this place, filthy *brujas*," he shouted. "We'll have none of your foul business here!" The balls of fire danced with mad vigor; the mindless laughter increased. Nahum was shocked at their brazen behavior. He felt his heart thumping, the fear sending electric shivers through his old limbs.

One of the fireballs assumed the shape of a voluptuous young woman; the form moved to the limestone outcropping as Nahum withdrew, shielding himself with his staff held forward at arm's length. The sheep scattered. The flaming figure placed a large square bottle on the limestone and indicated, with a seductive gesture, that Nahum should help himself. The mellow scent of aged whiskey wafted to the shepherd's nostrils. For a moment, he desired the whiskey more than life itself. The *bruja* laughed. "Taste, old man, taste and enjoy. It is better than you can imagine. Drink to your heart's delight; the bottle is always full!" Nahum hesitated for a moment, then bent over, picked up a chunk of basalt, and flung it at the decanter. The glass shattered, spilling lustrous streams of liquid over the limestone. The sweet odor was now almost overpowering, as if the scent itself might intoxicate him.

As the whiskey rivers flowed over the edge of the rock outcropping and spilled amber falls onto the clay, he heard the rumbling approach of the storm. The whirling fury stood before him, towering out of sight into the vault of heaven, but not a breath of wind could be felt in the pasture. Nahum trembled. The voice in the whirlwind spoke soothingly, gently, inviting the old Ute to . . . *communion*.

Nahum raised his staff above his head. He shouted into the churning malignancy of the abyss: "Go away from this place, *Kwasigeti. . . . Yaweh* is my shepherd—"

The whirlwind exploded with elemental ferocity.

Charlie Moon surveyed the landscape in silent wonder. The twisted bodies of sheep were scattered over the pasture like broken, discarded toys. Sturdy clumps of chamisa and sage had been pulled up by the roots and torn to splinters. The Ute tribal policeman removed his hat and scratched thoughtfully at his coarse black hair. He turned to look back at the small figure of Armilda Esquibel; the tiny woman had not been able to keep pace with his great strides.

Armilda hurried along, gasping for breath, grateful that the giant policeman had stopped. This Charlie Moon, she recalled, was the one the old Utes called Makes No Tracks. This one, the tribal elders whispered, had inherited his grandmother's ability to walk through the forest without touching the ground. The old woman smiled at this nonsense; his big boot heels were making heavy imprints in the moist clay. So much, Armilda thought, for the silly gossip of old Indian men. The exhausted woman paused in the shadow of the policeman's towering frame and clutched at

= 21 =

the lapels of her raincoat to protect her body from the chill wind whipping down the broad floodplain of the Animas.

The policeman found a ballpoint in his jacket pocket, glanced at his wristwatch, and jotted the time down in his notebook. "Okay, now. Tell me exactly what you saw and when you saw it." He hoped she would not embellish the facts, but Armilda was a spinner of fantastic yarns. Moon suspected that she added a touch of spice here and there to give her product a more delectable flavor.

She gulped in a breath that the wind almost sucked away. "I already told that girl at the police station . . . when I called."

"I know what you told the dispatcher. Just tell me what you saw, without any . . . ah . . . interpretation." He couldn't sup-press a brief smile.

The voice from the small figure in the plastic raincoat was surprisingly strong and salted with defiance. "Believe whatever you want. I'm old and don't give a damn. I saw what I saw. Maybe . . . maybe I should just keep it to myself." She paused to see the effect of this remark, but Charlie Moon, apparently oblivious to her presence, was leaning over to examine the shat-tered body of a spring lamb. Armilda tugged anxiously at his sleeve, annoyed to be ignored by this big brute. The Ute tribal policeman seemed not to notice. She elbowed him sharply in the ribs; Moon recovered from his apparent interest in the dead animal.

"Oh, yeah. Were you saying something, Mrs. Esquibel?"

"Learn to pay attention, young man, I don't dip the same snuff twice. Now write *this* down in your little book: Last night, see, I hear this big commotion, like a freight train straight from hell. Only it wasn't no train." She twirled her hand in a circular motion. "It was . . . like a tornado. Saw the whole thing from my bedroom." She nodded toward the small rise where her two-room adobe perched precariously on the edge of a crumbling arroyo. "I can see most of Nahum's north pasture from my window; it happened not too long after the moon came up over Bondad Hill."

Charlie Moon jotted a reminder in his notebook: "Check time—moon rise."

She continued, her voice shaking with emotion at the memory. "That awful storm, it could've killed us all, but God in his tender mercy delivered me." Her pious expression suggested that the Almighty knew very well who deserved deliverance.

Moon picked a dirty clump of wool off a flattened sage bush and sniffed the crisp morning air. The smell of whiskey covered the pasture like fog. Perhaps Nahum, after these many years of abstinence, was hitting the bottle again. "We understood about the storm from your telephone call. But the dispatcher didn't understand . . . um . . . everything you reported." That, he thought, was an understatement.

Armilda crossed herself hurriedly. "It was that big wind that killed these poor animals. It killed Nahum, too. I saw his body in the pasture, after the wind went away. He was about . . . over there, by that white rock." She pointed toward a limestone outcropping. "He would sit right there, on that rock, watching over them sheep of his. Sometimes, if it was light, he read books." Judging by her expression, she considered the latter activity to be somewhat eccentric.

The policeman turned to study Armilda's wrinkled face. "I can see there's been a bad wind here, ma'am. And there must be a dozen dead sheep. But there's no sign of Nahum." The old shepherd, Moon imagined, would be in Durango filing a claim with the insurance agency, maybe throwing down a stiff drink. Nahum claimed to be "cured," but you could never tell with alcoholics.

Armilda shook her head in frustration. "Well of course there's no sign of Nahum. He's not here. He's gone."

"Then where . . ."

"*They* took him." She crossed herself as she squinted up at the policeman. "Three of them, I saw them gather up his body and carry it away. And there was this music . . . sweet, sweet singing. . . ." Armilda paused, her voice trailing away into a whisper. She rubbed at her eyes and tried to swallow the hard knot in her throat.

Moon scribbled more notes; now he was getting somewhere. Even these days, it still happened. Relatives had removed the body for burial, probably singing ancient chants for the dead as they carried Nahum's remains away. It was the old Ute custom to hide the body. Nahum's corpse would be in one of the dry canyons to the east, secreted in a crevice in the yellow rock. Moon licked the tip of the ballpoint and held the instrument over the notebook page. "Which way did they go?"

"Up there," Armilda rasped, jerking her thumb upward toward the clouds.

Charlie Moon turned away and stifled a groan. Had this lonely old woman been influenced by those fantastic stories about inhabitants of cigar-shaped UFOs with a ravenous appetite for mutton? "So . . . he . . . they . . . went up there." He squinted upward thoughtfully, as if he accepted the story. "Who, exactly, took him up there, Mrs. Esquibel?" He dropped the ballpoint into his coat pocket and closed the notebook.

Armilda stared up at the policeman with frank astonishment that he did not have the capacity to grasp the obvious. Someone had to explain the facts to this big jughead. The old woman spoke slowly, hoping Makes No Tracks would finally comprehend the obvious. "*They* took him, of course, the *angels!*"

A perfect crystal of snow fell onto the sleeve of Charlie Moon's dark blue uniform. Unaccountably, this six-sided jewel of ice filled his soul with a deep melancholy. This first snowflake of winter.

4

Priscilla arrived a full hour before the scheduled Electromagnetics lab; she needed the extra time to prepare the demonstration experiment for the sophomore class. The graduate student lit the gas on a greasy Bunsen burner and brewed a cup of green Japanese tea, laced it with five cubes of sugar, and settled down to prepare herself for the mundane task. It was not easy to concentrate on the alternating current motor-generator experiment, not when there were so many terribly important matters to consider. She would keep up appearances, at least until the end of this semester. Before her doctorate was awarded, Priscilla expected to be wealthy. Not merely president of General Motors wealthy—Arab oil prince wealthy!

It would be necessary to do everything just so and the young woman did not intend to miss a trick. She had kept a detailed description (in indelible ink) of her experiments in a bound notebook. Nothing would be left to chance. Priscilla had taken great care to record every stage of her experimental procedure. The precise amount of each chemical used in preparing the precursor compound was listed, along with the temperature level during the sintering procedure. There were charts of heating rates, oxygen pressures, final temperatures, time-at temperature, and, last but not least, the cooling rate. Each plot was taped into the book, both the recent successful runs and the early tests that had, in spite of their production of unstable samples, provided intriguing clues. It was excellent scientific procedure; her record was complete.

The only important item missing from the notebook was the signature of one or two knowledgeable witnesses. It was an important omission, but it couldn't be helped. To be useful in any future legal proceedings, a credible witness should be someone who understood the nature of the invention. Once she revealed her astounding accomplishment to a single fellow scientist, the secret would be too good to keep. Much better to line up a buyer before the word was out, an investor with deep, deep pockets. There would be no lack of buyers; there would be a bidding war! Then, the results of her discovery would gradually revolutionize the way millions lived. The world would never be the same.

The young scientist was lost in these thoughts when the intercom buzzer on her telephone jarred her back to the present reality. Priscilla pulled off a clip-on earring and pressed the receiver to her ear.

The caller did not wait for her to speak. "That you, Priscilla?"

She smiled as she recognized the voice of Kristin Waters. "Yeah, Kristin, it's myself. What's on your mind this morning?"

Kristin Waters, secretary to the entire Physics Department, had never married. The middle-aged woman took a special interest in the welfare of the graduate students. Particularly the female students. "As usual, it's Professor Thomson, sweetheart. He's working on the air force contract renewal forms, needs to talk to you. After you're through with Thomson, see Professor Dexter. The chairman wants to discuss next semester's schedule, your teaching assignments. I think he wants you to take over the undergraduate thermodynamics class."

"I'll be right there." Priscilla was not surprised. When it came time to generate the paperwork for a contract renewal, Thomson was even more agitated than usual. She picked up her files on the honeycomb armor contract from the physics lab and was at Thomson's office door in less than a minute.

He glanced up from the pile of papers that covered his desk, blinked under his bushy brows, and smiled. This jarred Priscilla momentarily; she had never seen a genuine smile visit the features of Professor Waldo Thomson.

She stepped inside his office. "You wanted to see me?"

He appeared distracted for a moment and then seemed to remember. "Oh, yes, of course. Come in and sit down. Make yourself comfortable." He waved his hand to indicate where she should sit.

This was the second surprise. All of his students, even his graduate assistants, knew that you stood at attention when summoned into the master's presence. Priscilla seated herself in the uncushioned wooden chair and waited for the next surprise.

Thomson leaned back in his swivel chair. "How are things going for you, Miss Song?" He tried to smile again. The effort strained his facial muscles.

She returned the smile. "Just fine. I have the latest data on compression strength and fracture resistance for the honeycomb structure. I think you'll be pleased at the progress we see with the forty-micron silicon carbide fibers embedded in—"

He interrupted. "I'm certain I will. You've been doing an excellent job. Understand you've been working very hard lately. That's what I want to talk to you about."

This was strange. "I do hope that you're satisfied with my work."

"Oh my yes. Quite satisfied. In fact, I've learned you're rather an eager beaver, not satisfied to put in only eight or ten hours a day!"

Priscilla's mouth went dry. It had been inevitable that someone would eventually notice her late hours. But he knew nothing more than that. After all, what *could* he know?

Thomson clasped his hands as if in prayer. The forced intermittent smile was replaced by a smug expression "Now let's discuss your recent . . . ah . . . extracurricular activities."

* * *

Julio Pacheco shuffled along the hallway, lugging his heavy tool-box. If it wasn't one damn thing, it was a dozen damn things. What had the gringo woman said on the telephone? "Someone smelled something . . . like a gas leak. You'd better come over and check out the whole building." Pacheco had checked dusty offices and cluttered laboratories, rest rooms that smelled of urine and bleach, musty classrooms with odors of chalk dust that made him sneeze. He had found nothing. A few more stops on the third floor and he would be finished with this foolishness. It was a good thing, too. Half the places he stopped had some half-assed little job to take up his time. A loose hinge on the chairman's door, a leaking flush valve in the women's rest room. Do this, fix that! What did they think he was? He slipped his master key into the slot, then realized that the laboratory door was unlocked. He pushed the door open and was pleased with what he saw. Priscilla was at her desk. The Oriental girl was small and well shaped. Beautiful dark eyes, arching brows, moist full lips . . . this was good fortune. She was wiping her eyes with a tissue. Had the pretty girl been crying?

Priscilla looked up at the sound of familiar footsteps. It was Julio, the Mexican with the steel taps on his shoes. The Mexican always smelled of cheap cologne, but he was good-looking in a rough sort of way. She dropped the tissue into her purse; the meeting had shaken her, but she didn't want to advertise the fact that she had been driven to tears.

"Hullo there, *chica*," Pacheco grunted. "Got to check the place out. Somebody smelled gas, so they call your man Julio to have a look. You smell anything?"

As he came close, she did smell the sour odor of beer. "No, Julio. But have a look around. Help yourself."

The repairman leered at her as he produced the miniature gas sniffer from his pocket and waved the rubber-covered sensor wand in her direction. "I appreciate the invitation, little girl. Maybe I will help myself." He chuckled.

Priscilla blushed and returned her attentions to the computer keyboard. It would be best to ignore him.

Pacheco was persistent. "It's time we got together, had a serious talk, you and me. Unless you think you're too busy to bother with—"

"We can talk anytime you want." She whirled in her chair and glared at him. "Exactly what do you want to talk about?"

"Oh, lots of things." Pacheco crawled along the floor and tested the heat vents for signs of escaping gas, but the sensor was silent. "You been busy lately; don't see you much anymore." He opened his toolbox and removed a heavy pipe wrench. "I better tighten up the gas pipes a little, just to take good care of you." She had turned away. He winked at her back as she pretended not to hear. "Don't want nothin' should happen to little Priscilla. Know what I mean?"

This interchange was interrupted by the sudden appearance of Professor Harry Presley, whose tall, skinny frame appeared in the hall door as if he had materialized there. Students referred to Presley either as "Elvis" or "Snake Hips." He sniffed the air like a giraffe wary of hyenas, regarded the Mexican with frank distaste, then smiled at Priscilla. "What's going on in here, my dear? Is there a problem?"

"Nothing," she said coolly, "that I can't handle." He took note of the curt dismissal, lost the smile, and departed as silently as he had appeared. Pacheco muttered an obscenity, then turned his attention to a loose fitting on an archaic gas valve.

Priscilla forgot about Pacheco's presence; she had more urgent matters on her mind. This would be her last day at Rocky Mountain Polytechnic. There were so many loose ends to tie up, but the bastard might be watching her. Tonight, she knew, she would have the lab to herself.

On Friday evenings, the Physics Building was deserted. The sharp clicks of her high heels echoed hollowly off the plaster walls as she marched down the empty hall. On such nights, the place reminded her of a museum. Full of dusty old artifacts, hidden mummies, and other mute testimony to the victory of decay over progress. Priscilla turned her key in the lock and opened the door to "her" laboratory for the last time. There would be no experiments, no data analysis tonight. The precious logbook was now under the temporary protection of employees of the United States government. This evening, she would search the lab, her computer files, every conceivable place where any scrap of evidence might remain of her experimental work. There must be nothing left for anyone to examine, not the least clue to the recipe for her compound.

She started to flush three small jars of chemicals down the sink and hesitated. These compounds were important clues to her research, but it was poor environmental practice to dump them into the sewer. It occurred to her that a thorough inventory of her supplies was probable. If the weasel was only moderately clever, he would be waiting to discover what she had removed from the lab! Considering the neat row of highly purified bottled elements on the shelf above the oven, Priscilla smiled mischievously at the thought of how she could confuse her adversary. She removed four small bottles of powdered elements that were *not* used in her compound and dropped them into her purse. If he noticed their absence, that would give the bastard a few false trails to follow!

After she had used the DEC terminal to clear all of her files on the VAX mainframe, the young woman pressed the power button on the Macintosh computer. When the screen had turned a bright blue, she opened her daily log and scanned each page until she reached the final entries. There was nothing in that file to worry about—it was all routine stuff, no mention of after-hours research. The data on her sensitive research was still on the hard disk, but it was safe from prying eyes. The file was encrypted with the best technique available; without the code word, the most clever hacker in the world couldn't read her notes. Even so, it was time to erase the encrypted file from the disk.

She had just placed her fingers on the computer keyboard when she heard footsteps in the hall. Odd. Who would be in the building so late? Probably a campus guard making his lonely rounds. No. The gait—the sound of the footsteps were unmistakably familiar . . . but surely not! The footsteps stopped outside the laboratory door. Priscilla watched the doorknob turn.

It was late and Arnold Dexter was utterly exhausted from his work. Nevertheless, the chairman of the Physics Department was particular about his appearance. He straightened his platinum-plated cuff links just so. He tilted his head slightly and inspected his reflection in the office window; he was smoothing the knot on his narrow red tie when he heard the screams echo down the empty halls. The animal sound was terrifying; the chairman felt ripples of horror propagate along his spine. The Mexican was shrieking in his native tongue, but Dexter understood less than a dozen words in Spanish. The physicist grabbed the telephone receiver and dialed 911. The answer was immediate.

"Granite Creek Police. How may we help you?" He recognized the choppy speech pattern of a Ute. Must be the Tavishuts woman. Dexter's hands were trembling; he tried hard to control himself. "Hello? My name is Dexter, Professor Arnold Dexter. I believe a violent crime is in progress. . . . I can hear screams. . . . I don't know what to do . . . please . . ."

Clara Tavishuts was rock steady. "Understand. Tell me where you are . . . and whatever you do, don't hang up the phone."

"I'm here in my office," he whined desperately. "Please send help. I think someone is being killed. . . ."

"Where is your office? You at the university?"

"Yes, yes. Physics Building, third floor. Just across Willow Avenue from the gymnasium. Please hurry. . . ."

"Got it. Now hold on, sir. Don't hang up."

He could hear her calling for help. "Car Three. Car Three. Emergency." There was a brief pause before he heard Clara's voice again. "E.C., drop that jelly doughnut and answer this call right now or I'll kick your fat butt into the next zip code!"

The next voice Dexter heard crackled over the squelch on the shortwave police radio.

"Hold your panties on, Minnie-Ha-Ha. I'm right here. Whatsamatta?"

"See the man at the university. Physics Building, across the street from the Sports Complex. Report of a fight or something. Sounds like serious business. You better peel rubber, E.C."

E. C. "Piggy" Slocum's reply was sober. "Ten-four, base. ETA three minutes."

Clara was back on the telephone. "Help is on the way, Mr. Dexter. Now listen closely. Leave your phone off the hook. Get out of the building and onto the street pronto. Avoid the area where you hear the screams; take a back door out if there is one. You got that?"

"Yes, but what about—"

"No *buts*. Get out of the building and wait on the Willow Avenue side. Our man will be there in nothing flat. You tell him where the disturbance is, but don't get involved yourself. Now get moving."

Arnold Dexter did precisely as he was told. He had barely reached the street when he heard the wail of the approaching siren. Julio had heard it, too. The handyman was walking, somewhat unsteadily, from the building as E. C. "Piggy" Slocum screeched to a halt. Dexter pointed at Julio's figure and screamed at the policeman. "That's him, Officer. Stop him. Don't let him get away!"

Instinctively, Julio raised his hands above his head. This evident gesture of guilt was enough for Piggy, who had already removed his .357 Magnum from its holster. For most of his life, Piggy had lived for this moment. He leveled the bulky pistol at the hapless repairman and called up the best Clint Eastwood imitation he could muster. "Freeze, you little cockroach, or I'll drop you like a bad habit." Piggy cocked the hammer.

Julio's visual field narrowed, tunnel-like, to focus on the chrome-plated revolver in the policeman's trembling hands. Few things were as unsettling as a nervous man with a loaded gun. Impulsively, he turned and sprinted toward a grove of lodgepole pine at the end of the building. Piggy's stubby finger squeezed the trigger; the pistol nearly jumped from his plump hands. A brick exploded in the wall a yard behind Julio's head, and this inspired the terrified man to accelerate. Piggy emptied the remaining five chambers in rapid succession, but each shot was a worse miss than the previous one. Several more bricks and a window were demolished by the cannonade.

Julio's form melted into the darkness as Piggy made a valiant attempt to chase after the vanished Mexican. It was no contest. The policeman, whose form resembled his nickname, was sixty pounds overweight, and the Mexican was lean and terrified. Piggy, puffing and wheezing, waddled back to the squad car and pressed the button on his mike. "Clara . . . ahh . . . oh damn . . . this is Slocum. Put out an APB on . . . ahh . . . whew . . . following suspect for resisting arrest. About five seven or five eight, medium build, dark complexion, heavy mustache. Wearin' jeans and a leather jacket. Cowboy boots, too, I think."

Dexter cautiously approached the wheezing policeman. "May I help, Officer?"

"Help away, fella. You"—he stopped to draw a gasping breath—"know somethin' about that guy?"

"He's Julio Pacheco, a university employee. Lives over on Denver Street, in that run-down apartment building near the YMCA. The one that used to be the High Country Motel. That"—Dexter pointed—"is his university vehicle."

Piggy glanced at the handyman's truck, then squinted his little porcine eyes at Dexter. "You know anything else, mister?"

Dexter's normally bland face was a picture of dread. "You'd better have a look on the third floor. From the screams I heard, it sounded as if he was attempting to . . . to molest someone."

5

Scott Parris, clad in boxer shorts and a White Sox T-shirt, had been watching the late sports news from a Denver station. He was muttering in disbelief at footage of the Broncos' most recent loss when the telephone jangled.

Clara Tavishuts was already talking when he put the receiver to his ear. "I sent Slocum out on a call from the campus, Chief, a report of some kind of fracas. There's been an assault, maybe a homicide. Piggy wasn't too clear. Victim is a young woman, probably a student. No ID yet."

"Do we have a suspect?"

"I already put out an all points on a Mexican suspect who resisted arrest. Lieutenant Leggett has taken charge and Sergeant Knox is on the way to the campus. Thought you'd want to get there right away while the scene is fresh."

Parris groaned. He could feel it. This was the reason for the visit by the Dread. "Thanks for the heads-up. It'll take me a few minutes to get dressed, then I'll check it out."

"What you need to know," she added, "is that Piggy unloaded all six chambers of his big horse pistol at the suspect, who fled on foot. Doesn't sound like E.C. killed anything, though, except a window—glass." Parris wondered what trouble Patrolman E. C. Slocum might have landed the department in this time. "Tell me what you know," he said. "Was it a righteous shoot, or did our pistol-happy cowboy go bananas when he had a live body to aim at?"

"I don't know," she replied, "but there was a witness to the shooting. A Professor Dexter. He's the guy who called nine-one-one to report the assault; he was on the scene later when Piggy fired his piece."

"Oh great," Parris said, "a witness, and ten to one the suspect wasn't armed."

When Parris arrived, cars Seven, Four, and Three were on the scene, along with the country coroner's unmarked gray van. An ambulance was leaving without a customer. The hospital would be of no help to this particular victim. The medical examiner would be with the corpse, and that scene was not one that appealed to Parris. He had avoided the homicide squad during his entire tenure in Chicago. Vice, burglary, and auto theft details had been sufficiently grim; the bodies of murder victims gave him the shivers.

Sgt. Eddie "Rocks" Knox was busy directing occasional traffic and keeping a few curious onlookers at bay. Parris stopped to question Piggy, who, oblivious to the cold, was sitting on the hood of his patrol car, his short legs dangling over the radiator grille. Eddie Knox backed off to allow the chief some privacy. Piggy shrieked when Parris asked about the victim. "Is she dead? Hell *yes* she's dead! You'd be dead, too, if you had that thing stuck in your . . ." The fat policeman paused to blow his bulbous nose into a filthy red bandanna. Piggy began sobbing like a small child. It was too much for Parris, who turned away in embarrassment.

"I understand the suspect ran when you arrived. Was he armed?"

Piggy dropped his head and muttered something incoherent.

Parris left Piggy and headed for Car Seven, where Eddie Knox was notifying Clara Tavishuts that Parris was on the scene. He dropped the mike and grinned at the chief. "Don't you just love police work?"

"What went down here?"

Eddie Knox's features harbored a perpetual hint of insolence, a barely concealed insubordination. The "Rocks," so the story went, was afraid of nothing and nobody. And that went double for a new chief from an eastern city. Eddie chewed thoughtfully on a jawfull of Red Man, then spat carelessly on the pavement, just far enough from Parris's shoe to avoid insult.

"I know less than nothin'. Showed up here about ten minutes before you did. Didn't go inside. Just doin' crowd control." He jerked a thumb toward the lighted windows on the third floor. "Leggett's up there with the body. Doc Simpson's there, too."

"Slocum is pretty shaken up. I understand you two get along pretty well. Would you keep an eye on him for me?"

Eddie Knox's eyes lost their insolence at this request. "Well, I guess you know, I'm probably the only real buddy Piggy has in the whole department. Old E.C. never did have much in the way of friends. Why, did you know . . . well, no, I expect I shouldn't shoot my mouth off so much. Just gossip anyhow."

Parris was still new on this job; he was eager to know everything about his staff. "Whatever it is, Sergeant Knox, I think you can share it with me."

Eddie Knox hesitated, then gave in with a shrug. "Well," he replied between chews on the wad of tobacco, "I'm probably the onliest one what knows about it, but poor old Piggy never did have *any* buddies, even when he was a little boy this high"—Knox held his hand knee-high to illustrate a boy-sized Piggy—" 'cause he was always such a little twerp. The way I hear it"—he leaned closer to stage-whisper into Parris's ear—"Piggy's momma had to hang a pork chop around his fat little neck just to get his dog to play with 'im!"

Eddie Knox watched Parris's mouth drop open before he snickered. The snicker grew to a chortle, which gave birth to a genuine belly laugh, and the laugh erupted into a loud series of snorting mulelike haw-haws. Parris turned on his heel and walked away as Knox choked and gagged on a swallow of tobacco juice.

Parris climbed the stairs to the third floor slowly, like a small boy approaches the principal's office. Lieutenant Leggett was stationed in the hall outside the physics laboratory; he had already set up four plastic stands to hold the yellow Mylar tape that announced DO NOT ENTER—POLICE—DO NOT ENTER, and so on.

Parris nodded at the lieutenant. "Bring me up to date." Anything to delay looking at the body. Leggett, who had the appearance of a casting director's policeman in his immaculate blue uniform, flipped his notebook open. "Here's what we have so far. University employee, name of Arnold Dexter, better make that *Professor* Arnold Dexter"—Leggett grinned—"called on nine-one-one at twenty-five to ten. Clara took the call. It's all on the tape. This professor reports some kind of rhubarb, says he can hear screams. Piggy . . . uh . . . Patrolman Slocum was close by and got here pretty quick. When he arrived on the scene, this Dexter guy met him at the curb and pointed out the suspect, who was leaving the building. Officer Slocum ordered the suspect to halt, but he hotfooted it, sir."

Parris grimaced. "And Officer Slocum felt compelled to fire his piece?"

Leggett hesitated. "Six times. Suspect wasn't hit. Did some damage to the building, though." The young policeman could not suppress a weak smile. He turned his head and covered it with a cough.

The chief laughed. It felt good; laughter drove the dark spirits back into the shadows. "I saw the shattered bricks. I'd have thought the shrapnel alone would've killed the suspect." Parris paused to regain his composure. "Does the Physics Department use the whole building?"

"No," Leggett said. "Just the third floor. Chemistry Department has the second floor, Electrical Engineering and Computer Science occupy the ground floor."

"Everybody's talking about a Mexican. Do we know the suspect is a Mexican? Is this speculation or fact?"

Leggett flipped back one page in his shirt-pocket-sized notebook. "Our suspected perp is one Julio Pacheco. Works for University Maintenance. Had the job for just under three years. Clara woke up some guy in Personnel and got Pacheco's folder; some of the boys have already checked the suspect's apartment, but he's long gone, of course. Our guys found a green card that looks like a fake. We'll get a search warrant tomorrow morning, give his digs a thorough going-over."

"Clara said she put out an APB."

"That's right," Leggett said. "State cops should have roadblocks up in a half dozen spots from Gunnison over to Pueblo, and Alamosa up to Leadville."

Parris glanced apprehensively at the laboratory door. "What about the, uh, corpse?"

"Female. Graduate student. Really gruesome. Simpson's in there now. Once he's done with the body, I'll bag all of the evidence, check for prints and fibers, the whole ball of wax."

Parris beamed at the young man. Leggett had completed the FBI's eleven-week National Police Academy course with high marks. If only he had a half dozen bright fellows like Leggett, Piggy took early retirement, and Eddie Knox landed a job doing stand-up comedy. It was one of his dearest fantasies. He slapped Leggett on the back with a force that rattled the young officer's teeth. "Good work, Lieutenant. With the exception of the folks from the coroner's office, don't let anyone else, including Officer Slocum, near the crime scene. I don't want anyone entering that room until further notice. Put a department padlock on it before you leave. Ditto on the suspect's apartment."

Parris attempted to prepare himself mentally for the ordeal; he pushed the lab door open and was assailed by mixed odors—the corpse's blood and the medical examiner's raw alcohol. Walter Simpson was between him and the body, evidently studying it thoughtfully. The physician heard the footsteps and turned to glare under his bushy eyebrows at whoever might be intruding on his domain. The medical examiner's gruff appearance dissipated when he recognized Scott Parris. They had met only a few months earlier but were already good friends.

Simpson grimaced and raised his hand to hold the chief at bay. "You won't like this, Scott." He had firsthand knowledge of Parris's distaste for corpse viewing. They had worked a bad accident on a steep jeep road only a month earlier. Parris had been searching a dark ravine for a body when he stepped in something slippery. He had wiped some of the shiny material off his boot sole for a closer inspection. It was a splattering of human brain. The chief had been sick and Simpson had been thoughtful enough to keep this piece of information to himself.

Parris steeled himself as he moved past Simpson. He was totally unprepared for the sight that had turned Piggy into a blubbering child. For a fleeting moment, his mind could not accept what he saw. He wondered, irrationally, if this could be real. It was a scene from a grade-B horror film. The young woman's body was nude; her jaw shifted sideways, as if it was completely unhinged from her skull. Her clothing was scattered across the floor in a random fashion—a yellow dress splattered with blood, black spike heels, panty hose. An implement that appeared to be a heavy screwdriver was buried almost to the handle in her left eye socket. The socket was filled with blood that had spilled out and soaked into her lustrous dark hair. Her abdomen had been ripped open by a half dozen slashes; entrails were exposed, spilling out onto the floor. His mind reeled under the impact. This looked less like a human being than a small animal that had been ripped apart by a wild beast.

He couldn't tear his gaze from her face; the right eye was open, staring cyclops-fashion at the ceiling. This blank uninjured eye was, somehow, more obscene than the nude, mutilated body. Parris's knees wobbled; he steadied himself on a file cabinet and felt an irrational burst of anger. Why the hell didn't Simpson close the undamaged eye?

Parris finally turned his back, unwilling to look at the pitiful, pale wreck of a body, its small, delicate face framed by a swath of blood-soaked raven black hair. He realized that he did not think of the corpse as "her," but as "it."

Simpson was on his knees, humming something that sounded vaguely like a Strauss waltz. Yes, "Tales from the Vienna Woods." With professional detachment, he removed a ten-inch mercury thermometer from the rectum of the corpse. He squinted at the instrument. "Temperature is thirty-five point one degrees Celsius. Victim probably died just about the time the crime was reported. May be able to tell you more after I do a complete workup." The old man grunted an arthritic's grunt as he pushed himself to his feet.

Parris closed his eyes and fought to suppress the nausea. "Was she raped?"

Simpson was inserting the mercury thermometer into a leather case. "Don't know. I understand old Sure-Shot Slocum got here pretty damn fast; maybe he interrupted the criminal. Be able to tell you more late tomorrow. Drop by around five-thirty or six."

Parris watched the medical examiner gather up the tools of his trade and pack them neatly into his black leather satchel. He wondered idly whether Simpson used these same instruments on his living patients, but thought it impolitic to ask. Simpson appeared to be bone-tired as he headed for the door. "Let my boys know when you coppers are through with your photographs and all that fine detecting you do. They'll pick up the body."

After Simpson had left, Parris found a tattered lab jacket and draped it over the pale body. The instrument in her eye socket held the white smock up, tentlike, above the victim's face. Parris bellowed for Leggett, whose face immediately appeared in the lab door.

"That fellow who called in the disturbance, the teacher . . . is he around someplace?"

"I stashed him in his office. Figured you'd want to do the interrogation. He's just down the hall."

"Did he identify the body?"

A faint shadow of professional concern passed across Leggett's face. "Well, no. Poor guy's pretty shaken up; didn't want to view the corpse. I told him a young woman was dead in the lab, but he said he couldn't bear to look at a dead body. Considering the shape the corpse was in, I didn't want to push him. He sort of looked like . . . well, like he might keel over."

Parris felt strong empathy for anyone who didn't wish to view a corpse. "So how do we know who she is . . . was?"

"There was a driver's license in her purse. Had her photo on it. Victim's name is Priscilla Song. Professor Dexter said she was a graduate student."

Parris examined the room, keeping his eyes away from the small form under the lab coat. The cotton smock was soaking up blood like a sponge. He knelt down to study each piece of clothing that had once covered the victim's body. He could see nothing that helped shed light on this crime, except that the killer had evidently been in a hurry. Her yellow dress was ripped into shreds. He stood upright and noticed that the computer screen was emitting an unnatural hue of blue light.

Leggett nodded toward the display. "It was on when I got here."

"Maybe," Parris said, "she was working on the computer when the bad guy showed up."

"Let's have a look-see." Leggett stepped over the covered body and seated himself in the creaky swivel chair at the desk. "We're lucky. It's one of those Macintosh jobs. Transparent operating system. Easy to use. My wife bought one for her real estate business, so I know a little about it."

Leggett, Parris knew, was modest to a fault. If he admitted he "knew a little," it meant he could write a manual on the infernal thing.

The lieutenant paused before his fingers were on the keyboard. "Want me to check on it now or save it for the experts?"

"If you can have a look without altering anything, have a go at it."

"Looks like," he said, "she was using a word processor. Only there's no file open. I hope it was saved."

"Can you find the last file she was working on?"

Leggett rubbed his hands as if he were preparing to play a piano concerto. "I'll do some checking. I think we have a shot at it."

"Forget the 'we' stuff, kid," Parris said amiably. "I don't know one end of a computer from the other. You'll have to manage on your own. I'll go have a chat with our witness while you deal with the machine."

Parris found Arnold Dexter in his office, pacing back and forth like a caged panther, nervously wiping his freckled hands over a balding head. The policeman flashed his badge and identified himself. "You the guy who reported this sorry business?"

The slender, pale man nodded. "Professor Arnold Dexter. Chairman of the Physics Department." He seemed close to tears.

"Tell me about it," Parris said gently.

"I was at my desk. Heard the awful screams. I wanted to help, but I'm not a *physical* person." He appeared to be embarrassed by the appearance of cowardice. "Even so, if I had known it was Priscilla who was in danger . . ." He peered at the policeman through thick spectacles, silently appealing for understanding.

"You know . . . knew the victim, then?"

Dexter collapsed dramatically into his desk chair and buried his face in his hands. "Of course. Priscilla was one of our most promising graduate students. I was her thesis adviser until Waldo took over the ceramic armor project last semester."

Parris had his notebook open. "Waldo?"

"Professor Waldo Thomson. He took over as her thesis adviser several months ago when I accepted the chairman's position. Being department chairman doesn't leave me as much time to work with the students as I would like. There's so much paperwork when you become an administrator."

Parris chuckled and tried to express his sympathy. "Tell me about it. I haven't had time to write a parking ticket in months." Dexter seemed puzzled by this remark. This little guy was dull as a butter knife, a nerd's nerd. Parris dismissed any further thoughts of light conversation and assumed his official tone. "Okay. So what was she doing here so late? I thought the university shut down with the sunset."

"I'm not certain," Dexter said, "but I imagine she was working on Waldo's . . . Professor Thomson's air force armor contract."

There was just the least hint in his voice that the department chairman was worried that Priscilla might have been involved in something less innocent than her adviser's armor project. Parris pulled a wooden chair from a corner and straddled it, leaning forward on the back of the chair. "What were you doing here tonight? Is it customary for you to put in such late hours?"

Dexter rubbed at his eyes with a handkerchief. "Depends on the work load. I'm planning next semester's schedule. What courses will be offered, when they'll be taught, who will teach, estimates of how many students will sign up. It's difficult to get it done during regular hours; there are so many distractions. Classes to teach, lectures to prepare, students continually barging in. I came in this evening to get the job finished."

"I understand," Parris said. "Do some night work myself from time to time; good way to catch up." He smiled to reassure the shaken academic. "I understand you identified the suspect."

The chairman avoided eye contact with the policeman. "It was Julio Pacheco; he's with University Maintenance. Pacheco was in the building only this morning, to look for a gas leak. I believe he was in that lab with Priscilla for a time. Loathsome fellow. There is some gossip that he . . . well, flirted with Priscilla on occasion. I suppose he came back tonight to . . ." Dexter paused as if unable to contemplate what had happened to his student.

"Yeah," the chief replied. "That's usually the way it works.

He may have been following her around for weeks, waiting until she was vulnerable. Anyone else in the building tonight?"

The question seemed to surprise Dexter. "Well, not that I know of. I was in my office until I heard the disturbance, so I can't say for certain." After a few more routine questions, Parris advised the pathetic figure to go home and try to sleep.

Leggett, completely oblivious to the body under the lab coat, was busily checking files on the computer. As Parris entered the laboratory, he heard the young officer exclaim, "Hot damn!" Leggett turned to gawk wide-eyed at his boss. "Take a look at this. I think I found it."

Parris stepped gingerly over the shrouded body and peered over Leggett's shoulder. The file name was "Work-Log." According to the information the computer had automatically recorded, the document had last been saved at 9:23 that same evening. Leggett double-clicked the cursor on the file icon and waited for the stored document to appear on the computer screen.

Parris blinked at the computer. "Remind me. When did the professor call for the police?"

"Nine thirty-five," Leggett said. "Twelve minutes after the file was stored."

The heading read, "Records—Fall Semester"; the file appeared to be a journal of Priscilla Song's daily activities at the university. Leggett scrolled through the document page by page. There were accounts of meetings with students, comments about homework assignments, names of students who had been absent from the Electromagnetics laboratory, and more trivia.

Parris muttered, almost to himself, "Lots of stuff to sort through."

"That's right," Leggett said, "but this word processor can find the last position of the cursor, just before the file was saved. That'll be where she made her last entry." He opened a section of the menu labeled "Utilities" and used the mouse to slide the arrow down five spaces until it was over "Go Back." He released the button. There was a brief whirring from the hard disk; a new page appeared on the screen. At the top of the page were columnar listings of undergraduate students' grades for an Electromagnetics laboratory class. At the bottom of the screen, just to the left of the cursor, there was an inexplicable entry:

z f r c y r t

Paris peered over Leggett's shoulder and scowled. "What in blazes is that?"

Leggett spoke without looking away from the cathode-ray tube. "Maybe," he offered solemnly, "it was the last thing she had a chance to say."

On the desk beside the computer, a few books and catalogs were held upright between heavy onyx carvings. Parris scanned the titles, then removed a small volume. He passed it to Leggett, who raised an eyebrow at the title: *A Layman's Guide to Codes and Ciphers.*

6

Parris arrived at RMP late in the morning; the Physics Department was in a state of collective shock. Faculty and students were gathered in small groups to discuss the horrific murder. A few wept openly. As he passed, they would either interrupt their conversation or speak in whispers. He stopped at the department secretary's office; a young Hispanic woman was tapping at a keyboard. Parris removed his hat and opened a leather case to display his gold shield. "I'm Scott Parris, chief of police. You must be Ms. Waters."

The suggestion seemed to upset the young woman. "Oh my, no!" Kristin . . . Miss Waters called in sick today. I'm from the secretarial pool."

"I need to have a chat with Priscilla Song's adviser, Professor Thomson."

The secretary took him to Thomson's office, pointed at the door, and then left without bothering to introduce him. A brass plate on the door was etched with the name of the occupant: WALDO THOMSON, PH.D.

Waldo Thomson was at his desk, reading the *Wall Street Journal*. From long habit, Parris made mental notes of the man's appearance: expensive suit, very expensive shoes. Broad shoulders, thinning sandy-colored hair circling a large bald spot, pale blue eyes set under bushy brows. Thomson was a few years younger than Arnold Dexter, and he was considerably more robust than the department chairman. There was a hint of middle-aged bulge under the silk shirt, but Thomson showed ample evidence of hard muscles; he had the leathery-skinned look of an outdoorsman. Even so, the man seemed to fit quite naturally into his bookish environment. Were these academics all of a type? That was absurd. Did all cops have flat feet? This hypothetical question reminded him of his own feet. A duck had better arches.

Parris entered the office without knocking and flipped open the small leather case that held his shield. The physicist stood up, stubbed a cigarette into a crystal ashtray, and glowered at the badge. "So. A member of the Protect and Serve squad. So much for protection. Now that one of our students is already dead, the cops arrive to put on a show. I suppose you have a lot of questions? Like did she know the Mexican? Did he hang around here? Did he show any interest in her? Did—"

Parris was tired and short of temper, and Thomson was clearly a smart ass. The policeman pointed at the empty chair the professor had just vacated. "Park it there. I'll ask the questions. Your job is to give me straight, civil answers. You understand?" Parris was surprised at the hint of menace in his voice.

Thomson sat down, but his jaw was set and his hands clenched. Parris wondered whether the man would clam up now. He could have cared less. They knew who had killed the student; this visit was little more than going through the motions. Maybe that was why Thomson's accusation had cut so deep. You had to show up and question everyone who knew the victim—it was expected. If the police showed no interest in anyone except Pacheco, the Mexican's defense attorney would make hay of it (assuming they caught Pacheco!), and the DA would have the chief of police for lunch.

Parris forced a thin smile by way of apology. "I understand you are . . . were Priscilla Song's adviser."

Thomson's mouth was a thin line. "That is correct."

The guy wasn't going to offer anything. Snapping at him had

been a dumb move, but it had felt good. "What kind of student was she . . . I mean, was she bright?"

"She was . . ." Thomson paused. "Above average."

"She have any bad habits? Drugs, for instance?"

Thomson's tone was sarcastic. "She didn't share that sort of information with me."

"Does . . . did your student normally work late hours, or was last night unusual?"

His answer was brief; the words were clipped. "She worked when she saw fit. Priscilla had a key to the lab."

"What was she doing last night . . . what type of work, I mean?"

Thomson's eyes now darted left and right, avoiding contact with Parris's gaze. He took a cigarette from a silver box and lit it. "Maybe she was collating data on our air force contract. Lightweight ceramic armor. Maybe she was baking cookies. I damn well don't know what she was doing." He deliberately blew smoke toward the policeman's face. "I understand you're an administrator, a paper-pusher. Does the chief of police usually perform interrogations?"

Parris bared his teeth in a grin; the effect was not pleasant, nor was it intended to be. "Not usually, Professor, but we're short-handed this week. I have a clever lieutenant who's interviewing the important folks; I take care of the small-fry." Time to twist his tail. "Where were you," Parris asked coldly, "say between nine and ten last evening?"

The man paled at the veiled accusation. "Why the hell do you care? You got the Mexican cold, so why poke into my affairs?"

Parris was poker-faced as he drew tiny interlocking triangles in his notebook. "Affairs, Professor Thomson? You were having an affair? With the victim?"

That did the trick. "Now look here, you have no right . . . I was at home last night. Alone, if you must know. My wife left me a few months ago, so I spend my evenings alone."

Parris suddenly felt like a heel. Helen had left, too. Now he spent his evenings alone. He tried to smile; it wasn't easy. "I guess we got off on the wrong foot. Let's start all over. You be civil, I'll be downright sweet."

"Just keep it short," Thomson said sullenly. "I've got a busy schedule."

Parris was leaving the building when he heard the whisper. "Here . . . I say . . . over here!" He turned to see a tall, pale man looking up and down the hall as he gestured for the policeman to enter an empty classroom. The skinny man quickly closed the door behind him. He pushed a bony hand into Parris's grasp. "I'm Harry Presley, Professor Harry Presley. Physics Department. Understand you're here investigating Priscilla's death."

Parris strained to keep from smiling at the odd figure. Presley was about six foot two and thin to the point of emaciation, like the victim of a famine or a World War II concentration camp. His magnified eyes appeared to bulge behind the thick-lensed spectacles, his ears protruded like pink flaps from a skull covered with stretched, transparent skin. Presley's belt barely managed to hold his rumpled tweed trousers around a sticklike waist that was the same circumference as his chest. His Adam's apple jiggled when he spoke. "Nasty business," Presley said. "So brutal, such a terrible waste."

"Certainly was," Parris said. "You acquainted with the victim?"

"Well, not exactly *acquainted*. It's a small department; everyone knows everyone else."

Parris produced his notebook. "Anything you'd like to tell me?"

"Well, everyone knew that Pacheco sniffed around her like she was a bitch in heat. If you ask me, I'd say it was a crime of *passion*." Presley was licking his lips. "There's been talk of drugs, and you know what some girls will trade for drugs. . . ."

"You have any information about illegal drug activity on the campus?"

Presley pursed his lips thoughtfully before he began. "Well, it's only talk, you understand, but it's common knowledge that someone is using the campus as a distribution center for drugs. Also some talk about someone making designer drugs for distribution to the West Coast. For all I know, Priscilla may have been involved with this Mexican fellow in some sort of sordid drug-sex relationship. If I were you, I'd look into that."

"If I were *you* . . ." The policeman forced himself to terminate the response; he had already made one enemy in the Physics Department. Presley was a slug in man's clothing. You often found these types hanging around the edge of a homicide. They knew nothing of value but were eager to talk to the police in the hope of picking up juicy details about the crime. He folded the notebook and tried to hide the disgust in his voice.

"If you think of anything specific, give me a call." He offered his card to the disappointed professor, who had evidently expected to share his darkest suspicions with the policeman. As he turned to leave, Parris heard Presley's last shot. "She was a tease. Wanted all the men to . . . to notice her. Young or old, it didn't matter to Priscilla Song."

Parris stopped abruptly and stared at Presley until the man blinked. "Old, yeah, that reminds me. We have a solid report," he lied, "that some old geezer has been seen following Miss Song around. I don't have a name yet, but"—his eyes swept Presley from head to toe—"we know what the guy looks like."

Presley seemed to shrink. "That seems irrelevant, since it was obviously Pacheco who murdered Pris—Miss Song."

"All we know for sure," Parris continued with an innocent expression, "is that Pacheco ran away from the scene. *Anybody* might have killed her."

The physicist swallowed hard; his Adam's apple bobbled.

"Who knows"—Parris fought to keep a straight face—"maybe this old guy works right here at the university. Might even be someone you know." He glanced at his wristwatch. "Well, gotta go do some paperwork. But I'll be back." Presley watched the policeman march away; he wiped at beads of perspiration forming on his forehead.

Baiting the old gossip, Parris mused as he found the stairwell, had been a pointless thing to do. He had made an enemy of Waldo Thomson and frightened Harry Presley, all in a morning's work. There was nothing to gain by annoying potential sources of information. Tomorrow, he knew he would reflect on his actions and feel foolish. Parris smiled as he pushed the door open and sniffed the crisp mountain air. But tomorrow was far away. This was today!

7

Parris opened the shoe box Leggett had found in Priscilla's closet. There was a photocopy of her RMP entrance application. A stack of of publications from her time at Arizona State was impressive for one so young; she was co-author on a half dozen scholarly articles. Parris made no attempt to read the erudite papers, but the titles dealt with such arcane subjects as diamagnetism, laser spectroscopy, and superconductivity. One publication in the *Journal of Clinical Neurology* fell outside the pattern: "Synergistic Effect of Specific Impurities in Lysergic Acid Diethylamide." It was evidently a cross-departmental collaboration; the other authors were associated with the Biology Department.

There were snapshots. After viewing the mutilated corpse, it was a surprise to learn she had been lovely. It was a sorry business, being a policeman—picking up bits of bodies at accident sites, examining records of lives lost. And calling relatives: That was the truly nasty part. The university registrar had reported that Priscilla Song's parents were deceased; there were no other known relatives. It was time to search for friends.

A sealed manila envelope contained a surprise: a matched pair of "fill in the blank" Last Will and Testament forms you could buy for fifty cents in any stationery store. The first began:

> *Last Will and Testament*
> *of* Priscilla Marie Song

In the Name of God, Amen. I Priscilla Marie Song, *of
the County of* Atascosa, *and State of* Colorado, *being
of sound and disposing mind . . .*

The sole heir was the same person listed on her university
admission form under "Who to Contact in Case of Emergency":
William C. Thorpe. The address was a rural route near Questa,
New Mexico. There was also a telephone number. The second
document was identical except that William C. Thorpe had
designated Priscilla M. Song as his sole heir. The documents had
been signed only a few weeks earlier. Why would one so young,
with so little property, draw up a will . . . and why *now?*

The kosher thing to do would be to fax the New Mexico State
Police and leave the notification of William Thorpe to them. It
was their jurisdiction; it might as well be their headache. But he
had an impulse. No . . . not this time. He dialed the New Mexico
telephone number Priscilla had penned under Thorpe's name.
The machine rang a dozen times; he was about to hang up when
a gruff voice answered.

"Thorpe Ranch."

"My name is Scott Parris. May I speak to Mr. William
Thorpe?"

"Ain't here. What's your business with him? If you're selling
something, we either can't afford it or don't have no use for it
nohow."

Parris knew this man, or at least this type of man. "Not selling
anything. It's personal business and it's very important."

"My boy's been up to Fort Collins." There was a slight pause.
"On business. Expect him back anytime now."

"Could I drop by, say . . . around noon tomorrow?"

Thorpe provided detailed directions for finding the ranch.

Julio Pacheco shivered under the pile of rubble in the concrete
tube that diverted spring runoff under the mountain road. He
had spent the night alternating between fitful naps and periods

of dull fear following any unexpected noise in the forest or along the road. Every time an automobile had rumbled over the high-way above, his muscles had tensed. Would the local cops have the dogs out sniffing for his scent? Julio was not a man who generally feared the creatures of this world, but the vision of hounds on his trail evoked a combination of loathing and terror. When he was a small child, his uncle's pit bull had attacked him without provocation. The boy had almost lost a leg; the infec-tion puffed the limb up until it seemed the skin would surely split under the strain. His mother and aunts had lit candles and prayed to Jesus and the saints, and, to the amazement of the doctor from Tuxtepec, the boy had lived and kept his leg. The ugly scars from the brutish canine's teeth were still there to remind him. He had faced determined men with sharp blades, even guns, without flinching, but he solemnly prayed to God that he would not be confronted by a pack of dogs.

His muscles ached. Julio was terribly thirsty, but the water that rippled through the culvert during the spring melt and summer rains was long gone; the streambed was powder dry. Always optimistic about his misfortunes, Julio mused that this was probably lucky; if it had been summer, a thunderstorm might have dumped enough water to wash him away as he slept. His romantic imagination embellished the headlines. JULIO PA-CHECO, UNGRATEFUL MEXICAN WRETCH, the American newspa-pers would shriek, SAVED BY THE SAINTS FROM THE PIT BULL, NOW DROWNED LIKE A RAT IN A SEWER! What would his mother, his uncles, and his nieces think of such a tale? He had only one goal in mind: to return to Mexico and tell his family what had hap-pened. A man might kill his wife or mistress, if she deserved it. That was certainly acceptable. Once he explained, even his mother would understand his predicament.

First things first, though. He must find water. The Mexican pushed away a large piece of cardboard and blinked at the first amber rays of the morning sun illuminating the eastern end of the four-foot-diameter culvert. No one had been over the road for a half hour, but the rising sun would surely bring travelers. He crawled out of the concrete tunnel, stretched, grunted, and urinated on a tree. Thus relieved, he left the roadside and trudged, parallel to the small highway, through the pine thicket, where he could quickly find shelter in the brush if anyone passed by. He kept the early-morning sun to his left. Even if the road turned, he would move south. Always south.

After he had walked another five miles and dropped to altitudes under six thousand feet, the tall pines were gradually replaced by juniper, piñon, and scrub oak. There was still no water; he was approaching the stage of dehydration where his lips would crack and his tongue would swell. He paused, shaded his brown eyes with his hand, and scanned the horizon. He spotted a windmill less than a mile to the southwest. Where there was a working windmill, there should be a water tank. The hardy Mexican threw his jacket over one shoulder and directed his tireless pace toward the windmill. As he approached within a hundred yards, he saw the pickup truck behind the livestock tank. A gaunt old man was pitching small bales of hay from the truck to a dozen black Angus whose ribs could be counted. Thirsty as he was, Julio decided to move into the grove of juniper and wait until the man left. As he turned, he heard the dog bark. Julio instinctively moved his hand to the ever-present hunting knife in the sheath on his belt; he was rooted to the place where he stood until he realized that the blue-eyed Australian sheepdog was small and apparently not vicious. He continued his steady pace toward the aged rancher, who eyed him warily.

"Well howdy," the old man offered between deliberate chews on a wad of tobacco.

"Howdy yourself," Julio replied through parched lips. "Been walking a long time. Saw your tank from up yonder. Spare me a drink?"

"Help yourself," the old man responded as he waved a hand toward the water tank. "There's a-plenty for everbody."

Julio was relieved. "Don't mind if I do." He dipped up shallow handfuls of the warm liquid and drank slowly so that he would not become ill. Julio had spent considerable time in the vast Mexican desert between Chihuahua and Piedras Negras, some of it on the run from the *federales*. He had learned how a man must deal with thirst.

Julio looked up and saw the old gringo watching him with great interest. Had the rancher heard broadcasts; were the radio announcers describing the Mexican who ran from the place where the young woman's body had been found? Was there a reward? Perhaps he would soon find out.

The old man hesitated before he spoke, then seemed to put away his doubts about this dusty intruder as he noticed Julio's calloused hands. After all, the Mexican did look like a working man, not one of those two-bit drug runners. "You looking for work? I'm getting too long in the tooth to do everything by myself."

Julio grinned in relief. Evidently, the rancher had not listened to the radio today. It would be best to go along until opportunity presented itself. "Maybe. Could use a few dollars and a place to bed down. What do you pay?"

The rancher answered cautiously, almost whining. "Well, that depends on what you can do. Times is hard in the beef business. Can't offer too much. There's a bunk and wood stove in the tractor shed and the grub is whatever I eat myself. Maybe two dollars an hour?"

The Mexican assumed a downcast look.

The rancher entered into the bargaining. "Maybe two-fifty, if'n you're willing to work hard."

This old man could spot an illegal a mile away. It was not the first time he had hired himself cheap Mexican labor.

"Well," Julio replied with pretended interest, "first, let's check out the grub." He flashed a smile. "If I don't choke and puke, then we'll see."

The old man eased himself off the pickup bed and climbed into the cab. The sheepdog followed. The rancher pushed the door open on the opposite side and motioned to the Mexican. "Pile your ass in here, Pancho. We'll go have us some eats and see if we can work out a deal."

Julio watched the dog as the pickup bounced along the pitted gravel road; the animal sat between them with its tongue hanging from its mouth. The dog stared expectantly ahead, seemingly unconcerned about Julio's presence.

It was time. He dare not wait until they reached a paved road. "Pull over here."

The old man seemed not to hear, so Julio raised his voice over the sound of the clicking valves in the worn-out GMC V-8. "Here. Pull over here!"

The rancher heard him clearly this time. "What? Why? It's more'n a mile 'til we get to the blacktop."

Julio reached across, shut off the ignition, and removed the key. The old man cursed and slammed on the brakes. "You crazy Mexican, you altogether loco or what?"

The dog seemed to be confused, and offered no raised hackles or bared teeth. For this, Julio was grateful. "This is adios, old grandfather. You and the mutt get out."

The rancher reached for the glove compartment, but Julio grabbed his wrist and pushed it back to the steering wheel. The Mexican pressed the latch on the glove compartment; the door fell open to reveal a .22-caliber single-action revolver housed in a worn leather holster. Julio removed the revolver from the holster and cocked the hammer. "Out of the truck now . . . don't borrow trouble."

The rancher was hoarse with rage. "It's my truck and my land. I ain't lettin' nobody, 'specially no wetback, order me around. You get out."

Julio sighed. The old man was just like his father; he had plenty of grit. It was too bad; he could have liked the hardheaded old cowman. With no warning, Julio swung the revolver barrel and struck the rancher with a sharp blow to his temple. The old man yelped, then slumped against the door. The sheepdog growled and attached its sharp teeth to Julio's sleeve. He slammed the gun barrel down hard, just behind the animal's head; the dog died instantly. He didn't feel bad about the small beast, but the old man really had balls. It was a shame to leave him on foot, but a man on the run from the law had few options. Julio carried the rancher several yards off the road and gently propped his limp form against a large piñon tree. The outlaw climbed into the old pickup and checked the gas gauge. It was just a notch above three-quarters; that was good luck. Perhaps the saints were watching over him. It was a good eight hours before dark, and he had a long way to go over unpaved back roads that would, he prayed, not be watched by the American policemen. He would point his nose south. Always south.

8

"Take a load off," Simpson said. "I'm about done with my final report." He glanced sideways at his haggard visitor. "You look kind of run-down." The dampness in Simpson's basement morgue seeped into his joints. Scott Parris straddled an uncomfortable metal chair. "I've been better."

"We'll have to make that fishing trip down to the Animas, get your soul refreshed. After we get our limit in native browns, I'll take you to the dining room at the Strater Hotel in Durango. My treat." Simpson's eyes twinkled. "For breakfast, they dish out pan-fried trout and eggs that'll make you say, 'Why thank you, ma'am, I'll be back for more soon as I get over this.' "

The policeman didn't look at the small form on the marble slab that was, thankfully, covered by a coarse pea green sheet. Simpson pushed the button on his Sony cassette recorder and cleared his throat. "Pulmonary condition marked. Plural and abdominal cavities contain normal amounts of fluid. Lower edge of liver is one point five centimeters below the costal margin on the midclavicular line. Heart weighs two hundred and ten grams, appears normal in all respects. Right lung weighs six hundred and twenty grams, left lung five hundred and ninety grams. Both lungs are edematous, moderate congestion. Trochesbronchial tree exhibits no foreign material or obstructive bodies. Liver weighs one thousand two hundred and thirty grams, also exhibits congestion, and has dark purple color."

Parris waited patiently for the bottom line as the medical examiner continued his monotone report to the rotating magnetic tape.

"Vertical fracture of left mandible. Caused by horizontal blow, judging from associated bruising pattern. Removed Phillips screwdriver from left orbit. Implement has shaft with five-millimeter diameter, eleven-centimeter length. Tip of screwdriver has a sharp point. Penetration was approximately eight point five centimeters, depth referenced to initial penetration in lacrimal bone, on nasal side of globe, which was not grossly damaged. Death ascribed to extensive cranial hemorrhage in left frontal and left temporal lobe, which was complicated by asphyxia immediately subsequent to strangulation."

He paused and glanced at Parris, who was somewhat pale. "Want a cup of coffee? Got a fresh pot upstairs; you know where to find a cup and everything."

"I'm okay. Been missing a lot of sleep."

The medical examiner cleared his throat and returned to his professional monotone. "Five wounds on abdomen followed death, penetrations of stomach and large intestine. Incisions appear to have been made by the blade of hunting or butcher knife, probably at least four inches in length." He detailed the location and depth of each incision. "One shallow laceration in liver, two more in large intestine, which is distended and empty. Stomach pierced by three-inch incision, some contents spilled into abdominal cavity. Kidneys weigh three hundred and twenty grams and are normal. Spleen weighs one hundred and ninety grams and is congested; bone marrow is dark red in color." He paused, Parris thought for dramatic effect, and continued. "No fluid material found in the vaginal canal, but two vaginal-smear swabs were prepared and will be submitted for analysis. External genitalia show no signs of contusion or abrasion."

Simpson pushed the OFF button and turned to see how his friend was receiving this report. "You want the layman's version?"

"Give it to me in two-bit words."

"The assailant grabbed his victim by the neck, probably with his left hand, and slugged her left jaw with his right hand. Must have hit her hard, because the blow broke her jaw. After this, he strangled her until she was unconscious or at least until she was weak enough so she couldn't put up a fight. Then, while her heart was still beating, he stabbed her through the left eye socket with the Phillips screwdriver to finish the job off. After she was dead—that is, when her heart was no longer pumping blood—he made several long incisions into her abdomen. It'll all be in the report."

The policeman felt a nervous twitch in his jaw, imagined the sensation of pain as the steel rod penetrated her eye. "He apparently took the knife with him," Parris said. "We've combed the building and grounds, turned up nothing. Can you help me on motive?"

Doc scribbled on a yellow pad. "No evidence of sexual contact."

"Then what do we have?"

The medical examiner peered over his spectacles at the policeman. "Could be sexual, in a twisted way. Maybe he gets his jollies from cutting up his victim. It's been known to happen. Then, it may be something more simple. May have something to do with drugs."

"You're suggesting the murderer was freaked out on crack or LSD? Is that why he butchered . . ."

Simpson discussed murder the way a gardener discussed compost. "Could be he was freaked out. Could also be that he was sober as a Mormon; could have been an argument over drugs. Sometimes, when a deal goes sour, the doper cuts the victim up as a warning. Keeps the other troops in line and all that."

"You think the Song girl might have been part of this campus drug ring we keep hearing about?"

"Maybe. Or maybe she was a DEA undercover agent and the Mexican made her. On the other hand, perhaps the girl was working on a new designer drug. There's been a persistent story about something like that making the rounds of the campus rumor mill. There's serious money in that kind of business; maybe this Mexican had a deal to buy the formula from the girl. Maybe she changed her mind or maybe she was unsuccessful and he thought she was holding out. Maybe, maybe, maybe. You're the investigator; go out and investigate. You tell me, then we'll both know."

Parris bowed his head and closed his eyes. A murder that had initially seemed so simple was now becoming complex. That was bad news for the prosecution. Any defense attorney worth his pay would pick at every tiny inconsistency to raise doubts in the minds of the jury about the most inconsequential matters the prosecution couldn't explain. He felt sad for himself, sad for the victim. He had an impulsive urge to pray for all of the Priscilla Songs in the world, even for the world itself.

He looked up at the coroner. "Why strangle *and* stab the victim? After he'd broken her jaw, why not simply strangle her? And the screwdriver . . . it doesn't make sense to leave a murder weapon behind. It's not something a pro would do."

"Maybe he heard Slocum's siren and lost his cool. Even professionals panic and screw up. The very thought of Piggy carrying a loaded revolver should frighten all of us." Simpson frowned as he removed his rubber gloves and stepped on the lever to raise the top on the stainless steel wastebasket. "You can never tell what they'll do or why. We had one in Denver, back in 'sixty-eight, where this hobo beat his traveling buddy to death with a frying pan, then carved his Social Security number on his victim's chest. He was picked up the same day."

"What about the screwdriver," Parris asked, "any decent prints?"

"Had a look with my reading glass; lifted two good latents. Made enlargements and faxed them to the FBI last night. If they match anything on file, you should have the results in a couple of days. The murder weapon is over there"—Simpson pointed toward a brown paper bag on the floor—"along with fingernail scrapings, victim's hair samples, stomach contents, and originals of the fingerprints."

"We lifted prints from Pacheco's apartment and truck," Parris said. "We'll compare them to the latents on the screwdriver. Leggett's requesting prints from everyone who works in the building where she died."

Simpson raised an eyebrow. "You've only been in Granite Creek a few months; you don't know those folks at the university. They won't like the notion of being fingerprinted. Touchy bunch, those academics."

Parris chuckled. "Tough cheese."

Walter Simpson sighed. "If I was young again, I might take up police work. Wear a smart uniform, blow my siren at pretty girls, eat jelly doughnuts. Wait for the friendly medical examiner to explain what happened. Yessir, sounds like the soft life, all right."

The chief started to respond to this, but he was tired of conversation. He planned to sleep at least eight hours before he left for the Thorpe Ranch. Parris gingerly picked up the paper bag that contained the instrument of murder. He had already turned for the door when he remembered. "Almost forgot. My boys found another body for you a couple of hours ago. Some old rancher from south of town. Lone Pine. He's been hit pretty hard, too."

"Who is he?" Simpson had been around long enough to have lots of friends.

"Sikes," Parris said, "don't remember his first name."

This was evidently not one of the medical examiner's friends. "Well, that's another fat fee from the county. If this cash flow keeps up, I'll be able to take down my shingle and retire to the fishing hole in a year or so." Simpson's eyes twinkled as he looked accusingly at his friend. "How come I haven't had a homicide victim to look at in over three years and now I have two in as many days? You gonna put a stop to this crime spree, or should I hire an assistant to help with the work load?"

Parris rubbed his chin thoughtfully and realized he hadn't shaved in two days. "Looks like it was Pacheco again; he took the dead man's pickup. Leggett made plaster casts of some boot prints at the scene; they're a good match to the ones the Mexican left on the lawn at the university when he was dodging Slocum's bullets. We sent the description of the stolen truck to every cop within six hundred miles. If Pacheco's smart, he'll ditch the pickup first chance and steal something else. We'll either have the bastard in custody within forty-eight hours or we'll never catch him. He'll disappear in Mexico or one of the big Latino neighborhoods in L.A. or Dallas."

The chief headed for the door but was halted by Simpson's voice.

"You didn't ask me if there was anything unusual about the corpse, so I guess you prefer to wait and read it in the written report."

Parris wheeled and grimaced with mock anger. "What are you holding out on me, you old coot? Did she have the Mexican's identity bracelet in her hand?"

Doc chuckled. "No such luck for you, copper. But she did have something else. There were two abrasions in the roof of her mouth. Never seen anything quite like it on a corpse before. Another thing—I found traces of a white adhesive material between her breasts; looks like she might have had something taped there."

Parris was backing out of Simpson's driveway when his radio crackled to life. It was Clara Tavishuts. He keyed the microphone. "Car Six here. What's the problem, Clara?"

"Chief? Been trying to get you. Why don't you answer your calls? You ought to wear that beeper when you're away from the car, or at least tell me where you're going to be. . . ."

Parris was tired and somewhat annoyed. "I will not wear an

infernal beeper on my belt, and I don't want to be getting telephone calls everywhere I stop. Get to the point. I'm going home for some shut-eye."

"Better stop by the station first. You have a visitor and she's been parked here for a couple of hours." When Parris heard who his visitor was, he was both pleased and worried. It was a special lady he had wanted to meet, but someone who could be a royal pain under the present circumstances.

Parris saw her as soon as he entered the station door. She was sitting, with her long legs crossed, on one of the hideous green vinyl couches that flanked the entry hall. Before she looked up, he paused, removed his hat, smoothed his hair, and checked to see that his dark blue shirt was neatly stuffed into his trousers. He sucked his gut in and walked through the swinging glass doors into her presence. The woman was stunningly beautiful. When she heard his footsteps, she turned her head. Long red hair rippled in shimmering waves around her shoulders. He wondered whether the ivory color of her skin was accomplished with makeup, but he preferred to believe that it was natural. The slender woman smiled as she retrieved a small purse and got to her feet. Parris's heart skipped a beat and he felt foolish. He also felt ten years younger. He removed a glove and accepted her small hand as she introduced herself. Her hand was warm and soft; he held it in his grasp for a moment longer than proper etiquette would have deemed appropriate.

Her voice was smooth and sweet; milk and honey. "I'm Anne Foster. I work for the newspaper."

There was the least hesitation before he found his voice. "I know who you are. Read your column every Sunday. Your picture's right by it." He groaned inwardly; it was a safe bet she knew that. "You write . . . uh . . . pretty good." That sounded lame. He wanted to bite his tongue, but she didn't seem to notice that the new chief of police was uneasy in her presence. Or perhaps she did.

She flashed a dazzling smile and he was completely disarmed.

"It's very sweet of you to say so." Parris grinned like an idiot and didn't care. Very sweet indeed!

When she got no response from the grinning chief of police, Anne took him by the arm and guided him as if he were slightly tipsy. "May we talk somewhere more private, Chief?" When he seemed disoriented, she led him to his office. As he opened his office door, Parris noticed Clara Tavishuts peeking over her radio console. He could feel his pulse thumping in his neck. The Ute woman winked at him suggestively and Parris turned blood-red as he hurried Anne inside and closed the door. Clara was definitely becoming a discipline problem, but that could wait. He hung his worn London Fog raincoat and archaic felt hat on the wall pegs while Anne made herself comfortable in a rocking chair in the corner of his office. He hardly knew what to say, but he coughed with self-consciousness and tried (with limited success) to avoid staring at her legs. Parris was almost overcome by an irrational fear that he would break wind or hiccup in her presence. He did his best to assume an official tone. "And what can I do for you, Miss Foster?"

He was rewarded with the dazzling smile again as she smoothed her skirt. His gaze was fixed dumbly on her knees when she answered. "Considering our professions, we'll probably be seeing lots of each other. Why don't you call me Anne."

He opened his mouth to reply, but his throat was suddenly dry. Parris cleared his throat and tried again. "Fine. You can call me Scott. Or Scotty."

He couldn't believe what he had said. Only Helen and his father had ever called him Scotty; he *hated* being addressed as Scotty. He felt guilty, as if Helen's ghost might be looking over his shoulder at this radiant woman.

Anne began to rock ever so slightly. She was wearing a black silk skirt. It was snug around her hips. Her gray sweater was loose. "All right. Let's see if we can do some business together," she said, pausing deliberately, "Scotty."

Parris, with great effort, began to exercise control of his behavior. No woman, not even Helen, had ever had this effect on him. "What type of business . . . Anne?"

She stopped rocking and leaned forward slightly. "The Song murder. It's my job to report it and I'm having trouble getting anything useful out of your staff."

Aha! That was her game. It delighted him, the knowledge that he had something she wanted. "All the information is in the official record," he lied. "Usual stuff, identity of victim, time of death, identity of suspect, the whole ball of yarn."

Her expression was now not quite so friendly. "I know that Priscilla Song was murdered in the physics laboratory at the university. I also know that you have an APB out for one Julio Pacheco, a university employee who turns out to be a Mexican national with faked ID and a forged green card."

"That's about it. You know pretty much what I know."

She got up from the chair. "What I want to know, Scotty, is *everything* you know." Anne Foster placed her hands flat on his desk and leaned dangerously forward. The sweater hung loosely. "I want," she said firmly, "to see the autopsy report."

He answered automatically; the voice he heard seemed disconnected from himself. "The final report isn't quite ready yet, but I'm sure the medical examiner is doing his breast." Parris wondered why she smiled at this remark; his hands felt cold, almost numb. "You must know how particular Simpson is about crossing the *i*'s and dotting the *t*'s on his reports."

"I think I know what you mean." She returned to the rocking chair and made a few shorthand entries in her notebook. "How about the police photographs of the murder scene? Those prints must be developed by now."

Parris unconsciously wiped his brow with his shirt sleeve. "They are . . . but there is . . . uh . . . some evidence that we must withhold. If we're fortunate enough to extract . . . I mean . . . get a detailed confession from Pacheco, we can't take the chance that some smart defense lawyer will have his client recant and claim that he read about the details of the murder in your newspaper.

And even though it's unlikely out here in the boondocks where everyone is near normal, I need some way to screen out false confessions from weirdos." Parris had now regained some of his lost composure. "You're a pro, Miss Foster. I'm sure you're familiar with that aspect of police procedure."

She scribbled more notes and smiled sweetly. Too sweetly, he thought. "You can't blame me for trying, chief, but whatever happened to 'Anne'?"

He returned the smile. "Whatever happened to 'Scotty'?"

"Let's start again," she said.

Parris felt himself relaxing. "I'm going to give you something that's not on the official record yet. We picked up another body earlier this afternoon. Old rancher, lived south of town near Lone Pine. We found boot prints. Looks like he was knocked off by the same guy who killed the young woman. Pacheco evidently stole the victim's pickup truck, so now we know what to look for." Parris assumed the most professional demeanor he could muster. "I hadn't intended to release this until tomorrow, but I'm going to trust you with a first draft of the preliminary homicide report on the rancher."

He removed a document from his right-hand drawer file and slid it over the glass desk top toward Anne Foster. She dropped the report in her purse after a glance at the cover.

"You," she said as she brushed her fingers over his sleeve, "are not half as nasty as everyone says." The effect of her touch was like a mild electric shock; he struggled to hide his reaction to her closeness. Her perfume . . . was it a fragrant marriage of lilac and honeysuckle?

"Have to go now," she said, "got a deadline to meet."

He didn't want her to leave. "The Song girl had a will," he offered.

Her eyebrows arched. "Really?"

"Left everything to some fellow in New Mexico," Parris said. "Her boyfriend. I'm going down to break the news to him. Tomorrow."

"Could I possibly come along! I promise I'll be no trouble."

"Twist my arm?"

"Consider it twisted."

After she left, he remained very still for several minutes and tried to remember every word she had spoken, the slight nuances of expression on her lovely face. He could still sense the presence of lilac and honeysuckle. All the fatigue of the past two days had vanished like the memory of winter on a fresh spring morning. He felt like singing but suppressed the urge, determined to preserve any shreds of dignity that might be left. He suspected that everyone in the station realized how he had been so easily vanquished by this woman with the strawberry hair.

When he finally left his office for home, he paused to speak to Clara Tavishuts. "I won't be in tomorrow. Tell Leggett he's acting chief. I'm off to New Mexico to see Priscilla Song's boyfriend. I'll fill out a travel voucher when I get back. One other thing, Clara, make a note in the log. I gave that newspaper reporter, Anne . . . uh . . . Miss Foster . . . a copy of the preliminary report on the Sikes homicide."

Clara looked up from her radio console with a puzzled expression. "Wonder why she wanted that?"

Parris glowered at the woman. "Why shouldn't she want it? She's a journalist, she collects the news, and the Sikes murder is certainly news!"

"But, Chief," Clara responded with a knowing smile, "Piggy gave her a copy of that report while she was waiting to see you. You know Piggy," she continued with a sparkle in her eyes, "that dumb cop's a sucker for a pretty face."

Daisy Perika trudged slowly along the rocky path at the base of Chimney Rock, her sore feet yearning for rest. The Ute woman was heading home after an afternoon digging wild potatoes. Her small basket was almost filled with the golf ball–sized tubers of *Solanum jamesii*. The recipe, borrowed from the Navajos, was stored in her memory. Add three pinches of salt, a bit of food clay to cover the bitter taste of the wild vegetable, boil for a half hour—they would make a tasty supper. She paused on the shady side of a stunted oak, hung her basket on a branch, and used her digging stick to support her weight as she carefully lowered herself into a sitting position against a sandstone boulder. Daisy leaned her head against a hollow in the boulder and considered whether to scramble an egg to go with the wild potatoes. Her home in the narrow canyon was a long way from the Ignacio Shur Valu, and it would be almost two weeks before Clara would come to take her shopping; eggs must be rationed.

Her thoughts drifted to Nahum Yaciiti. Was the old man truly dead? Armilda Esquibel insisted that she had seen his body, but then Armilda also reported she had seen angels carry him up to heaven. Charlie Moon, who had a level head, figured that Nahum was unconscious when Armilda saw him after the storm passed. The Ute policeman guessed that the old shepherd had regained consciousness and wandered away. Some among the Utes whispered that Nahum might be wandering in the badlands east of the Animas; others suspected that the old alcoholic had fallen into the river. A careful search of the area had yielded neither body nor tracks.

No one, of course, paid the least attention to Armilda's fantastic story about the "shining beings" that, like the Sweet Chariot, had carried Nahum's body into the night sky. Most of the Utes considered the local Mexicans to be somewhat gullible. The priest at St. Ignatius had consulted privately with Armilda about her story, but the Jesuit was a discreet man and would not comment about his view of her incredible report.

Only last night, Daisy had been awakened from a deep sleep by the unmistakable sound of Nahum's Dodge pickup grinding up her dirt lane. She had distinctly heard the rumbling sound of the leaky muffler, the grinding of gears as Nahum shifted into low. When she opened her bedroom door, there was no sign of the bowlegged shepherd or his pickup. The shaman called his name. Her voice echoed back across a deep, fathomless void.

A cool breeze wafted through the junipers; she felt so comfortable, so terribly sleepy. Within moments, Daisy was dozing peacefully, dreaming of her mother. This sweet vision was interrupted by whistling, crackling, rushing sounds. She found herself on her feet. She tried hard, very hard, not to look toward Chimney Rock. The shaman feared what she would see. Curiosity was far more compelling than common sense; she turned to take a quick look at the base of Chimney Rock. The balls of red fire were there on the talus slope—about a dozen of them? Daisy counted thirteen souls; it was a full coven. They danced around in circles, stretching into other shapes, leaping in unnatural pirouettes, whistling a rhythmic sound, blowing the dust aside in great puffs. She hid herself behind the stunted oak and, after she had taken a deep breath, used her digging stick to push a branch aside. She peered through the branches at the frightening spectacle. The fireballs would briefly change into humanlike shapes, kiss lustfully with tongues of flame, then dance away. Following these greetings, they all headed for the same destination; the spheres of fire were climbing the steep pyramidal slope toward the base of the chimney. She remembered her grandmother's whispered warnings: The chimney was "the devil's hitching post, a place where powerful witches gather."

Daisy closed her eyes and mumbled a brief prayer to protect herself from soul loss. This act quelled her growing fear, but only slightly. When she opened her eyes, the fireballs were dancing in a circle on the very crest of Chimney Rock. As she watched in awe, the spheres of flame were extinguished and in their places she could see the naked human bodies of *brujas* and *brujos*, both female and male witches. Those in the mad celebration joined hands and began to intone their blasphemous incantations; she could hear the harsh sounds sweep against the wind and across the clearing to her hiding place behind the small tree. Daisy could not understand all the words, and that was all the better. But she could see the dancers clearly, as if she was viewing the scene through a telescope. She was debating whether to stay or flee when one of the *brujas,* a fat Pagosa woman she recognized, turned to look toward Daisy's hiding place. The witch pointed a stubby finger and began to laugh, a mocking, cruel laughter. "Old hag," she heard the fat *bruja* call out, "our master has special plans for *you!*" The threat sent arrows of ice into Daisy's racing heart. Another witch looked familiar . . . yes . . . this *brujo* was a famous scholar from the university in Granite Creek. Daisy had seen him at the last Sun Dance, where the pompous man had discussed Ute ceremonial rites with great authority. The naked man snorted and made obscene gestures toward Daisy. "Want to ride on this, old squaw?" The other *brujos* began to imitate the obscenities while the *brujas* laughed hysterically at the vulgar sport. In all of her life, Daisy had not experienced such an evil presence or been so filled with paralyzing fear. She wanted to run, but in nightmarish fashion her old legs were like quaking aspen, rooted to the earth as her entire body trembled. More than anything, she wished that Nahum were with her. In her bitter frustration, Daisy wept. She felt that she would surely die. The woman from Pagosa Springs pretended to tremble while the others cackled with unwholesome delight. The witches, nourished by her fear, screamed mocking insults: "Where is your 'power' now, old sack of shit? Who will protect you from our circle . . . will you call upon the dwarf?"

"Nahum," Daisy muttered, her voice breaking, "why did you go away? I am afraid. What should I do?" Almost unconsciously, the Ute shaman's hand moved to her forehead and made the sign of the cross. The witches abruptly ceased their loud mocking cries, their obscene gestures. Daisy made the sign again, this time deliberately, with a urgency born of fear. The voices of the witches became muffled; their wild laughter subsided. All sounds from the pinnacle of Chimney Rock were swept away in a sudden gust of dry wind. When she looked again, the gathering was standing in a circle, immobile and silent, hands solemnly joined around the dreaded presence: A whirlwind of fire, towering out of sight into the twilight sky, rotating ominously in their midst. The presence in the whirlwind called. Daisy cupped her palms over her ears and screamed to drown out the sound of the summons. Immediately, the old shaman found that she could move. As she hurried along the path away from the cursed place, Daisy pulled her shawl between her face and the pinnacle of rock. If *Kwasigeti* decided to show himself, she would not look upon the beast who rode the whirlwind.

9

At Tres Piedras, Parris turned east on Route 64 and headed across the high, barren plateau toward Taos. They were approaching the Rio Grande Gorge when Anne noticed the dilapidated pickup truck on the opposite side of the road. "Pull over," she said, "that poor old man needs help."

Parris steered the Volvo onto the shoulder and rolled the window down. An aged Indian impassively watched a wisp of steam rise from the pickup radiator. "Got yourself some trouble?"

"It could use a drink of water," the old man said.

Parris found the plastic jug in the Volvo's trunk and filled the radiator. "Doesn't seem to be leaking. You should make Tres Piedras without any problem."

The old man left Parris at the pickup; he approached the Volvo in a bowlegged gait. He leaned on the door and grinned at Anne. "Watch real close," he said, presenting an empty right hand.

She watched with wide eyes.

The Indian closed his arthritic hand into a gnarled fist. "What would you like?"

Anne furrowed her brow in mock concentration. "Something nice, I think."

He muttered an incantation, then blew on his hand. "How about something good?"

She flashed her dazzling smile. "That would do nicely."

He opened his hand to reveal a flat pink stone suspended on a leather cord.

"Oh, you're a magician!"

"Only part-time." He winked. "Mostly, I'm a prophet. A minor prophet."

"It's a privilege to meet a prophet. Even from the minor leagues."

He chuckled and dropped the pendant into her lap. "This is for you," he said. "Put it on your neck right now; don't take it off before you should!"

So! The man was a peddler of Indian jewelry who used magic tricks and a line of blarney to disarm his customers. Anne fumbled in her purse to find her wallet. "It's simply beautiful, but I don't have much cash with me. . . ."

"No, no," the old man said, waving away a handful of greenbacks, "this sort of merchandise can't be bought with money." With this pronouncement, he turned abruptly and hobbled back to the pickup. He cranked the engine, released the clutch with a grinding clash of gears, and lurched away toward Tres Piedras.

Parris slid under the wheel. "That old heap needs a muffler. If he was in my jurisdiction . . ."

"I'm sure he's not," Anne said. "See my beautiful pendant? It looks like rose quartz."

"Uh-huh. What'd the old guy charge you for that bauble?"

"This kind of bauble," she said, "can't be bought with money."

As Parris pulled away from the shoulder, he glanced into his rearview mirror. The highway was arrow-straight for miles. "Now that's peculiar," he muttered. "How'd he get away so fast in that old Dodge?"

Anne turned and stared at the empty road behind them. "He's a magician. Part-time."

"Wonder what does he do full-time?"

Anne was slipping the pendant around her neck. "God only knows," she whispered.

The sun was near its zenith when Parris found the entrance to the Thorpe Ranch. The sign was freshly painted and the fences along the lane leading to the adobe ranch house were in good repair, but the blue grama looked very sparse to one who had walked in the knee-deep grass on the black loam of the Illinois prairie. He parked the Volvo a respectful distance from the house and asked Anne to wait until he had a chance to break the ice with the Thorpes. He buttoned his coat, partially against the frigid wind and partially because he didn't want the old man on the front porch to see the shoulder holster, which would immediately suggest cop or gangster.

A thin, stooped man in a western-cut white shirt, new denim jacket, and faded jeans emerged from the shadows on the L-shaped porch that was attached to the west and the south sides of the house. The rancher pulled his wool-lined jacket more tightly around his shoulders and descended the porch steps. Parris approached and stuck a hand out. "I called yesterday. Scott Parris."

The rancher returned the firm grip and nodded toward the house. "Buster's inside."

"Buster?"

"That's his nickname. He always said, since he was a little tad, that he was gonna be a champeen broncobuster, so we started calling him Buster way back then." The old man pushed a hand through his thinning shock of white hair and blinked his hard gray eyes at Parris. "Seems like a long spell ago."

Parris tried to smile but couldn't. "Did he? Become a broncobuster?"

The rancher pretended to study the storm clouds. "Reckon he did. Fair calf roper and passable bull rider, too. What's your business with Buster? Is it . . . trouble?"

He found it difficult to look at the old man's weatherworn

face. "Afraid so. But I need to see him first, then I'll tell you everything . . . if you like."

Thorpe clamped a hard hand on Parris's shoulder and looked him straight in the eye. "Understand. Go on inside and get it done with. I'll go out to the car and visit with the lady."

Parris climbed the porch steps and turned the knob on the heavy Mexican door. The young man was standing, arms folded and legs apart, in front of a massive stone fireplace. While the silhouette of his form was clear against the pile of blazing logs, Parris's eyes had not adjusted from the bright outside light. He could barely see the profile of the young man's face. But the tension was palpable, a stretched wire ready to snap. The Thorpes knew. How did they know? Did he look and smell that much like a cop?

It would be best to get it over with in a hurry, then get the hell away from here. He cleared his throat. "I'm Scott Parris. Appreciate the chance to meet with you."

The young man turned and nodded, but didn't offer his hand. He removed a cloth sack of loose tobacco from the pocket in his rawhide vest and proceeded to pour this into a thin piece of paper with a hand that, almost imperceptibly, trembled. "Daddy said you was comin'."

Parris hardly knew how to begin. In all his years of police experience, he had not had this duty a half dozen times.

"You may wish to sit down, Mr. Thorpe."

"I'll stand. Most folks call me Buster."

Parris's vision was adjusting to the light. The cowboy's face was a page he couldn't read.

Buster licked the paper and sealed the cigarette. "You're a lawman, ain't you?"

"Chief of police in Granite Creek. How did you know . . . ?"

The cowboy placed the homemade cigarette between his lips and searched his pockets for a match. "Daddy said you talked like a policeman when you called. It's Pris, ain't it?"

"Yes."

"If she was just hurt real bad, you wouldn't come all the way down here to tell me."

"I'm afraid Miss Song is . . ." Parris couldn't say it.

The young man's voice was hoarse. "Then she's dead?"

"I'm sorry."

The cigarette dangled, unlit, from the cowboy's thin lips. "How'd she die?"

Parris tried to speak and the words hung in his throat. He felt like an idiot. Why hadn't he let the local officials handle this? He cleared his throat and tried again. The single word came in what was little more than a whisper. "Murdered."

There was an interminable silence. The young man muttered something unintelligible and stomped out a side door. The sound of his steps was slightly uneven; Buster had a gimpy leg. Standard equipment for rodeo cowboys.

Parris stepped off the front porch; he squinted at the bright light reflecting off the barren landscape. The old man was leaning against a fence post. Anne had an arm around his shoulders. So she had told him. Parris was exceedingly grateful to her for this service. She was more than lovely. She was wonderful.

Parris approached slowly, hands in his raincoat pockets. The wind was whipping in from the northwest and it carried the sharp chill of snow. Storms on the high plateau could bring nothing more than sleet pellets that barely covered the ground or they could drop a foot of heavy white stuff. Parris felt as old as the elder Thorpe looked. Small beads of tears clung to the rancher's sunburned cheeks; they seemed to be strangers there, as if the stern face could not afford the luxury of weeping.

Parris looked away. "I've told your son. Didn't seem like he was surprised."

The old man blew his nose in a handkerchief and stowed this in a hip pocket. He pulled his jacket collar over his thin neck. "He wasn't. We figured you was the law. Lawmen don't usually bring good news."

The young cowboy appeared unexpectedly. He threw his roll-your-own onto the hard clay and ground it under his boot heel. "Pris always said I should quit smoking these damn things." He paused. "Tell me how it happened."

"I'll give you the general picture," Parris said, "but I can't provide all the details; it could complicate our investigation and prosecution. You understand."

The cowboy's expression said that he didn't understand, but he let Parris continue. "She was evidently working in the laboratory at the university. Two nights ago, around nine-thirty. Someone entered the room and . . . and killed her. I'm sure she died quickly." It was a deliberate lie, but he wasn't ashamed. The survivors always wanted to hear it.

Buster was, Parris thought, surprisingly calm. "You know who did it?"

"We have a suspect."

"Somebody she knew?"

This question surprised Parris. "Probably knew him casually. He's a repairman; worked for the university. One of our men found him at the scene and he ran. I expect we'll pick him up in a day or so. Why did you think it might be someone she knew?"

Buster looked away. "They say it's usually someone you know. Who kills you."

Parris reminded himself that you never knew how they would react. Buster seemed to be rambling. Probably in shock. "Yeah. I guess it usually is."

The cowboy held out his hand to display a heavy silver ring with a polished oval sky blue turquoise set in a rough dark stone. "This just came in the mail. Pris sent it for my birthday."

Anne touched the ring. "The turquoise is beautiful in the dark setting. It's really very pretty."

Buster didn't acknowledge the compliment.

Parris was watching every nuance of expression on the cowboy's face. "When did you last see her?" he asked.

"Three or four weeks ago, I guess. Talked to her on the phone . . . musta been last week."

"Was she having any problems?"

"Nope. Workin' hard, though. Stayin' up late at night. Missin' sleep."

Parris tried to sound casual. "What was she working on?"

"Dunno." Buster's expression was grim. "She would tell me, but I didn't understand much of it."

He wondered how much this seemingly backward cowboy really knew. About Priscilla's work. About a drug ring on campus. "Try to remember," Parris said. "Anything she said might be important."

"Pris talked a lot about crystals and electrons and such. Before she transferred from Arizona over to RMP, she was interested in makin' better plastics, usin' corn whiskey for gasoline, you name it." Buster was squinting his eyes, keeping his face to the north, away from the sunshine. The cowboy's pupils were slightly dilated. "Then she got this assistantship to work on lightweight armor. I don't think she cared much about that work, but it paid the rent."

Parris opened his mouth but was interrupted by Anne. "Had she had any trouble with anyone at RMP?"

"Not so far as I know," the cowboy replied. He was watching the heavy gray clouds build in the northwest. "She didn't care for some of the folks there, but she never talked about it much." He grabbed the brim of his Stetson to prevent a sudden gust of wind from lifting it skyward, then turned to study Parris's face. "You think her work might have had something to do with her . . . her getting killed?"

"No," Parris answered quickly. "Almost certainly not. And don't worry. We'll pick the killer up pretty soon. I'll call you when we do." He had already turned to leave when he remembered. "Was she . . . was Priscilla interested in coded messages . . . that sort of thing?" The question sounded inane.

Buster's expression showed a hint of interest in this query. "Not so far as I know." He paused and Parris could practically hear the wheels turning as the young man considered the relevance of this question. "Why'd you ask?"

Parris pulled his wallet from his hip pocket and removed a slip of paper from a plastic window. "This was in a computer file she was working on right before . . . about the time she died. Mean anything to you?"

Buster cocked his head at the string of characters:

z f r c y r t

The cowboy scratched at a tuft of sideburn. "Naw. Might as well be chicken scratchin's. Is it important?"

Parris pocketed the script and shook his head wearily. "Probably not. Where did you meet Priscilla?"

"At RMP, couple of years ago. I was there when she transferred up from Arizona State."

"Were you a physics student, too?"

"Nope. Majored in electrical engineering." Buster dropped his gaze to the ground. "Kinda got burned out. Daddy needed some help, so I took a semester off."

Buster's father invited them for lunch. Parris, eager to leave, told the rancher that they had eaten a late breakfast and needed to get back before dark. The snowstorm was moving in and he had no chains for the Volvo. As he slipped a key into the ignition switch, Buster Thorpe leaned on the door and studied Parris's face earnestly.

"You don't have no doubt a'tall about who did it?"

The policeman tried to match the cowboy's earnest expression. "Not the least."

As the policeman cranked the six-cylinder engine to life, the young man backed away and considered Parris with an expression that was hard to read. "That's good," he said, "glad to hear it."

Parris lifted his foot and let the engine idle. "I found copies of Priscilla's will. And yours."

A muscle twitched in Buster's jaw. "We was talking about gettin' married. She thought the wills was a good idea, so I said, 'Hell yes, why not.' "

"What's the C stand for?"

The cowboy tilted his head sideways. "Come again?"

"Your middle name," Parris said.

He looked at his boots and kicked a pebble. "Chester, after my grandad. Pris didn't much like "Buster" or "Billy," so she called me Chester."

When they were ten minutes up the road, Anne spoke without looking at her companion. "What was that all about? Did you mean what you said?"

"Well," he answered sheepishly, "I guess I wasn't completely honest with the Thorpes. I shouldn't have claimed that we both had a big breakfast when you ate like a sparrow. Coffee and toast isn't enough to keep a horned toad alive."

She elbowed him lightly. "You know what I mean, silly. Are you really so sure Pacheco is the murderer? All you know for certain is that he was at the scene. . . ."

"We have Pacheco cold. He killed the girl and the old rancher at Lone Pine. May take a few more with him when they try to pick him up." He expected the journalist to pump him for information about the murder scene, but she didn't. Probably, he mused, she had already picked up all she needed to know from Piggy. Was she testing him? Trying to learn how much he would withhold?

"I think," she said cautiously, "you should keep an eye on Waldo Thomson."

Parris set the speed control to sixty-five. "The kindly professor? Why's that?"

"He spends more money than he makes. A lot more. And he travels."

Parris raised an eyebrow. "Travels?"

"To South America," she said. "And not on university business."

"You see some connection to the Song homicide?"

"Not yet," she said sleepily. "But I've been checking him out for a long time."

"What about Professor Presley? He suspects Priscilla and Pacheco may have had some kind of . . . relationship. Maybe involving drugs."

"Harry Presley," she said, "is the designated department gossip. Talks to anyone who'll listen. He's harmless." Anne slid across the seat, close to him, resting her head on his shoulder. "I'm cold."

Odd, he thought, he could feel the warmth radiating from her body. "I'll crank up the heater."

"No." She shivered. "Not that kind of cold. Put your arm around me."

He did and she relaxed. It brought back old memories of long, romantic drives when he had first dated Helen. There was a picture in his mind of a red 1954 Pontiac convertible. Long walks on the lakeshore during warm summer evenings. Weekend trips to the Wisconsin Dells. Oddly, the memories did not conjure up pangs of guilt. Helen was finally gone; he was getting comfortable with this lovely woman. That, he decided, was good. Very good indeed.

10

For the third time, Parris read the sheet on William Chester Thorpe. A half dozen arrests for public drunkenness over the past five years, one for driving under the influence, another for public disturbance in a Las Cruces bar. Young Thorpe had, if the report was to be believed, bitten the "posterior third of the left ear" off a staff sergeant from Holloman Air Force Base. The records indicated a court-ordered psychiatric evaluation at a mental hospital in Las Vegas, but there was no information on a diagnosis. Probably the standard exam for a budding alcoholic who chewed off another drunk's ear. Nothing on drug-related arrests. Maybe the dilation of the cowboy's eyes had nothing to do with drugs. Maybe.

As Parris considered the possibilities, the FBI report rolled off the fax. The prints on the screwdriver belonged to a man who had been arrested five years earlier in El Paso; a prostitute charged that he had broken her nose. The charges were dropped when the prostitute vanished before the trial date. The man's name was Julio Pacheco.

Julio Pacheco hated to admit it, but he was lost. He had no map and was weary of bouncing over the rutted back roads. The afternoon sky had become so overcast that even his sense of direction was failing him. When he came to the paved two-lane where the gravel road ended, there was no choice but to turn back or chance being spotted by the police. He switched the engine off and considered his options with some care. In these desolate regions, one state patrol car typically had to cover as much as two or three thousand square miles. The American *federales* would have his description by now, maybe even know about the truck if the old rancher had managed to hitch a ride and find a telephone. On the other hand, the cops had lots of other problems to occupy their time.

Julio twisted the ignition key and listened to the old engine crank three times and fire hesitantly before it finally roared to life. He turned left on the paved road and accelerated gradually until the speedometer needle hung just below fifty. He wouldn't take any chances of getting stopped for a minor infraction. He had killed the dog, and everyone knew that Saint Francis loved animals. The saints, like any group, hung together. If good Brother Francis was upset, the other saints would not be smiling on Julio Pacheco.

The thought of annoying the meek and mild Francis was an unsettling one. He needed some diversion. Julio turned the dashboard radio on; he twisted the tuning knob to find something to soothe his raw nerves. He dialed past a Spanish-language station without interest, chuckled when he tuned in the choppy, incomprehensible syllables of a Navajo announcer, then paused at a country-western broadcast. This porridge was not too hot or too cold; it was just right! The music gradually transported him into a deeply satisfying melancholy; the Mexican threw his head back and wailed along with Willie as tears welled up in his dark eyes: "Bluuue eyes a-cryin' in the raaaiiiin . . ."

Moments after the song was finished, while the announcer was enthusiastically urging his listeners to come by and "have yourself a look at Happy Jack's fine selection of brand-spankin' new Chevrolet trucks," Julio was overtaken by a white GMC Blazer with a pair of red lights mounted on its roof. The words JICA-RILLA APACHE POLICE circled the tribal logo painted on the door. The bronzed man under the Smokey hat gave him a quick once-over as he passed. Julio flashed his most disarming smile and nodded politely. He chewed on the tip of his mustache as the patrol car gradually pulled ahead and then disappeared over a rise. The Mexican, who had not been inside a church since he was a child, crossed himself with great ceremony and thanked all the saints whose names he could remember for his deliverance. He assured them that he had never really doubted them, not even when the policeman had appeared so soon after he decided to risk the paved road. He added, as a postscript, that he was truly sorry about the rancher's dog, just in case anyone in particular was upset. It was best, he knew, not to anger the saints, lest they become vindictive. A saint in a good mood could be a great help to a poor man in trouble, but cross them and you might as well say your prayers!

A mile ahead, the tribal policeman's brow was furrowed with concentration. He had seen most of the old beat-up pickups in this sector, but that one had Colorado plates. He had memorized the number and was in the process of scribbling it into his notebook. Most likely just someone passing through, but a small voice in his subconscious kept nagging. Did the number on the plate sound familiar? Then he remembered the morning briefing. He thumbed the key on his mike, put in his call, and waited to hear the dispatcher answer in a bored monotone. He made his request. "Uh-huh . . . find the bulletin on that guy wanted up in Colorado. That's right. The Mexican with the all-points on him. Read me the description on the stolen pickup and give me the plates." Seconds later, the policeman hit his brakes and did a screeching U-turn on the narrow two-lane.

He made another call and it was a done deal. The dispatcher would alert the state and county cops, and they would set up a roadblock. There were no side roads worth mentioning for twenty miles. The Indian policeman smiled at the prospect of some action. He had not fired his gun on duty since the fat Colombian had crash-landed the twin Cessna on the Jicarilla reservation and tried to escape with nearly $2 million in hundred-dollar bills in a pair of oversized duffel bags. The foreigner, once cornered, had dropped the duffel bags and tried to shoot it out with his Czech submachine gun. The Indian had fallen to a prone position, just as he had been trained in the Marine Corps. He had aligned the scope cross hairs on the fat man's red T-shirt and pulled the trigger slowly as the Colombian's slugs fell to earth a few yards in front of his position. The Apache policeman had dropped his target with a single 30-06 copper-plated slug through his left lung. It was more fun than hunting elk. Elk didn't shoot back.

He hoped this hunted Mexican would panic, make a run for the badlands. That would be great fun—an excuse to shoot his tires out, then hunt him on foot. In his growing excitement, the Jicarilla Apache policeman was talking to himself: "Whatever you try wetback, unless you can make a pickup truck fly, your ass is *mine!*"

He imagined the envy of his fellow officers and the pleasure of his captain when he brought in the desperado who had eluded the net thrown out by the state cops and the Bureau whiz kids in their three-piece suits. It would be especially satisfying to succeed where the FBI had failed and then rub their noses in it!

It was less than a minute before he met the old pickup. He hit the emergency flashers and swerved to block the road. He watched the pickup pull to the shoulder.

Pacheco shifted into neutral and put his foot on the brake; he pushed the latch button on the glove compartment and removed the rancher's single-action revolver and a half box of .22-caliber hollow-point cartridges. It would be bad enough to be taken by a posse, but it was unthinkable to be arrested by a single police-man. It would be embarrassing; his hardcase friends would laugh when they heard that Julio had been picked up by only one little *Indio federale*. He would give a good account of himself; his family and friends could expect no more than this.

Pacheco considered the situation as he checked to make sure the cylinder was fully loaded with long-rifle hollow-point cartridges. The Apache cop was evidently in no hurry. That meant one thing: Roadblocks were being set up. After the arrest, thirty years in an American *cárcel* with an assortment of lunatics, misfits, and queers. The Mexican sighed and resigned himself to whatever his immediate fate might be, but he promised himself that he would never go to prison. Never! He cocked the hammer on the single-action Ruger and shifted the worn transmission into low gear.

The Indian policeman keyed his mike to report the situation to the dispatcher, but the suspect's truck was now moving—accelerating! Surely, the Indian thought, that crazy Mexican didn't think he would get away, not in that old pile of rusty nuts and bolts. The Apache policeman unbuttoned the flap on his holster and removed his revolver with the thought of blowing a front tire off the old pickup. He was expecting the Mexican to make a turn and present a good profile of the tires when the pickup roared across the road and headed directly for the Blazer. The Indian cursed and ground the gears as he attempted to shift the Blazer into reverse. Too late. He was releasing the clutch as the pickup hit him head-on at twenty miles an hour. The policeman's head smacked into the windshield.

As his vision gradually cleared, the policeman blinked several times at the grinning outlaw, who had his head poked into the Blazer window. "I hate to be critical, *Indio policía*," the Mexican scolded with mock severity, "but you should practice the first rule of operating a motor vehicle: Fasten your seat belt. It's just as well you bumped your head, though; now the Bad Mexican may not have to send you to the happy hunting ground."

The policeman swept his hand over the seat in a futile attempt to locate his service revolver, then realized that the Mexican was cheerfully waving the weapon in front of his face.

"Next thing you got to learn, Sitting Bull, is a good *federale* should never lose his firearm."

The Indian glared at his opponent. "Sitting Bull was Hunkpapa Sioux, you Mexican thug. I'm an Apache."

The Mexican laughed heartily, then put on a sad expression. "Too bad we had to meet like this, Geronimo." With this, he stuck both revolvers under his belt, opened the car door, and dragged the Indian out by his heels, giving his head another sound thump when it hit the pavement. When the dazed tribal policeman attempted to get to his feet, Pacheco waited until he was on one knee, then felled him with a heavy left hook. For a brief moment, the Apache could see the blacktop rushing toward his face. Then his world went completely dark.

Pacheco backed the pickup away from the Blazer and was relieved to see that no serious damage had been done to either vehicle. He dropped into low gear and nosed the pickup off the highway into a dry ravine that was deep enough to hide it from road traffic. He dragged the Indian well off the road and, true to his habit, placed the man under a clump of brush that would provide moderate shade from the afternoon sun. He removed all the greenbacks, which totaled more than sixty dollars, from the policeman's wallet. The Mexican helped himself to his victim's wristwatch, pocketknife, and some loose change. For the first time, he noticed the name tag on the policeman's jacket. It announced that the officer was Sgt. K. T. MacPherson. That, he thought, didn't sound like an Indian name at all. "Sounds more like a Scotchman than a 'Pache," Pacheco muttered suspiciously, as if the Indian might be part of some dark conspiracy against him. In the Mexican's world, nothing was without meaning. Could this be an omen? He tried in vain to remember whether there were any saints that hailed from Scotland, saints who might disapprove of his shabby treatment of Sergeant MacPherson.

He removed the Indian's jacket, which had the tribal police shield pinned to its left breast pocket, and covered his victim with a rough, rank-smelling horse blanket from the bed of the pickup truck. Pacheco tried on the jacket and was pleased to discover that it might have been tailored for his own frame. A man who drove a policeman's car, after all, should look like a policeman! MacPherson's hat was two sizes too large and dropped to his ears.

Within five minutes, Pacheco, with his foot on the floorboard, was pushing the Blazer at seventy-five miles an hour in the opposite direction from the presumed roadblock. His good fortune was holding; the gas tank gauge read almost full. He listened to the police radio and chuckled at the dispatcher's urgent calls for Sergeant MacPherson. The Blazer had a compass mounted on the dashboard. The Mexican turned off the highway and headed south across the high plateau. He had enjoyed the encounter with the Indian. It had not been a good thing to slug the old rancher, but the young Indian had been a suitable adversary. He had outsmarted and outfought this descendent of Geronimo. For the first time in days, Pacheco was genuinely happy to be alive. He sang loudly and off-key as he drove across the rocky terrain. It was a sad Argentinian ballad about a young vaquero who found his wife sleeping with another man; honor compelled the betrayed husband to cut out his wife's heart and force-feed it to her unfortunate lover. The song brought enormous content-ment to the Mexican's heart.

"Hi que cabrón," he muttered. The unexpected sound had star-tled him. Pacheco was nearly forty miles from where he had left the Indian policeman, when he heard the throaty *whump-whump* echoing off the steep sides of the red-rock mesas. It was a famil-iar, if not welcome, sound. He had heard it the last time he had crossed the border near Las Palomas. Then, it had been a border patrol copter. Now, he expected, it would be the state police, maybe even the National Guard. He braked the Blazer to a crawl and stuck his head out the window. The copter was a good mile off to the northwest, hovering at a thousand feet above the floor of the high plateau. He shut off the engine; no point in wasting gas. Pacheco considered the situation. If the copter approached, he could take a shot with the Indian cop's revolver or the shot-gun mounted behind the seat, but there was no chance of doing any useful damage unless they were within a hundred yards. Anyway, if he had been spotted, they would have already radioed his position in. He could keep moving, changing directions, complicating their plans to intercept him until dark, which was still hours away. There would be no moon until past midnight. He might have a chance of losing himself in the badlands. If he left the car, the Americans might bring dogs to sniff him out. Julio shivered at the thought of bloodhounds, imagining sharp yellow canines under drooling black lips. He made his decision: no point in prolonging the run until he was exhausted and the dogs came. It would be better to fight the men while he still had some strength left. He suspected it would not be long until the encounter. Morning at the latest. Julio prayed to the saints to preserve him from the dogs. If they would do this one last thing, he promised, he would take on all the gringos and Indians with no further request for help. He felt confident that his prayers would be answered; with such a deal, how could the saints refuse? If Death came calling, he would die like a man. His relatives would have no cause for shame. Pacheco cranked the engine and headed southeast toward a shallow sandstone canyon, moving slowly to keep the dust trail at a minimum.

11

Julio Pacheco was, ever so gradually, relaxing. The hunted man had not heard the sound of the helicopter since the sun had dipped low over the Continental Divide, casting long, indistinct shadows behind stunted junipers and sandstone boulders. Maybe the pilot of the copter had not seen him. Perhaps the saints had heard his prayers and were in a generous mood. He had expected to be stopped when he crossed Interstate 40 at Acomita, but there was not a policeman in sight. Pacheco hoped that Death had more pressing business; perhaps another less fortunate soul would feel the sharp edge of his broad scythe tonight. With new confidence, he topped the tank off at a Shamrock station and bought a handful of candy bars. The hunted man had been alert for any unusual activity as he drove south across the Acoma reservation in the Apache policeman's Blazer, but he had seen less than a half dozen souls and was regarded with nothing more than casual glances. He was relieved when he drove over the dry wash of the Rio Colorado, which formed the southern boundary of the reservation. The Rio Salada was also dry, but this dusty riverbed marked the beginning of the truly desolate country. Perhaps the *Yanqui* lawmen had lost his trail. Julio began to entertain hopes that he would live to see his mother. Once it was dark, before the moon showed its orange face over the rough peaks of the Sierra Lucero, they would have little chance of finding him. Safety was only hours away; the

Mexican border was less than two hundred miles as the raven flies.

Julio pulled the Blazer off the rough road and shifted into low gear as he looked for a suitable place to conceal himself, to rest for a few hours. It would be best to wait until the moon was up, then drive without lights. He made his way with great care between stunted cedars and rough outcroppings of basalt until he found a small overhang of sandstone. The sandstone shaded a gentle slope that led to one of many dry washes that drained the Gallinas Mountains when the infrequent rains came. He got out, stretched his back, and sighed with contentment. The air felt crisp, clean, odorless. Julio Pacheco had never known boredom; life was a continuous, exciting adventure!

The Mexican made a long, circular hike that encompassed his campsite. Pausing frequently to listen, he could see no lights, hear no engines or voices or any unnatural sound. In this uninhabited wasteland, there was only the infrequent yip-yip of a distant coyote and an occasional short hoot from a speckled owl secreted in one of the junipers. Back at his makeshift camp, he curled up in the rear seat of the Blazer, intending to sleep until the moon rose over Ladrones peak.

Presently, Julio dreamed of his mother, and also of his nieces, and Uncle Fortunata. They were seated on wooden pews in the gray stone church in Tuxtepec that his mother attended faithfully three times every week and more often during holy feasts. He stood at the doors and looked in; there was a black coffin by the altar rail. A young priest was sprinkling holy water over the coffin as he read from a small white book. Pacheco walked slowly up the aisle between the mourners, but they did not notice his appearance among them. As the dreamer approached the coffin, the priest flung a vial of holy water toward the unwelcome guest. The water erupted from its silver container and was transformed into a raging, splashing torrent that washed the terrified Pacheco from the church. He could hear the priest's voice as he was swept away: "Repent Julio. The saints can no longer hear you. They weep for your soul. Repent!" Pacheco could feel himself drowning and was grateful to return to consciousness. Small beads of sweat dotted his forehead; seconds ticked by before he could remember where he was. He blinked at the eastern sky; the moon was at least four disks high. He cursed himself for his self-indulgence in sleeping so long; he should have been moving south as soon as the moon appeared on the horizon. The hands on the luminescent dial of the Apache policeman's watch indicated that it was already well past midnight.

Julio grunted with stiffness, rose to his feet, and stretched luxuriously. After urinating on the tire of the Blazer, he tore the paper open on a Mounds and popped one of the chocolate-covered bars into his mouth. He flicked half the wrapper aside and closed his eyes as he leaned against the Blazer and chewed slowly on the sweet grated coconut. Life was truly wonderful. How terrible it would be to cease living! What did the priest in the dream know? The saints were surely watching over him, and it was better to have one reliable saint for a friend than a hundred fickle priests.

His eyes were still closed when the pair of red laser beams pierced the night like silent arrows of blood. The moving beams first reflected uncertainly off the Blazer window and then found their intended target. They danced on Pacheco's broad chest like playful fireflies, but he was unaware of their presence. It was the man's voice, booming out of the pitch-darkness, that startled him.

"FBI. You're under arrest! Hands on your head. Do it *now!*"

Pacheco dropped the candy bar and instinctively reached for the revolver stuffed under his belt. His hand had barely touched the grips when he felt a heavy blow to his shoulder, then heard a great explosion. Within seconds, two men in camouflage fatigues were standing over his body, while a third man in a Forest Service uniform was applying a pressure bandage to the wound. The bandage was, in the bright light of their electric lantern, rapidly turning from white to bright crimson.

The special agent from the Albuquerque FBI office dropped to one knee for a closer look. He turned to grin at the Apache policeman, who aimed a revolver at Pacheco's head. "Say, Mac-Pherson, this fellow's wearing a 'Pache shield and a jacket just like the one you lost. You sure he's not one of your fellow officers?"

The Apache did not smile at the jibe; he cocked the revolver and prayed silently that Pacheco would give him an excuse. "Why don't you fellows go get the stretcher from the copter. I'll keep an eye on him." An involuntary twitch; a muscle spasm. Any little excuse.

The forest ranger left to get the stretcher. The FBI agent got to his feet and kicked at the candy wrapper. "I've learned to put up with gunrunners, kidnappers, and bank robbers, but one thing I simply can't abide," he drawled, "is a damned litterbug."

A uniformed policeman examined Parris's ID, then opened the door without a word. A nurse was attending Pacheco. The Mexican, whose left shoulder was wrapped in bandages, waved with his right hand. "Hello, gringo *federale.*"

"You know who I am?"

Julio smiled weakly under the thick mustache that framed his faultless teeth. "Seen you around town a couple of times. You're the Chicago cop who took over that hick police force in Granite Creek."

Parris pointed at the bandages. "Hear you caught one. You seem to be in pretty fair shape, considering you've been shot."

Pacheco coughed and grimaced with pain. "I'll get along. You come to take me back?"

"I've filed the papers for your extradition to Colorado. If you heal fast, you'll be ready to travel in a few days."

Pacheco was doing his best to exude machismo. "Hey, man, it's no big deal. Back in 'seventy-six, I was knifed by my second cousin; we got drunk and fought over a Cuban whore in a little dirt-floor bar in Ascenscíon. Cousin Paco, now he's a first-class knife artist; laid my belly open from crotch to ribs. Paco felt real bad when he got sober; cried like a baby, swore he'd kill himself if I died. But I lived, because the saints, they watch over me. You want to see the old scars on my belly?"

Parris placed a miniature tape recorder on the bedside table and pressed the RECORD button. He grinned at the scrappy Mexican. "Sounds like a rare treat, but I'll pass." He removed a card from his wallet and read the standard Miranda statement. "You understand your rights? If you can't afford a lawyer, the Court will . . ."

"I don't want no damn *abogado*, man. They just take your money and wave good-bye. Could you pass that pitcher of water over here? My mouth is full of cotton."

Parris poured the ice water into a plastic cup and waited while the Mexican drank deeply. "You speak pretty good English. Been in this country long?"

"I spent more time with you *Yanquís* than in my own country. Peso's no damn good for anything, but a man can buy what he needs with U.S. dollars. Worked a lot in hotels; had to learn good English to hold a job."

"Tell me about the rancher. The one you left up near Lone Pine."

Pacheco leaned back on his pillow and breathed deeply. "Mean old goat; I bet he's pissed. Tell that old man I'm sorry about his dog, but the stinkin' little mutt tried to bite me." He closed his eyes and shuddered. "I hate dogs."

"The rancher isn't worried about his dog. He's dead."

Before he responded, the Mexican searched Parris's face, as if this might be some kind of trick. When he decided it was true, he avoided the policeman's eyes. "I didn't mean for that to happen; just tapped him a little. Damned contrary old booger, why'd he have to . . ." Pacheco clasped a hand over his eyes. He was angry at his victim for having the poor taste to die after being "tapped." He gulped down another swallow of ice water and slammed the cup onto the table that extended over his bed. "What's the charge?"

"Murder one, most likely, considering you stole his truck. Killed your victim during the commission of a felony. Smart lawyer might make a deal for manslaughter, but I wouldn't make book on it. You might as well tell me everything. . . ."

Pacheco grimaced again as the pain flashed like summer lightning from his shoulder to his groin. "What else you got on your mind?"

This was the crucial moment. Parris cleared his throat and glanced at the recorder to verify that the tape was turning. Caution was the watchword. One wrong step and the suspect would clam up. "What can you tell me about Priscilla Song?"

The nurse returned and used a plastic hypodermic to inject a clear fluid into Pacheco's IV. Parris guessed this would be a narcotic to cut the sharp edges off the pain. Almost immediately, the Mexican smiled dreamily. "Priscilla. Good-lookin' little chica."

"Miss Song was a graduate student at RMP. You were employed there as a repairman?"

"Facilities engineer, man. I fixed whatever got broke. Pay was not too good, but I managed to get by."

"Why don't you tell me exactly what happened that night." The Mexican licked his lips but didn't answer. No, Parris thought, he's not going to admit to it. He's dreaming up some cock-and-bull story. It would be so much easier with a confession.

Pacheco finally spoke. "My head hurts. I feel a case of lockjaw comin' on."

Parris removed a manila folder from his briefcase. He emptied its contents on Pacheco's bed. There were a half dozen color prints, enlarged to eight-by-tens. He held a print up for Pacheco's inspection. It was a close-up of Priscilla Song's twisted, bloody face. The Phillips screwdriver was still in place. Pacheco grimaced and looked away. The nurse, who had remained silent during the entire interview, glanced at the photograph and put her hand over her mouth. She hurried into the adjoining bathroom and vomited into the toilet.

Pacheco had lost all of his bluster. "Why do I have to look at that garbage, man? Can't you see I'm sick?"

Parris felt his temple throbbing. "Mr. Pacheco, why did you assault this young woman?"

"I told you, I got nothing to say! You got wax in your ears, you don't hear so good?"

"Tell me about the drug trade on campus. I'd like to hear about your part in it."

Pacheco regarded his accuser in disbelief. He smiled weakly. "I get it, man. You got to be crazy. I don't know nothin' about no drugs. Go away and let me rest. Nurse! Where the hell is the nurse?" The nurse, her face drawn and pale, emerged from the bathroom.

Parris gripped the rail at the foot of the hospital bed; his knuckles turned white. "Your prints are on the murder weapon. What do you think about—"

"I think," Pacheco snarled, "I got nothing more to say to you. You want to put me in a cage, and I ain't gonna help you. So buzz off." Pacheco grinned maliciously and lifted his index finger. The nurse glanced at Parris with an expression of sympathy.

Parris switched the recorder off. "You," he said, "are one sorry excuse for a man."

Pacheco opened his mouth, then clamped it shut. In all his life, he had never been so wounded by an insult.

It was past midnight. Parris tossed and turned in the king-size motel bed; sleep was an elusive goal. Anne Foster's suspicions about Professor Waldo Thomson were an annoyance that wouldn't go away. Leggett had done some discreet checking. As Anne had claimed, Thomson did spend more than his university salary. The physicist drove a Porsche 930 turbo slant-nose and owned a two-bedroom condo at Snowmass. Moreover, he made frequent trips to Colombia and Peru, even during the rainy season. Anne's hunch could be right; there might be a connection to the illegal drug business. More than likely, though, it was all innocent. Thomson probably had an inheritance, or a good nose for the stock market. Maybe the professor liked the rainy season in the South American jungles.

Finally, Parris slipped into the dark, uncharted abyss of his unconscious. As he dreamed, his eyes darted back and forth under his lids as if he was surveying a grand scene in the imaginary worlds of his mind.

It was a fine autumn day as he paddled the feather-light birchbark canoe along the mirrored surface of a deep river. Honey-colored maples lined the bank like columns of tireless sentries. Fallen maple leaves drifted along with him as he moved effortlessly through the crystalline waters. The girl with the dark hair appeared from nowhere, a slim, pretty figure in a yellow dress. She walked through the knee-deep water and tossed her long hair over her shoulder with a dainty hand. The girl was pure and unearthly and lovely. The forest maiden with a black patch over one eye was Priscilla Song.

The young woman approached the canoe and extended both hands palms upward. Her lips moved, but the words were lost with a gust of wind that troubled the surface of the water. Her face was full of appeal as she spoke again, but he could not hear. She seemed to sense the futility of this attempt to divulge her secret to a man who was deaf.

Parris tried to speak, but the words came out with difficulty; the wooden paddle was transmuted to lead and slipped from his hands into the dark water. "What? What did you say?" He cupped a hand over his ear. "Please . . . I can't hear. . . ." She removed a heavy oversized ring from her thumb and offered it to the man in the canoe. Parris reached for the ring, but her hand was barely out of his grasp. The young woman's face was a picture of frustration.

She held her arms over her head; like the most graceful of

ballerinas, she began to turn effortlessly in the water, rotating like a corkscrew. A small whirlpool formed around her slender form as she sank out of sight amidst a foam of tiny bubbles. When she had disappeared into its depths, the surface of the water became still, a faultless mirror to the azure reflection of the sky.

Parris lurched off the pillow as if propelled by an electric shock. This dream, like all his dreams, was useless nonsense. Flickering shadows to disturb a man's sleep. Groaning, the policeman vainly attempted to reshape the distorted pillow. Sleep would not come easily after the ghostly figure's enigmatic visit. It was going to be a long, tedious night without rest. He dropped his head onto the pillow and, to entice sleep, contemplated fine seasons of years that had gone, days of soft breezes and warm sunshine.

A refrain from an old hymn drifted through his mind, mixing with his fantasies. "Precious memories . . . how they linger" . . . a log cabin in the deep forest . . . "how they satisfy" . . . a pristine rippling trout stream splashing over mossy boulders . . . "satisfy my soul" . . . a light breeze embracing the quaking aspens . . . Helen close by his side, whispering her warm breath in his ear. Or was it Anne? Or—he shivered in his half sleep— was it the girl in the yellow dress, the girl who wore a black patch over the hollow socket where an eye had once funneled light into her soul?

12

The sinuous road, picturesquely shaded with stately Douglas fir and conical blue spruce, was a zigzag of deep ruts and muddy pools; the heavy automobile responded with creaking groans as Parris dropped the gearshift into the L slot and eased his way along what he hoped would be the path of least damage to the disks between his vertebrae.

After a half mile that took ten minutes to navigate, the road ended abruptly in a sparse stand of luxuriant blue spruce and quivering aspen, flanked on the west by a dozen lofty ponderosa. Parris spotted his objective, or at least the domicile of his objective, illuminated by shafts of late-afternoon sunlight piercing branches of the tall pines. The old man's home was nestled at the northern edge of a small meadow of Johnson grass decorated with purple aster and Indian paintbrush. The Lilliputian cabin, dwarfed by its setting, was constructed of rough-hewn pine logs and topped off by a chimney of odd-sized and irregular-shaped stones. Wood smoke curled from the stone chimney and hung over the peaked shingle roof like a misty umbrella. A matched pair of wooden whiskey barrels had been placed at the corners of the cabin to catch water that spilled from the split-log gutters. There was no telephone line to connect the lone inhabitant with the outside world, nor was there any electricity available at this remote location.

Parris counted to thirty before he switched the ignition off; it would give the old recluse a chance to realize that he had company. "He has," Anne Foster had warned darkly, "been known to take a potshot at intruders. Keeps an old twelve-gauge to put cottontails in his stew pot. Best be careful up there." Anne's information on the hermit wasn't limited to his hunting practices. Potter-Evans, she confided, had left England in 1954 after a terrible scandal involving a woman. A married woman. Her husband, more than twenty years her senior, was a Member of Parliament. The brilliant young mathematician had emigrated and immediately landed a job at Cornell. He had been refused tenure after a brief affair with an undergraduate. Potter-Evans's professional life had gradually slid downhill after this episode. There had been a tedious series of undistinguished posts at backwater colleges, finally relieved by a penurious retirement and welcome oblivion in the San Juans.

The policeman had never met an honest-to-goodness hermit, and thought it best not to startle an unpredictable old eccentric who might be fingering the trigger of an equally unpredictable shotgun. Parris approached the front door warily, keeping his hands in full view. He called out, "Hello in the cabin. Anyone home?" His voice echoed off a basalt bluff behind the ponderosa. A light breeze shifted the burlap curtains that hung inside two small windows on each side of the door, but his answer was silence. He raised his hand to knock when he heard the voice that materialized from behind.

"No need to pound on my door; you'll get no answer."

He turned to see the man who had spoken with more than a trace of a British accent. The angular figure, somewhat over six feet in height, held a pair of cottontail rabbits by the ears in one hand. The other hand gripped a well-oiled double-barreled shotgun, carelessly pointed toward the policeman's knees. Leathery skin was stretched over his face as if it had gotten wet and shrunk on his skull; a soft crown of silver hair framed his head like a halo. He gave the appearance of being tired from a long walk in the forest, but not of being weak. The man broke the shotgun down and ejected a pair of spent cartridges. Parris could smell the faint odor of burned powder. It was an oddly pleasant smell, here in the deep forest, where a shotgun was more than a mere ornament to hang over the mantelpiece.

Parris extended his hand, which, after the old man dropped the rabbits, was accepted firmly but without enthusiasm. "Claude Potter-Evans, I presume?"

"That's me" was the curt reply. "From that pretty six-pointed star on your shirt, I may safely assume that you are a law-enforcement officer."

"Scott Parris, chief of police in Granite Creek. Need to have a talk with you." If Potter-Evans got nasty, he could always ask for a look at his hunting license.

The hunter hung the cottontails over the sawn-off branch of a small aspen and pulled the latch handle on the cabin door. "Come into my modest lodgings, Constable. I require refreshment. I'll brew a pot of tea . . . unless you are partial to coffee. I keep an instant-brew version of that stuff as well, for the infrequent guest."

"No," Parris lied, "tea will do just as well."

The cabin had a single room. It appeared somewhat barren, even with the clutter of worn, mismatched furniture. Parris found himself a seat at a wooden bench that, judging from the presence of an archaic typewriter, an array of dusty manuscripts, and an unmatched salt and pepper set, evidently served double duty as desk and dining table. The old man added a handful of dry branches to smoking embers in the fireplace. The kettle over the flames began to bubble. Potter-Evans dipped a pair of enameled tin cups into the kettle. "Water boils at a lower temperature at this altitude. Hope it's hot enough for you." The Englishman produced a pair of tea bags from a tightly covered can and dropped them into the cups. "What, precisely, shall we talk about?"

"Have a crime on my hands. Murdered student." Parris swallowed a mouthful of the tea, then swished the remaining liquid into a sloshing whirlpool by shaking the cup in an elliptical orbit. Potter-Evans grimaced at this lack of respect for the precious beverage but held his tongue. "She left a gobbledygook message on her computer," Parris continued. "On her desk, I found a book on codes. Need some help. Understand you know something about this sort of thing. From the big war, in England."

Potter-Evans closed his eyes as if to call up the ghosts of old memories. "England. Ah, I miss it constantly. But not today's England, thank you, no. I remember her in the thirties and forties." He abruptly dismissed the nostalgic remembrance. "But that England is dead and gone, like old Winnie." The recluse raised his cup in salute. "Now dear old Winnie, there was a prime minister. A truly great man, wouldn't you say?"

"Indeed," replied Parris, raising his tin mug. "To Winston Churchill."

Potter-Evans's pale blue eyes were moist as he raised his own cup in salute to the departed warrior-statesman. "Hear, hear."

There was a long silence, eventually broken by Parris. "This young woman left one word, seven letters, on a computer file just before the attack. May be nothing. May be important."

Potter-Evans raised an eyebrow. "Seven letters? And you expect me to decode it for you?" The old man lowered his head; his gaunt frame shook with silent laughter.

"Why . . ." Parris began.

"Oh, that just won't do, don't you see?" Potter-Evans took a tiny sip of tea from the blue enameled mug. "There is one fundamental principle about breaking codes. The longer the message, the easier the code breaker's job. Breaking a sophisticated code when there is only a seven-letter sample is next to impossible. Your only chance is that the victim used some very simple type of transposition or substitution scheme. What, by the way, were the seven mysterious letters?"

Parris produced a small notebook from his jacket pocket and tore out an unused page. He wrote the letters, now etched in his memory, on the paper and slid it across the table to his host.

Potter-Evans held the paper close to a kerosene lamp. He read the letters aloud. "Hmm, z, f, r, c, y, r, t. Ah yes. Hmm. Might be merely a phonic message."

Parris raised his eyebrows. "A phonic . . . you mean a sound?"

Potter-Evans expression was deadpan. "I say . . . rather sounds somewhat like a mule breaking wind."

"I'll take your word for it." Was everybody a comedian?

"Forgive me," the recluse said, "I realize this is a serious matter. You presumably hypothesize that this assemblage of letters might provide some clue to the identity of the murderer. I will try to be of some help, Constable, but you must provide me with the names of everyone at the university—students, faculty, office workers, janitorial staff, everyone."

"You," Parris replied, "have got to be kidding. There must be over four thousand students and at least a couple of hundred—"

"I jest not; I'll also need the victim's book on codes. I won't waste my time on this task unless I have your full cooperation."

Parris groaned inwardly. "I'll have one of my men bring you the list of faculty tomorrow; we already have that. A listing of students may be a bit more trouble."

"I must learn everything possible about the victim," Potter-Evans continued. "This may finally boil down to guessing a key word. Might be the victim's mother's maiden name, her favorite flower, the street where she grew up. I will also need a complete copy of your files on the homicide."

"Maybe," Parris interjected acidly, "you'd like to have my firstborn child, as well."

Potter-Evans paused thoughtfully. "No, I think not. I detest children."

"I will," Parris said, sighing, "do my best. You come up with something useful, I'll try to squeeze some consultant money from the city coffers. Maybe a few hundred bucks if you really hit the jackpot."

This brought a sparkle of interest to the old man's eyes, but he didn't respond.

"Oh, one other thing . . ." Parris retrieved the paper with the code and wrote another string of letters under the first, underlining the repeated letters.

z f <u>r</u> c y <u>r</u> t

p a <u>c</u> h e <u>c</u> o

"That," the policeman said, "is our suspect's name."

"You may," Potter-Evans said, "be on the right track. It could be a simple transposition code, where the c becomes an r. On the other hand, it may be a coincidence."

"See what you can do with it," Parris said. "If you can convince a jury that the last word the victim entered on her keyboard was *Pacheco*, that would tie this case up nicely."

"I'll try a few possibilities, see what falls out."

As the policeman was opening the Explorer door, he turned to say good-bye to the old man. The recluse, who had followed his visitor from the cabin, was distracted by the darkness slipping over the forest floor. The pines were covered with deep shadows that seemed to breathe in step with the rhythmic breeze. Parris caught Potter-Evans's eye. "You really like it up here? All by yourself?"

The Englishman paused thoughtfully before he answered. His reply was barely more than a whisper, an echo of the soft breeze through the pines. "It's rather quiet, you know. But it always moves; it's alive."

"Yeah," Parris muttered, almost to himself, "I know what you mean."

The old man stood under the stars, hardly noticing the cold breeze as the heavy, frigid air spilled down from the mountaintop. He listened to the distant growl of the policeman's automobile as the sound faded into the night. A small owl hooted, and he suddenly felt cold. And old. Very old. He closed and latched the cabin door and loaded the shotgun with fresh shells. He caressed the trigger, then sighed and leaned the shotgun in a corner.

Potter-Evans lifted the glass door that kept the dust off a small bookshelf and scanned the titles: Karel Rektorys' *Survey of Applicable Mathematics*; Athanasios Papoulis's *The Fourier Integral and Its Applications*; Michener's *Centennial*.

He removed a leather-bound volume. It was a first edition of W. W. Ball's *Mathematical Recreations and Essays*, printed in 1892. It was one of the select volumes he had kept all these years; the old man handled the book as if it were an irreplaceable treasure. It was. Reading and rereading this collection of essays was one of his greatest pleasures. He placed the volume on the table, cranked up the wick on the kerosene lamp, and turned to chapter XIV, "Cryptography and Cryptanalysis." It was a very elementary presentation, but it would help concentrate his thoughts, to call back memories of the arcane occupation he had practiced a half century earlier, a lifetime and worlds away. Perhaps he might even be of some help to this American policeman. It had been a long time since he had provided service to his country, and this former colony was gradually becoming his country. He liked Parris; the policeman didn't know how to enjoy a good cup of tea, but he did know how to do his job. Claude Potter-Evans appreciated those who took their work seriously.

"Now," he said aloud, "think about it, old boy, exercise the cerebral cortex. What sort of cipher would be simple enough . . . what technique could a frightened victim be expected to use?" This problem occupied his mind for some minutes. As he tried to picture the crime, a sinister possibility surfaced in his thoughts: What if the "message" was left not by the victim but by someone who wished to misdirect the investigation? Someone who left a book on codes conveniently nearby for the police to find. Someone with blood on his hands. Or perhaps . . . *her* hands? But that was police business. His task was to uncover the hidden meaning in this unlikely array of letters.

13

Pacheco was delivered to the Granite Creek Police Station in a Colorado State Police van. Except for a bulge of bandages under his shirt, the Mexican appeared to be fit. Knox and Leggett unloaded the cuffed murder suspect from the van, signed the release papers, and provided the state troopers with black coffee and doughnuts. Piggy watched the delivery of the "one that got away" from his botched attempt at arrest with ill-concealed resentment, nervously running his stubby fingertips over the stag handle of his .357 Magnum revolver. Pacheco was locked into one of the remodeled cells, where he would be continuously monitored by a television camera.

While the other officers were involved in the camaraderie of doughnuts and storytelling, Piggy Slocum swaggered to the cell, his thumbs hitched under his gun belt, and glared at Pacheco. He was infuriated when the Mexican seemed to take no notice of his giant shadow. Piggy leaned against the bars and fairly hissed, "Don't try anything cute, you little wetback, or I'll have you for breakfast!" Pacheco recoiled in wide-eyed mock horror, staring pointedly at Piggy's ample waistline, then at the empty cells around him. "Oh, I do believe you Señor Puerco. It looks like you've already eaten a whole jailful of prisoners!"

The shaman's resistance finally dissolved after two nights without sleep; it was clear that the unwelcome task could no longer be postponed. Daisy Perika left the warm comfort of her trailer home and shuffled along the deer path to the mouth of Cañon del Espiritu. After she passed through the narrow entrance to the canyon, the old woman abandoned the rough trail for the dry bed of Spirit Creek. Come spring, the stream would be churning with noisy water from the snowmelt on the rolling peaks of the San Juans. Even in the dry season, there were isolated pools where brown trout darted. The streambed was scattered with smooth stones of every shape. When she was a child, Daisy's grandmother had told her that the stones with peculiar shapes were inhabited with spirits of the water, but these spirits were not as strong as the spirit of Badger or Bear. Daisy considered the story about the odd-shaped stones having spirits to be suspect, but she had always avoided stepping on them. There were so many mysteries . . . one could never be sure.

Daisy left the streambed when she saw the gentle arch in the canyon wall where the Old Ones had scratched pictures into the stone. The Ute shaman stopped to lean on her oak walking staff until her breath would return. She directed her gaze toward the ancient petroglyphs on the beige sandstone of the canyon wall. There were three stickmen with large bulbous heads and sharp protruding ears. Shaman in buffalo masks. There was a horned serpent; this was a cruel god of human sacrifice who had been brought up from Mexico by the people who traded colored macaw feathers for tanned hide of deer and elk.

Far to the right of the stick figures and horned serpent was the tiny figure of a man with one hand reaching toward a spiral symbol of the sun. His other hand grasped a feathered staff. This was a representation of *pitukupf*; the dwarf was the most powerful force among the elemental spirits of the earth.

Daisy remembered the first time she had seen the little man. It had happened when she experienced her first menstruation. As was the custom, her mother and aunts had promptly built a menstrual hut. The conical *nakanipi* was fashioned from green willow branches stuck in the earth in a circle, tops bent over and lashed down. During her sojourn in the hut, Daisy had faithfully observed the taboo on consumption of meat or salt. She ate food from special baskets and drank endless cups of hot water to help the blood flow freely. She was warned not to touch her head or face with her hands; her long locks of dark hair might fall out if she broke this particular taboo. During this time in the menstrual hut, Daisy's latent powers gained strength. She dreamed of the *pitukupf,* who offered her his healing power in exchange for certain services. When she awakened, she peeked through a gap in the willow thatch and caught a glimpse of the small creature as he darted behind a boulder.

After this experience, Daisy listened more intently than ever to her grandmother and to her uncle, Green Humming Bird, who was also a respected shaman. From these sages, the girl learned that the dwarf dressed his small body in bright green; he expected gifts from the Dreamers among the Ute. Only a Dreamer could find the dwarf's home, and only after its location was revealed in a trance. Other passersby would believe the lair was that of a badger, but the Dreamer would see the faint wisps of smoke rising from the piñon-wood fire on the *pitukupf's* hearth. This smoke was usually invisible to other Utes, much less to *matukach,* the white people.

Only two years earlier, this particular *pitukupf* had killed a horse that grazed too close to his underground home. Daisy's cousin, Gorman Sweetwater, had received a permit from the tribal council to graze his pinto in Cañon del Espiritu; he planned to bring in a small herd of Hereford cattle once he purchased a fine bull. Gorman's daughter Benita found the pinto dead, but the cause of death was uncertain. The unfortunate horse was immobilized, its front legs wrapped in vines. This was a favorite trick of the dwarf from Lowerworld, to ensnare his victims with a cord of braided vine. Gorman didn't believe in the old ways; he foolishly insisted that his dumb pinto had gotten itself entangled in the vines and died a natural death. Sooner or later, Gorman would learn better.

The shaman turned first to the north, whispering, *"Nitukwu,"* and tapped the earth lightly with her staff. She faced the direction of the setting sun. *"Nitukuwa tapai-yakwiniti."* She repeated the ritual for the other quarters of the world. Daisy rummaged through her coat pocket and produced a package of Lucky Strike cigarettes and a short string of multicolored glass beads. She wrapped these in a paper napkin she had saved from her last meal at the McDonald's restaurant in Durango and tied the offering with black cotton thread. She laid the gift within inches of the hole in the earth and backed away. The *pitukupf* would not need matches for lighting the cigarettes. She had seen a thin column of smoke curling upward from the hole in the earth; the dwarf had his own source of fire to ignite the *sapatuti.*

The return path was mostly downhill, but it took her a full twenty minutes to trudge back to her house trailer. She locked the door behind her and leaned her staff against the television. When she was on her bed, Daisy closed her eyes and waited, listening for sound of the Lakota drum. During one of his infrequent trips to the Black Hills, her second husband had traded two tanned deerskins to an aged Sioux for the medicine drum. The Lakota man, Lawrence Short Hand, had solemnly guaranteed that this drum had the Power. Was it not decorated with the sacred red paint of Wovoka, the Paiute *Wanekia,* the originator of the Ghost Dance? The promise was true. The first time her husband had tapped the *papu-ti* to produce a monotonous rhythm, the resonant, hollow sound had swept Daisy into a deep trance. She had left her body and visited a bright land where all her ancestors lived in happiness. Her visit had been all too brief; though she had tried many times, the shaman had never been able to return to that good place.

Her husband had been gone these many years, but the drum still hung by its rawhide thong over her kitchen table. The shaman concentrated on the drum, remembering its low, thumping voice. She could barely hear it, far away at first, then nearer. Soon, the drum vibrated the frame of her bed. The monotonous rhythm filled her consciousness until she could hear nothing else, not even the sudden gust of wind that shook her fragile trailer home. Daisy felt her spirit body float through a damp gray mist, then enter the earth at the hole that led to the lair of the *pitukupf*. Her spirit body did not stop in the den of the dwarf, but continued to follow the long roots of the juniper tree, until the root became a shining tunnel. She felt herself falling ever more rapidly toward her destination in Lowerworld, so fast that she had to gasp for a breath of air. She had made this journey many times and was not afraid, even though the voyage often ended in a part of Lowerworld she had not seen before. She emerged into a humid world of yellow light filtered by swirling blue mists. Reptilian creatures scurried under luxuriant under-growth; robin-sized humming birds flitted nervously among the oversized ferns and gnarled cypress.

Daisy was young again, but she was not herself. This was puzzling; she was someone else, in an earlier time. She followed a muddy animal path, parted the ferns, and found her new self near the bank of a wide river. It was certainly not the Piños or the Piedra, nor was it the familiar Animas. It was a large river, in a foreign land that she had not seen in all her journeys to Lowerworld. She approached the bank, her bare feet stepping lightly over the smooth stones of mica-flecked granite. The air was cool and moist, and she found the effect to be strangely pleasant. At the bank, under an umbrella-shaped maple, a raft was tied to a stake in the blue clay. The raft was of Ute design, and this familiar sight gave her comfort. Three long cottonwood logs formed the basic structure; these were strengthened by smaller poles laid across them at right angles. The top of the raft was covered with willow branches, and the whole assembly was tied together with willow bark. A sturdy oak push pole, deco-rated with delicate bands of aspen bark, leaned against the tree.

Without warning, the *pitukupf*, arrayed in luminescent green silk, appeared on her left and elbowed her thigh to announce his presence. The dwarf, leaning on his crooked staff with the plume of green feathers, was happily puffing a Lucky Strike cigarette. She was startled and stepped back, but the diminutive creature seemed not to notice her mild alarm. The *pitukupf* pointed at the raft with a stubby finger. She watched eddies and whirlpools forming in the river; these were sure signs of dangerous currents.

"I could drown," she protested meekly. "The water looks deep."

The dwarf blew a puff of gray smoke over the waters and tapped the raft impatiently with his feathered staff. The shaman obeyed without further question; it was the utmost folly to ignore the command of the *pitukupf*. If she did not cooperate, she would certainly become ill, perhaps even die. Daisy was an old woman and her bones ached when it rained, but she was not ready to hear the owl call her name. Not today.

14

Parris was reading an outraged citizen's complaint about Patrolman E. C. Slocum. Piggy, as the elderly woman wrote in a precise hand, was observed "urinating on my gooseberry bush at half past four this morning." She doubted the bush would survive this insult; its fruit would certainly never grace another gooseberry pie. Slocum didn't try to evade such issues, because he never understood what all the hubbub was about. He had explained the reason for this latest outrage with disarming directness: "It hit me kinda sudden. Felt like I'd split wide open. Where would *you* take a quick piss when you're out on patrol an hour before daylight? In your hat?"

The intercom buzzed. Parris pressed the button and spoke to the machine. "Yes, Clara. What is it?"

"Are you busy? I have someone . . . a visitor."

"I can spare a minute."

Clara, who entered alone, was subdued. "It's my Aunt Daisy. She wants to talk to you."

Sooner or later, everyone wanted to consult the police. "Sure. Bring her in."

Clara was nervously pulling at her braided hair. "My aunt is . . . an old-fashioned Indian." Clara hesitated, then blurted it out. "She is a *piikati*, a person with power."

Parris raised his eyebrows. "What sort of power?"

"A *piikati* is a kind of a . . . what some people call a shaman.

Mostly, they heal the sick. They're connected to animal spirits with power, like the bear or buffalo. A particular animal gives them the power to heal a certain type of sickness. A woodpecker gives the power to stop bleeding; a badger, the power to heal problems with the feet. I wanted you to understand this before you met my aunt."

Parris resisted the temptation to ask what animal Aunt Daisy was connected with. "Bring her in."

Clara left, then returned immediately with a woman who walked with the short, measured steps of an arthritic. "This," she said as she ushered her relative to a seat, "is my aunt, Daisy Perika. She lives on the Southern Ute reservation. Aunt Daisy has a message for you." She smiled with honest affection and patted the elderly woman on the shoulder.

Daisy peered through a heavy pair of spectacles that magnified her eyes in a fashion that would have appeared comic on one with less dignity. He got up from his chair and smiled in a manner that was intended to be reassuring. "Good morning, Miss . . . uh . . . Mrs. Perika. What can I do for you?"

Daisy Perika blinked, and the effect was owl-like. "I had this vision," she said simply. She had no intention of telling this white man about the *pitukupf*; he would neither believe nor understand and it would embarrass her niece. "I have come to you with a message. Three nights ago, I left my body." She made this pronouncement with no pretense, like someone else would say, "Yesterday, I went to Farmington." Daisy stared at the white man, waiting patiently for a response.

If he didn't handle this just right, Clara Tavishuts would be impossible to work with. Parris sat down on the edge of his desk and pretended that this was a normal conversation. "What happened when you . . . uh . . . left your body?"

Daisy was rocking gently. "I was young, in a far land. On a raft of cottonwood logs, covered with willow branches, floating down a deep river." After this, she fell silent, as if she had drifted away. The old woman's eyes seemed to glaze, as if she had forgotten the purpose of her visit.

"Yes," Clara prompted, "and then what happened, Auntie?"

She blinked again and cleared her throat. "I floated along on the water for a long time, not seeing nobody. I felt lonesome, but I wasn't afraid. Then, there was this young girl on the bank. She had long dark hair and wore a yellow dress."

Parris remembered his dream of Priscilla Song . . . in a yellow dress. She had also worn a yellow dress on the night she was murdered. Mrs. Perika had undoubtedly picked this up from Clara.

"As I floated by, this young girl was plaiting flowers; they looked like purple asters or maybe chickory—I couldn't tell. She made these flowers into a garland and put it around her neck. Then she walked right into the water, toward my raft, and the raft became still, like the current had stopped. Her dress floated up to her waist, but she didn't sink. When she got close, I was sure the *uru-ci* had something to say to me."

Parris interrupted. "The *what?*"

Clara interpreted. "The ghost."

Parris was now riveted to every word. "Did she—the ghost—try to speak to you?"

Daisy tried to read his face. Why did the policeman say "*try* to speak"? This man, who seemed so ignorant, *knew something.* Did this *matukach* policeman have the gift—did he hear the whispers of the spirits? "Yes, she tried to say something, but I couldn't hear her." Daisy turned her attention to Clara. "You go away now. I want to talk to this man by myself." Clara departed without protest.

Parris was stunned. In his own dream, the girl in the yellow dress had tried to speak, but her words had been lost. Maybe the old woman had sensed something in the way he asked the question.

"She had," the shaman continued, "these four black stones. She held them in her hand so I could see, like this." Daisy held her hand out palm upward. "Then she drew a ring in the water with her finger, like this"—Daisy made a circle in the air—"and dropped one of those black rocks in the ring; it floated above the water. Then she ate the other three stones."

"She swallowed the stones?"

"Sure." Daisy nodded. "The *uru-ci*, she ate all three of them. She put her hand on her throat, then coughed like she was choking." Daisy illustrated by putting her hand on her neck, then over her lips. "After that, she vomited and two of the stones came out of her mouth and disappeared."

"What did the stones look like? I mean, did they have a special shape?"

Daisy seemed to be perplexed, then remembered. "Yes! Like medicine—you know, little black pills."

Parris started to say, "Like drugs," but caught himself.

Daisy shifted her weight in the chair and groaned; the trip to Granite Creek had exhausted her. "That's all the ghost did. My raft started floating again and I was gone around a bend in the river. By and by, I was awake and back inside my body. I read about that dead girl in the newspaper, and told Clara about my dream. Clara said to come and tell you." She pushed herself out of the chair. Before Parris could protest, Daisy gently placed her fingers on his temples. He felt a buzzing in his head, then a distant thumping—hollow, resonant. Like a drumbeat. It must, he thought, be my heart beating.

"You dream dreams," she said. It was not a question. "You see things . . . know things. But you don't believe what you know." She removed her fingers from his temples and regarded him quizzically. Someday, maybe, she would tell this one about the *pitukupf*.

The thumping in his head was still there. Had the old woman hypnotized him?

Daisy Perika removed a scrap of paper from her purse and offered it to Parris. "I don't have no telephone. This is directions to my house. If you want to talk, you come by and see me." The policeman folded the paper and put it in his wallet.

The shaman paused at his office door. "You know what I think?"

He rubbed his temples to make the thumping go away. "Tell me."

The shaman closed her eyes. "That deep river I saw in my vision. It was the one that separates us from the dead people."

"Yeah," he whispered hoarsely, "I know about that river."

Daisy departed as silently as she had arrived. He switched off the lights and watched the sun slip behind the rolling peaks on the western range. What did this mean? Did the old woman have some kind of gift? Was she able to communicate with . . . He dismissed the absurd thought. It was time to get back to the real world, solve real problems.

15

Slocum's sour expression revealed his displeasure; Piggy had a serious grievance to communicate to the chief of police. The Mexican prisoner, Slocum insisted, was "unsubordinate." There was no doubt that Julio Pacheco was taking verbal liberties; he continued to make disparaging remarks about Officer Slocum's oversized girth and prodigious appetite. Some of his observations had been repeated in the officers' locker room: "Hey, Porky. I read in the newspaper that three goats are missing from Mrs. Snipes's backyard. You have them for breakfast?"

Piggy's request was simple and direct. "Lissen, Chief. I'll come in at midnight, take Sonny's spot on third shift. I'll open that little bastard's cell and kick the vinegar out of him from here to Tuesday. That's the onliest way to handle them smart-mouthed little jumpin' beans!"

It was impossible to reason with Piggy when he was angry. Scott Parris responded with a poker face. "That, Officer Slocum, is undoubtedly the most ludicrous proposal I've ever heard."

Piggy was jubilant. "Knew you'd see it my way. I'll give Sonny a call and we'll switch shifts."

"Not so fast," Parris interrupted. "These things must be done according to proper procedure. You have a ten-seventy-eight form?"

Piggy's expression shifted to puzzlement; it was a familiar configuration for his facial muscles, because Piggy was continually puzzled at all manner of developments. "Do I got a . . . ten what?"

"First, you fill out a ten-seventy-eight form, reporting the prisoner's abusive language; make sure you list his insults in some detail. Make six copies for distribution. It'll be just one more nail in Pacheco's coffin!"

"Well . . . I don' . . . don' . . . don't know," Piggy stuttered.

"Then," Parris continued coolly, "submit a detailed outline of your proposal for remedial action. Describe the exact form of punishment—where you'll kick him, how many times, how hard, that sort of thing. Rules say you can't kick a prisoner in the groin or face; I'm not sure about kidneys. Ribs and shins should be acceptable. We'll need that report in triplicate. One for your personnel folder, another for department files. I'll turn the third copy over to the DA for approval. Once all the paperwork's done, you can stomp him to a pulp. We could make a videotape for training new officers."

Piggy frowned and muttered something about looking into it and backed out of the chief's office, where he bumped into Eddie Knox.

"How's it hangin', Toe-Jam?" Eddie asked innocently.

Piggy recounted the essence of his encounter with Parris. "I ain't altogether for sure," he said after he finished his tale. "I s'pose them city cops hafta do things different up there in Chicago, but the boss, he sure got some funny notions."

"Noticed it right from the first day he got here," Knox said through a jawful of Red Man tobacco spittle. "We better keep a close eye on that silly sumbitch, or he'll get us all into deep shit."

Piggy was deeply engrossed in a Batman comic book when he glanced up at the array of television monitors. It was Cell Seven. The inmate's body was hanging from the light fixture, rotating ever so slowly. "Oh my God *Almighty*," he prayed earnestly, "please don't let him be dead!" For one so heavy, Piggy managed a fast sprint to the cell door. His hands trembled as he fumbled with the key ring. "Oh, Sweet Nelly, the chief will have my badge for this." He finally felt the latch slide, and opened the cell door just far enough to squeeze through. Piggy waddled to the feet of the suspended body, clinched his chubby fists, and shrieked in his frustration. "Damn you anyway, you smart-mouth little wetback! If you hadda stretch your neck, why couldn't you of done it somewheres else?"

The suspended body responded to this query with a swift boot in the policeman's left temple. Piggy took a short step backward; his eyes rolled upward until only the whites were visible before he toppled to the floor with a dull thud, rattling the bars on Cell Seven. Julio dropped to the floor, removed Piggy's Magnum from an engraved leather holster, and helped himself to a supply of bullets from the policeman's cartridge belt. He found the most important item hanging on a ring from Slocum's leather belt: a key to Car Three.

Piggy, lost in utter blackness, couldn't hear the Mexican's taunting farewell. "So long, big man. Hope this don't ruin your appetite."

Piggy was rushed by helicopter to a hospital in Boulder for a CAT scan. When Parris announced to the force that Slocum had suffered no apparent brain damage from being kicked in the head, Sgt. "Rocks" Knox snickered and bellowed, "How could they tell?" Parris used all his reserves to avoid joining in the nervous laughter that followed.

The authorities in nine states were alerted to be on the look-out for Julio Pacheco, but Parris had no doubt where the Mexican was headed. South. It was assumed that the Mexican, who was not stupid, would already have dumped Car Three and replaced it with a less conspicuous stolen vehicle. Every report on a stolen car was hot news.

At 9:00 A.M., Parris dialed the DA's office. Slayton Cobb was on vacation, the secretary informed him. "Bad news," he told her. "Julio Pacheco escaped last night. We'll probably pick him up again, but we can't be certain."

Her tone was icy. "I will inform the district attorney when he returns." Parris hung up, grateful that Cobb was out of the office. He found himself staring blankly out the window into a thick grove of pines. Pacheco was gone, and he was responsible. Sgt. "Rocks" Knox came in to pitch the duty roster on Parris's desk and noticed the despondent expression on his boss's face. Knox's normally cheerful expression was replaced by uncertainty, even a hint of concern. "You doin' okay, chief?"

Parris hadn't noticed Knox's presence until that moment. "Okay? Yeah, just contemplating the situation."

"Situation?" Knox cocked his head to one side.

"That's right. I can't hold a two-bit hoodlum in this tin-can jail. Officer Slocum remains alive and able to wreak havoc over the earth. Wondering whether I should shoot myself or jump out the window."

Knox thought about it. "Drop from that window ain't more than twelve feet. Likely, you'd just bust a leg. I'd say shootin' is the ticket, boss."

16

SILVER SPRING, MARYLAND

Waldo Thomson nosed the rented Town Car into one of the hotel slots marked GUEST, slipped the gearshift into PARK and stepped on the emergency brake. Before unlocking the door, he placed his palm over the slight bulge just above his belt buckle. He had repeated this ritual more than a dozen times since leaving Denver, as if the booty might somehow vanish. The precious samples were still there, wrapped in a plastic bag, zipped into the canvas money belt. He would take no chances of being robbed, of losing this treasure to some doped-up mugger looking for a few bucks for a fresh fix. Before he left the relative safety of the Lincoln, the physicist removed the pistol from the suitcase and slipped it into his inside coat pocket. No one would interfere with his game plan. Absolutely no one.

On the flight toward the gathering darkness on the East Coast, Anne had tried to dismiss the absurd feeling that she was being followed. Waldo Thomson, after all, was already in Washington; *she* was doing the following! But eyes seemed to bore into the back of her neck. She turned and glanced at the passengers behind her: a woman traveling with her small child; a matched pair of nuns reading Hillerman paperbacks; a cowboy dozing under his Stetson. She dismissed this paranoia and focused her thoughts on Thomson. Was she a fool for following him all the way to Washington on the basis of the tip from her contact at the travel agency? But it was peculiar; Thomson was leaving days early for the North American Physical Society meeting in Silver Spring. She had tried to pick up something from the Physics Department. Kristin Waters had told her that Thomson had taken a few days of vacation before the NAPS meeting started. The department secretary proudly pointed out that Thomson and Arnold Dexter would be delivering joint papers on the ceramic armor research. Anne had asked to speak to the department chairman about his paper, but Professor Dexter was at home recovering from a bout of intestinal flu. Kristin thoughtfully asked if Anne wanted to speak with another member of the staff who would be attending the NAPS meeting. Professor Harry Presley was available. The journalist, who found the man particularly repugnant, graciously declined.

A storm was slipping down the coast from Maine; Thomson wouldn't use up precious vacation days to endure a blizzard in Washington. No. The physicist was going to the capital on business and she was determined to discover just what that business was.

She had just stepped out of the shower when someone tapped on her door. Anne slipped on a soft cotton robe and opened the door until the brass chain caught. It was, as she had expected, Freddie, the bellman. She regarded his flaccid freckled face with a forced expression of assurance. "You have something for me, Freddie?"

He grinned and gawked at the part in her robe. She tugged at the garment, closing the gap, and he reluctantly switched his attention to a scrap of paper in his hand. "It's that guy you asked about, Thomson. Occupant of room twelve-thirteen."

"So? What did you learn?"

"Checked in yesterday afternoon at three-fifteen. Checkout date is open, but he expects to be here at least a week. Arrived from National Airport in a Hertz rental—Lincoln Town Car. Asked for seven A.M. wake-up call. Wants breakfast sent to his room at eight A.M. sharp. Ham and scrambled eggs, wheat toast and marmalade, decaf coffee." He held out a pudgy hand. "You got that Mr. Jackson for me?"

She fumbled in her wallet, found the bill, and passed it to him with two fingers, cringing at the thought of touching his hand. "I need to know who he calls. You bring me the numbers as soon as they're posted on the computer. No delays. If I don't get the word within twenty minutes of the call, no reward."

The bellman slipped the greenback in his hip pocket and faked an expression of uncertainty. "Hey lady, I don't know. I don't normally have access to the telephone billing terminal. This kind of thing could cost me my job."

"No problem. If you can't manage it, I have other means." It was a bluff, but Freddie was unsure. He appraised her thoughtfully and decided not to pass up the bucks.

"Okay. I'll try, but I don't come on duty until noon. Maybe I can get a buddy to cover for me tomorrow morning. One Mr. Jackson per phone number, deal?"

"Deal. Unless Thomson calls for pizza. Don't try to pull any fast ones. I know this guy's business, who he's likely to call. I just don't know when. You pass me a fake number and I'll know it. The outfit I work for won't like it. Fool around and we'll feed you to the hotel management."

Freddie's mouth dropped open; his Adam's apple pulsed. Anne wondered if she had overdone it. Easy does it. Too tough and you'll scare him off. "Deal straight with me and I'll have more work for you." Anne closed the door before the man could respond, shuddering as she turned the security bolt. This guy was generic pond scum. She couldn't wait to get the job finished and return to Colorado. She counted the greenbacks left in her wallet. Most of her expenses would be on plastic and could be put off for a month. If the bellman came up with more than a half dozen phone numbers, her hard cash would be gone. That, Anne decided, was a future bridge to cross. She fervently hoped that her quarry was up to no good—enough no good for a wire story that would be picked up by the major papers. If Thomson was clean, this expensive little escapade would take a long time to pay for and much longer to forget.

The freckled bellman muttered darkly as he punched the button for the elevator. "Smart-assed bitch. I'll teach her to mess around with Freddie." He grinned with self-satisfaction. He knew exactly what to do!

Waldo Thomson slept with the samples under his pillow and the small revolver on the small table by his bedside. He did not sleep soundly; he dreamed of noisy violence, pools of congealed blood, and dark chambers of unknown horror. He got up twice to check the security lock on the door. Several times during the long night, he anxiously groped under the pillow for the plastic bag that contained the broken halves of the dime-sized disk. After his wake-up call jarred him to consciousness, he repacked the precious samples into the money belt. He hung the belt over the plastic shower door while he stood under the needle spray. Thomson was fully dressed when his breakfast arrived, but he poked at the scrambled eggs with little interest and managed to consume only a few bites of the salty "Farm-Fresh Virginia Country Ham," which had surely arrived at the hotel restaurant in a can.

At 8:40 the following morning, Anne heard a tapping. She opened the door with the safety chain in place until she saw the uniform of a bellman. This one was black and looked to be a few notches higher on the food chain than Freddie. This young man had a sullen expression as he offered her a blue envelope emblazoned with the hotel's return address in raised lettering. "Freddie say I should bring this."

She found a small sheet of pale blue paper in the envelope; two telephone numbers were scrawled in ballpoint. One had been made at 8:22, another at 8:28 A.M. Anne studied the young man's face. "This better not be a rip-off. I already explained to Freddie . . ."

He raised his palms in protest. "I dunno what it is, lady. I don't axe nuthin'. Freddie say bring it, so I bring it."

She passed him a pair of twenties and hoped this wasn't a scam. If it was, there was little she could do about it. When the door was closed, she removed an earring and dialed the first number on the scrap of paper. There were three rings before a woman answered: "Zimmelhauf Enterprises. How may we help you?"

Waldo Thomson was ushered into the president's office by a receptionist. The balding middle-aged man behind the desk got up and held a limp hand out to his guest. "Zimmelhauf, Fritz Zimmelhauf. Pleasure to meet with you."

Thomson dropped the man's hand after a perfunctory shake. "I'm pressed for time. Let's get down to business."

"Certainly. I understand you have a rush job."

"You got it right," the physicist snapped. "You tell me precisely what this stuff is made of within forty-eight hours and, in addition to your usual fee, you'll get a ten-thousand-dollar bonus. In cash. Off the record."

Zimmelhauf bit his stubby cigar in half, then threw it away. He grabbed Thomson's hand in an enthusiastic grip. "If we don't produce that information for you in forty-eight hours, you can kick my ass from here to Baltimore!"

"Baltimore," Thomson said with a cruel grin, "isn't nearly far enough."

Anne Foster watched from behind dark sunglasses. Two men finally appeared at the front door and shook hands. Thomson slid under the wheel of the Lincoln while the shorter man made a few parting remarks. She waited until the Town Car was lost in traffic before she dared approach the entrance to Zimmelhauf

Enterprises. The receptionist, who seemed to be very busy, was nevertheless polite.

Anne removed the dark glasses and presented a dazzling smile that had no effect whatever. "I'm Anne . . . Forbes," she said, "with the *Post.*"

This took a moment to register. "You're a reporter? With the *Washington Post?*" The receptionist patted her hair into place, as if the visitor might produce a camera at any moment.

"You'll just have to forgive me for barging in like this. I know I should have called and made an appointment, but I'm interviewing everyone who has a business in the Industrial Park, and I finished my morning appointment early. Thought I'd fit you in before lunch. We're going to have a report in the Business Section in a couple of Sundays, describing the wide range of high-tech business in this area. Is there someone here who could describe your operation? I'd be so grateful, and I'd hate to leave Zimmelhauf Enterprises out of our story."

The receptionist was practically wringing her hands in frustration. "Oh dear, not today, I'm afraid. We have an important contract, and the boss has put most of the staff on overtime. I just know Dr. Zimmelhauf won't have time to speak to you today. Maybe if you come back next week . . ."

"An important contract? Maybe I could do a sidebar. Could you tell me—"

"Oh gracious no!" The receptionist paled. "I shouldn't have said a word. We get lots of *government* jobs, you know, and some are very hush-hush. Please don't let on that I ever mentioned it. Dr. Zimmelhauf would be just livid!"

Anne smiled a conspirator's smile. "I'll promise not to mention where I heard it if you'll tell me one thing. Does this job have anything to do with the gentleman who left a few minutes ago?"

The receptionist bit her lip, glanced to her left and right, and then whispered, "Yes. Now please forget that we talked about it."

17

Thomson was ushered into the attorney's plush corner office at precisely three o'clock. The young man, whose slender athletic form was clothed in an expensive tailored suit, shook his hand with just the appropriate measure of enthusiasm. A tray of silver decanters, china cups, gourmet crackers, and small cubes of imported cheese were on a conference table. The attorney poured his visitor a cup of Celestial Seasonings Red Zinger tea into a delicate cup decorated with a swarm of tiny blue butterflies.

"I recall, from our telephone conversation, that you believe . . . that this is about a breakthrough of some sort."

The physicist accepted the fragile cup and sniffed at the fragrant aroma. "The patent application must be filed immediately."

The attorney leaned forward, clasped his hands, and placed his elbows on the thick plate glass that protected the varnished surface of his immaculate walnut desk. "You realize that we have a huge backlog of work. . . ."

The visitor swallowed a sip of the hot red brew. "Sure I do. But you're going to move this job to the front of the queue."

The attorney cleared his throat nervously. "I rather doubt that would be possible."

The physicist removed a thick manila envelope from his briefcase and tossed it onto the attorney's desk. The young man blinked at the envelope; a dark vein in his forehead began to pulsate. "That," Thomson said, "is stuffed with brand-new twenty-dollar bills. Five hundred twenty-dollar bills."

The young man touched the envelope; his hand trembled. "We don't normally take our fee in cash. . . ."

"That," Thomson said dryly, "isn't your fee. Let's call it a tip. Anybody asks me, I know nothing about it."

"I should imagine," the attorney said as he dropped the envelope into a desk drawer and turned a key in the lock, "I could work on this at night."

"I thought," the physicist replied without expression, "you'd see the logic of it."

Thomson had barely turned the latch on his hotel room door when someone knocked. He opened the door, to find a uniformed bellman who was twisting his hands in agitation. "Hi. I'm Freddie." The bellman glanced nervously up and down the hall; his pale face was wet with perspiration. "Can we talk, sir?"

Thomson took one step backward. "Talk? You and I? Whatever about?"

The bellman, not waiting for an invitation, brushed past the scientist and pushed the door shut.

The professor's voice was shrill. "Now see here . . . what is this all about?"

"Maybe," Freddie began, "we can do some business. I picked up some information you might be interested in."

Thomson eyed the brazen intruder cautiously. "What kind of information?"

Freddie grinned his toothy possum's grin. "It's this redhead on the third floor. Good-lookin' fox. Been askin' a lot of questions about you. Make it worth my while, I'll tell you what I know about her."

Thomson hardly noticed the bellman's silent departure. The physicist stared at the name on the paper without comprehension. Ms. Anne Foster, 211 Copper Lane, Granite Creek, Colorado. The name was vaguely familiar; his mind raced through its memory files to match the name to a person. The appropriate array of neurons fired. Everything clicked into place. Of course, Anne Foster. The name over the Sunday column in the *Granite Creek Adviser*. The attractive redhead who had interviewed everyone in the Physics Department about Priscilla Song's untimely demise.

He had followed the instructions; everything had been going so well. Thomson sat down heavily on the bed and glared at the paper as if, by some wizardry of concentration, he could force it to yield more information. What was a reporter from a small-town newspaper doing in Washington? The check-in time on the photocopy indicated that she had arrived a day after he had. Was it an incredible coincidence that she was here, in the same hotel, at the same time? He calmed himself and considered the probabilities. The woman was probably here to cover some news event; it surely must be a coincidence. The reporter had seen him in the lobby, had her professional curiosity aroused, and bribed the bellman to get some information. But why? She couldn't possibly have any idea of his real purpose in Washington, so she must be fishing. And what if she did manage to learn something about his business? In a short time, it would all be public knowledge, anyway. A few days after the patent was filed, there would be no more reason for skulking around. It would be time for the big announcement! But in spite of these rationalizations, the physicist had a sense that something was terribly wrong.

When he entered the hotel dining room, Thomson was delighted to see the small contingent from Rocky Mountain Polytechnic having an early dinner. Arnold Dexter was dominating the conversation; Harry Presley was attempting to crack the shell of a lobster. Thomson had been so completely preoccupied with his urgent business that he had forgotten about the North American Physical Society meeting. The NAPS registration booth was already signing in some early arrivals and the plenary session would begin precisely at eight the next morning. As Thomson approached their table, Presley looked up and grinned his corpselike smile. Arnold Dexter got to his feet, made a perfunctory comment, and offered his hand. Presley swallowed a mouthful of red wine and waved a thin yellow hand in greeting. "Good to see you, Waldo. How are things going?"

"Things," Thomson replied without conviction, "are going well."

It had been a slow day. Parris was in his stocking feet. He had opened a new can of saddle soap and was applying the soft cream liberally to his stiff new boots. It was a simple pleasure, working the yellow soap deep into the leather, producing a soft boot that would expand to fit itself to the shape of his oversized foot.

"Chief!"

He looked up in dismay to see the ample figure of E. C. "Piggy" Slocum blocking the doorway into his office. "What is it?"

Piggy mumbled something about a phone call and left, slamming the door behind him. Slocum was acting as dispatcher; he preferred coming to the chief's office rather than using the intercom, because the array of buttons confused him.

Parris pushed the lighted button on the telephone console and pressed the receiver to his ear. "Yeah?"

"Yeah? Some kind of greeting. Thought I'd get more than that."

The voice shot whippets of electricity through his body. "Anne! I've been leaving messages on your machine. . . ."

"I'm in Washington. Well, not exactly. I'm in Maryland, but inside the Beltway."

Parris leaned back and propped his stockinged feet on his desk. "Washington? Whatever takes you to that cauldron of confusion?"

There was a pregnant pause before she answered. Parris could feel something coming. Something he wouldn't like. Did she have a new job? A job that would separate them almost as absolutely as he was separated from Helen? Was this call the kiss-off?

"I'm here on business."

"So. Business, huh? Find yourself a better job?" He tried to sound as if it didn't matter.

"New job? Don't be silly." She laughed, and he felt relief flowing over him like a waterfall. "I came here intending to follow Waldo Thomson, thought he might be a player in this drug thing at the university. Had hopes he would meet with a sinister Colombian, but nothing so interesting," she continued playfully. "He visited a couple of local firms and met with ordinary citizens. It's probably a snipe hunt, but I'm going to do a little more digging before I head west."

He felt it, a hint of the Dread. Cold fingers, bony fingers, lightly touching the back of his neck. "Look, sweetheart, you've got no business chasing after someone who might be involved in the international drug traffic. Leave that sort of nonsense to the professionals."

This brought a slight edge to her voice. "I *am* a professional. Anyway, it looks like he's here on some type of ordinary business. I'll explain it all when I see you."

The Dread settled into his abdomen; he fought against the desire to yell into the mouthpiece, but his voice was hard as flint when he responded. "You don't seem to understand. If Thomson *is* involved in some kind of drug deal, you could get yourself—"

"Don't fret about me. I'm the soul of caution. I'll check things out a bit more, then head home."

He was on his feet now. Forgetting his bare feet, he kicked his desk in frustration and then yelped with pain.

Anne was alarmed. "What is it? What happened? Are you hurt?"

Parris sat down and rubbed his big toe. "Old football injury," he muttered darkly, "nothing compared to what'll happen when I get hold of you."

"So," she replied in a mock-seductive whisper, "are you going to spank me?"

In spite of his anger and the dull throbbing in his bent toe, he grinned. "You're a nutcase. You know that? I want a full report when you get back, but take care. . . ."

"Well, worrywart, now I know who not to call when I need a cheerful word. You certainly know how to ruin a girl's day."

He closed his eyes and tried to paint an image of her face. "Come on home. We'll have a nice dinner, spend some time together."

Her voice dropped to a whisper. "You know . . . that's all I've been thinking about. See you in a couple of days."

He touched the flame to a fresh cigarette and took a deep draw. It was bitterly, painfully cold. He was buttoning his coat at his neck when he sensed its presence. The Voice was usually inside his head, but now it seemed to originate near his left shoulder, as if the formless presence drifted along beside him. He glanced to his left and imagined a brief glimpse of a misty figure, but this vision disappeared in the whirling flakes of crystalline snow. He did not interrupt his brisk pace along the frigid street; he was eager to get back to the hotel. "She's here," he told the Voice. "I've seen her."

The malignant presence told him exactly what to do about Anne Foster.

Now that he owned his victim's priceless property, he was reluctant to take unnecessary risks. He exhaled a puff of smoke. "What if I'm caught?"

The Voice reminded him that he had experienced doubts before he killed Priscilla, but now the police were looking for the Mexican. It was true. Hadn't the Voice told him which screwdriver would have Pacheco's prints on the handle and how to manage the theft from the toolbox while the repairman was distracted?

"Her property is mine now," he said. "Don't want to take any more chances, maybe end up in prison." He dropped the cigarette butt onto the ice-encrusted pavement and ground it under his heel. Once this was all settled, he promised himself he would stop smoking again, for good this time.

The Voice shifted to a soothing cadence, offered to provide proof of its ability to protect him.

"Proof," he muttered to himself, "that would be good."

It had been a long day. The Jiffy Shop manager hoped to leave early and get a jump on the storm that would shortly turn the District into an ice-skating rink. There were few customers now and that was good luck. If the store emptied in the next twenty minutes, she could close the shop early. The young black woman, bored with her dull job, exercised her intelligent mind by studying each customer. She attempted to guess what their purchases were for, tried to imagine how each item might be used in their daily attempt to survive in the city. She watched her latest customer. The man obviously had time to kill. He wandered up and down the aisles, making a selection here, another there. He had less than a dozen items in the red plastic shopping basket when he shoved it onto her checkout counter. The assortment didn't fit any familiar pattern. She slid each purchase over the laser beam that interrogated the bar code, calculated the price, and adjusted the inventory data. Cigarettes. A can of fancy cashews. A roll of nylon cord. A map of the District and Maryland. It was no surprise that he was a tourist; his jacket had a distinctly western cut. And, of course, there was the string tie.

She paused when she came to the last item and offered a shy smile to her customer. "Well now. Mostly sell these during picnic season; didn't know there was any still on the shelf." His lips grew taut. The clerk kept her gaze away from his face as she dropped the last item into the plastic bag. Some folks, she had learned, were hard to figure. Won't open their mouth to say a friendly word; wouldn't spit on you if you were on fire. And the strange things they buy! Why would anybody, she wondered, need an ice pick at this time of year?

18

The tired young woman pulled her thin canvas raincoat over the woolen ski sweater and draped a heavy purse over her arm. When she locked the Jiffy Shop door and turned to face the deserted street, a frigid wind sucked her breath away. She buttoned her raincoat collar around her neck and headed south toward the Takoma Metro station. The cold slush penetrated her red imitation-leather shoes and filled the spaces between her toes, which immediately began to ache. No stranger to the harsh Washington autumns, she forged ahead stoically; the brown pillar marking the Red Line Metro station was only five blocks away. A half hour later, she would be home. She imagined a steaming bowl of chicken noodle soup, the comfort of a warm bath. But her greatest desire was for sleep. Sleep without dreams.

She would have heard his approach had it not been for the wind. The tempest howled and shrieked like a choir of demons, drowning out the normal sounds of the city. She felt the heavy cord as it dropped over her face, and thought a pull string had fallen from her raincoat hood. She attempted to brush it away with a gloved hand. When the cord tightened around her neck, she attempted to cry out but could not. It would not have mattered; the wind would have swallowed up her screams.

As she struggled, a motorcycle policeman appeared at the next intersection, only yards away. The officer braked at the traffic signal and turned his head in her direction as he adjusted a helmet strap. He seemed to be blind, completely unaware that a citizen was being attacked within a stone's throw. Her mind screamed out *Why can't you see me? I'm in the light, here under the lamppost!* The traffic light switched to green. The cop calmly squeezed the accelerator on his handlebar, lifted his black boot from the pavement, and sped away in a swirl of snowflakes. The terrified woman swung her purse overhead in a vain attempt to strike her assailant; its contents were scattered at the curb.

The cord tightened until it was impossible to breathe; she felt cartilage snap in her throat. The woman lost consciousness within seconds, and this was fortunate. She did not feel the thin cylinder of steel as it passed between her ribs and punctured the wall of her racing heart.

Now the tired woman had sleep. Sleep without dreams.

The madman stood exultant over the twisted body; a commonplace artist who had finally produced a masterpiece. Lost in ecstasy, he was unaware of the tears that left wet traces down his face. The policeman had looked directly at him while he strangled his victim, but the officer had seen nothing. Now he was certain: The Voice was not a symptom of madness. The Voice was a source of power—immense power.

He no longer entertained the least fear of being apprehended. With an utterly calm demeanor, he squatted and pulled the nylon cord from around her thin neck. The woman's head rolled to one side, doll-like; her eyes stared dumbly into the darkness. He carefully wrapped the nylon cord into a ball and pushed it into his coat pocket. He pulled the ice pick from her chest and wiped it on the corpse's face to remove the blood. He did this several times, leaving patterns on the cheeks that reminded him of Indian war paint. This suddenly struck him as immensely funny. He chuckled silently at first, and then, as the hilarity of the situation overcame him, laughed out loud.

It was a great relief—to know that the Voice was an objective reality. To know for certain that he was not insane.

*   *   *

Her job in Washington was finished, but it had been impossible to book a connection to Denver before morning. Anne made a reservation for dinner at a four-star Italian restaurant in Arlington. From the time she left the hotel garage, when she crossed the Potomac on the Teddy Roosevelt Bridge, even when she parked the rental car at the restaurant, she had felt it. Someone was watching her. Someone was following.

She sat in the car and watched. And waited. An occasional car plowed through the slush on the street, but no one followed her into the parking lot. Anne closed her eyes and tried to rein in her runaway imagination. It was merely a case of nerves. Why would anyone be following her? Thomson certainly had no idea she was in Washington. She removed the key from the ignition and dropped it into her purse, then opened the door and gingerly stepped onto the asphalt. She was, she told herself, perfectly safe. Unless she slipped on this filthy oil-impregnated ice!

Anne didn't hear the man who approached from the shadows. It was all over within the space of a few heartbeats.

Parris was asleep; he was also dreaming. He was sitting in a small rowboat on a lake with a mirror surface like green glass. Not a ripple. Not a worry. The sun was warm on his face as he cast the line near giant lily pads. The rod bent into a U shape. The reel buzzed as the fish took the orange floating Rapala deep into the still waters. He tried to turn the crank, but the line continued to slip away. The trout had taken the lure, but the reel wasn't working. The reel began to ring intermittently. Why, he thought idly, would a reel make such odd sounds? Fishing reels buzz or click, but reels don't ring. Telephones ring.

He rolled over onto his back. Damn the telephone! Tomorrow, he'd call Mountain Bell and demand an unlisted number. No, that wouldn't be appropriate, not for the chief of police. There were other ways. He would unplug the infernal machine at bedtime. If they needed him at the station, they could damn well send a car and knock on his door! Parris squinted at the red digits on the clock radio and groaned. It was almost 2:00 A.M. He pushed the telephone receiver against his ear and grunted.

"That you, Chief? This is Knox. Sorry to call so late, but . . ."

Parris was instantly awake. Even the insolent Knox wouldn't call his boss at this hour to have a casual chat. He pushed himself up on one elbow. "What is it?"

"Some cop from back East is on the line. Thought he better talk to you, so I got him on a conference hookup." Knox's tone was unusually professional.

He sat up and dropped his feet to the carpet. "Go ahead, Knox."

"Roger." There was a clicking sound as Knox pressed the buttons.

Parris's hand trembled slightly as he gripped the telephone receiver. "Hello. Anybody on the line?"

The connection was perfect; the voice could have been originating from next door. "Hello, Chief Parris? Officer Jerome Sloan, District of Columbia Police."

Parris felt his hands go cold as the blood drained from his fingertips. "You're calling . . . from Washington?"

"Right. Look, one of your citizens was delivered to the hospital over at Howard University Medical School. Bad news. Strangled and stabbed." It was standard operating procedure to contact the police in the hometown so they could notify the victim's family. Parris knew why Knox had referred the call to him. He knew, but he had to ask. "Who's the victim?"

"Well," Sloan cleared his throat nervously, "she's sure not talkin', but her ID says she's Anne Foster. Officer Knox says you . . . ah . . . know her."

The receiver almost slipped from his grasp; he fought to speak without a quaver. "Yeah." Parris felt a cold emptiness growing inside his gut. "I know her."

* * *

The man who was filled with darkness lifted his foot from the accelerator and pressed it lightly on the brake pedal. The car gradually slowed to a crawl. He pressed the brake pedal again and pushed a button on the door panel to roll down the right-front window. He glanced up at his rearview mirror. No head-lights were visible through the swirl of snow behind him; a truck approached from the opposite direction and passed.

He was dead center on the Arlington Memorial Bridge. He unbuttoned his shoulder strap, picked up the ice pick by its metal tip, and tossed it out the window into the black waters of the Potomac. This small physical exertion gave him great plea-sure. The cold air rushing into the warm automobile was in-vigorating. He had never felt so physically sure of himself. He removed the roll of nylon rope from his coat pocket and pitched it out the window.

He hadn't heard the Voice since he drove the ice pick into Anne Foster's chest. That was no problem. He sensed that he was in complete control of his life; he presently had no need for his adviser. When he did have a need, he knew the Voice would be there.

The sympathetic policeman met Parris at National Airport and chauffeured him to the hospital at Howard University. They were halfway to their destination before either spoke.

Sergeant Sloan kept his eyes glued to the slushy streets. "Of-ficer Knox, he said you and this Foster woman . . ." His voice died, trailing off into the humming noise of the late-night traffic.

"Yeah." Parris clenched his fists. He wanted to break some-thing. Anything.

"Sorry, man. That's rough."

"Have any ideas about the assailant?" Parris had his own notions, but it would be best to find out how the locals figured this.

The officer was relieved to shift the subject to business. "No suspects; we have it down as a random attack. MO identical to another attack on the same night, up in Silver Spring. First victim was a black woman, late twenties, clerk in some two-bit store. Larynx crushed, left ventricle punctured. Died almost instantly."

"You're sure it was the same . . ."

"Sure as death and more taxes. Both victims strangled with a nylon cord. We got fiber samples from both assaults, probably from the perp's overcoat. Good match. Both victims stabbed in the chest with an ice pick or something that'd pass for an ice pick. No attempt at robbery or rape. There was no more than a two-hour interval between the assaults." After a few moments passed, the young officer offered another comment. "My cap'n is worried about this one. If the papers tie these attacks together, they'll start yellin' 'Serial Killer in the Beltway.' Son of Sam, devil cults, you know the kinda stuff. We'll never hear the end of it."

It was an oblique plea for Parris to avoid any public statements that might set off a public panic. He didn't bother to answer; the D.C. captain's concerns about adverse publicity were trivial compared to the heavy weight on his chest.

Parris tried to think, but he hadn't slept three hours out of the last forty-eight. Two women. Strangled and stabbed. Like Priscilla Song. Only it wasn't exactly the same. Priscilla's assailant had strangled with his hands, not with a cord. Priscilla was stabbed in the eye. The clerk . . . and Anne . . . they had been stabbed in the chest. It seemed so similar and yet what would Sloan think if he suggested the possibility that a visiting professor of physics was responsible for these crimes? But why would the scientist kill a woman who worked in a convenience store? Only a lunatic would kill a stranger for no reason. Thomson might make a few dollars on drugs, but he wasn't a lunatic. Sergeant Sloan must be right. It was random. A coincidence that Anne, in pursuit of a supposed drug dealer, had encountered a crazed killer. Metropolitan Washington had no shortage of killers. Anne was simply the latest casualty.

Parris followed Sergeant Sloan into the deep recesses of the Howard University teaching hospital. Most of the staff, from medical students to nurses and physicians, were black. The physician who had filed the police report on Anne was a short, plump Puerto Rican who spoke with a barely discernible lisp. With clinical detachment, he described the cord marks on the neck and the tiny hole that had penetrated the chest a full twelve centimeters. The physician paused after he had finished his report on the clinical details. "We made the preliminary ID from her driver's license. Maybe you could give us a positive . . ."

Parris nodded dumbly. This encounter, the doctor's lilting accent—it had the hollow quality of a dream. A very bad dream.

The policemen left the physician to attend to an accident victim and eventually paused before a heavy green door. Officer Jerome Sloan stood to one side, his gaze fixed on the cracked linoleum floor. "If you don't mind, man, I'd as soon wait out here." He shuddered. "Never did like these places."

Parris didn't answer. He pushed the green door open. When his eyes had adjusted to the dim lighting, he saw her prone figure draped in a light blue sheet at the far end of the windowless room. His boot heels clicked hollowly as he approached her immobile form. Parris forced his hand forward and grasped the sheet; he pulled it down just below her shoulders. She appeared much as he had expected; her eyes were closed as in a dreamless slumber. A long, arcing bruise circled the tender whiteness of her throat like a dark blue necklace. He touched her face, stroking her cheek with two fingers.

Anne's eyelids flickered, then opened. "Hello, copper," she whispered.

He squeezed her pale hand. "The doc said you were sedated, probably wouldn't wake up until tomorrow morning. Thought I'd hang around and keep an eye on you."

"Shut up," she said weakly, "and kiss me. On the mouth."

He did.

The Puerto Rican physician padded softly into the room. He coughed to announce his presence and grinned. "I'm only her doctor, but I think our patient needs some rest."

Parris kissed Anne lightly on the forehead and followed the plump man to the door. "I understand this was a close thing."

"She's lucky to be with the living," the physician replied. "The penetration missed her heart by less than a centimeter." He held his finger barely off the tip of his thumb to demonstrate.

"We can be thankful the bastard had bad aim."

The surgeon smiled proudly, like a small boy who knew a wonderful secret. "Nothing wrong with his aim; he was dead center over the heart." He removed something from his pocket and dropped it into Parris's hand. "She was wearing this around her neck. See that little metal tracing on that stone? It deflected the weapon just enough . . ."

Parris tilted the rose quartz pendant to achieve just the right reflection from the fluorescent lights. There it was—a hairline tracing of steel where the tip of the ice pick had slid across the polished surface of the hard quartz. Anne's survival was no accident. Her life was a gift from the old Indian with the radiator problem; the minor prophet who had vanished into the thin desert air on Route 64.

19

Claude Potter-Evans was mentally exhausted; he leaned back in his rocking chair and rubbed his eyes. He had used the computer in the county library, programmed it to try dozens of potential key words. He had tested the "z f r c y r t" message on transposition and substitution systems, diagraphs, triagraphs, Vigenére squares, and Playfair ciphers. Every attempt had been a failure. This whole undertaking was a waste of precious hours. He had told the policeman that it was absurd. You couldn't break a serious code with only seven letters to work with. Particularly at his age, there were better ways to spend one's time—walking in the forest, making rabbit stew, reading a good book. A nighttime visit to Madeline's apartment. But no time to waste with fool's errands. The old man pushed himself from the chair and pulled back the curtain on a small window to survey his "estate." A light breeze whispered through the spruce; a blue jay fussed at a tufted-ear squirrel; marshmallow clouds were impaled on the summit of Salt Mountain. But he couldn't get it out of his mind. If the girl had enciphered a message while she was under stress, it had to be something simple. Something *very* simple. She was under enormous pressure, perhaps knowing that death was near. How could she remain calm under such circumstances, calm enough to encode her last message to those who would ponder her fate?

The riddle had nagged at him, robbed him of sleep, ruined his normally hearty appetite. It was like the war days, when he had been so close to a solution but unable to see it. He bowed his head in frustration. "I'm a fool. . . . It was a bloody mistake to get involved in this nonsense. If only I could put my finger on it. . . ." He paused and looked at his hands. Mistake . . . finger on it. He remembered a seemingly unimportant entry from her high school transcript. Priscilla Song had taken two semesters of typing. The victim, was a touch-typist. A touch-typist didn't look at the keyboard like a hunt-and-peck typist. Hunt-and-peckers might get a letter wrong here or there, but an expert touch-typist would generate several words of total garble before she realized her fingertips were misplaced on the keyboard. Potter-Evans's mouth dropped open and he cried out, "Oh surely not . . . how could I have overlooked something so simple!" What if it was never a code? . . . What if it was a damned bloody *mistake!*

The old man hurried to his workbench. He purposely misplaced his hands one row high on the keyboard of the antique typewriter, closed his eyes, and typed "z f r c y r t" as if his fingers were in the correct position. This produced a meaningless garble of letters, as did the second, third, and fourth trial positions. On the fifth trial, he started in the canonical position, then misplaced his fingers one position to the right; the z became an x. More garble. On the next trial, he offset his position one key to the left. This would "decode" the mysterious message if the victim had, whether by accident or design, misplaced her fingers one position to the *right*. He typed "z f r c y r t." The z was replaced by pressure on the shift key. Of course—to capitalize the first letter of a proper name! It would be a reflex action for a touch-typist, even if she were under great stress. Instead of the seven letters of the "coded message," only six letters appeared. A name. No need to check the long list; this was a very familiar name.

"Aha . . . Aha! Great Jupiter!" the old man roared as he

danced on the plank flooring. The sounds of his exultation echoed through the forest. "I've done it! I've jolly well *done* it!"

They arrived in Granite Creek at sundown. Anne's ivory skin was more pale than usual, but aside from a general weakness of limb and shortness of breath, her recovery was remarkable. She had Parris stop at the supermarket, where she selected a pair of New York–cut steaks, Idaho potatoes, and a copy of her employer's newspaper. They were in her kitchen, the steaks were in the oven, and Parris had just switched the oven to broil when Anne began to scan the newspaper. At the bottom of the editorial page, she spotted the brief announcement. "Scotty," she said, "look at this!"

Parris felt a tingling sensation on the back of his neck as he read the single paragraph:

Rumor Has it . . .

While the *Adviser* hesitates to publish unsubstantiated stories, we have decided to report a rumor that is already common knowledge on the campus of Rocky Mountain Polytechnic. According to our sources, a member of the Physics Department has made a major scientific discovery. While the exact nature of the breakthrough is a closely held secret, we are told that the excitement revolves around an important new development in superconductivity. Stay tuned!

Parris closed his eyes and concentrated. "Something sounds awfully familiar. Wait a minute! In that box of stuff from her apartment—I remember now. She was listed as an author on some technical publications, before she came to RMP. There was something about magnetism . . . and *superconductors.*"

Wheels were turning in Anne's head. "Could be," she said, "Thomson's early visit to Washington wasn't about drugs, after all."

"You figure," he said, "the Song girl made some kind of

breakthrough . . . then Thomson took the opportunity, after Pacheco murdered the girl, to steal her superconductor discovery?" It sounded awfully thin.

Anne was nervously twisting the rose-quartz pendant. "I assumed Thomson visited Zimmelhauf Enterprises to have a drug formulation analyzed, but what if that scoundrel was there with a superconductor sample?" She slapped herself on the forehead. "I wondered about the visit to the law firm. When I called, the man said they specialized in intellectual property."

Parris was a little behind the curve. "Intellectual property . . . ?"

"He intends to file a patent application. That scum! He's going to patent the dead girl's superconductor discovery as his own."

"Well," he began uneasily as he noticed the hard glint in her eyes, "we don't know that Thomson is going to claim anything that isn't his own property. Maybe he discovered this superwhatsit all by himself!"

Anne removed a fat wallet from her purse and withdrew a crisp twenty-dollar bill from its innards. She held the bill daintily between two scarlet fingernails, waved it before his face, then dropped the bank note on the table. "I'll wager my Mr. Jackson against your Mr. Hamilton that Professor Thomson announces a superconductor discovery and that he's in court within, let's say, twelve months, trying to prove that he didn't steal the research from the murdered girl. Put up or shut up."

Parris grinned and pushed the bill away. "A sworn officer of the law can't indulge in this sort of vice."

Something else was gnawing at his insides. The case against Pacheco was so sweet, so solid. What could a clever attorney for the defense accomplish by suggesting that Thomson was profiting from the Song girl's death? He still hadn't established a motive for Pacheco; a sexual crime had seemed plausible, but Simpson's final report specified that the girl had not been raped. A drug deal gone sour was a possibility, but their best efforts to tie Pacheco or Priscilla to the drug scene had come up empty. All it might take to queer the prosecution of the drug pusher was an unexpected twist. A greedy university professor who saw the untimely death as an opportunity for theft would do just fine. Parris closed his eyes and dropped his face into his hands. Why couldn't something, just for once, be simple? Anne was at his side, stroking her long fingers through his hair. "What is it?"

"Heartburn."

20

Scott Parris was sipping a steaming cup of acidic coffee as he gazed through the plate-glass window at the pine-studded canyon between the Los Alamos town site and the National Laboratory territory. The laboratory cafeteria was quiet at midmorning; the policeman was certain that he was completely alone when the tall man materialized at his side and tapped his shoulder.

The policeman lurched involuntarily, spilling scalding coffee on his hand.

"You," the owner of the finger said, "must be our visitor."

"Jeepers," Parris muttered as he wiped at his wrist with a paper napkin, "where did you come from?"

The man made an undulating manta-ray motion with his hand. "Just tunneled in through the quantum fuzz," he chirped gleefully. When he saw Parris's puzzled expression, he was mildly apologetic. "Sorry. That's kind of an inside joke."

The policeman studied the tall, gaunt figure in wrinkled khaki shorts that, unfortunately, came just short of hiding a bulbous set of knees. His black T-shirt was emblazoned in luminescent orange with the announcement DANCING IS MY LIFE. The scientist was looming over him expectantly, peering at Parris as though the policeman was an interesting specimen.

"I'm Scott Parris. You are . . . ?"

"Otto D. Proctor. Had a call about you, from Protocol. Understand you have some questions about something or other."

The physicist put a plastic tray on the table, then offered a hand, which Parris accepted. The tray held a peculiar assortment of items that, given the hour, Parris assumed must be the man's breakfast.

"I'm chief of police at Granite Creek in Colorado. Rocky Mountain town, a bit of silver mining, some tourism. Biggest industry is Rocky Mountain Polytechnic."

Proctor sat down, spread hot Mexican salsa on a bagel, and nodded. "I've been there a couple of times. Nice little town."

The policeman touched his fingertips together in a prayerful manner and studied Proctor as he spoke, "What I want to discuss is . . . sensitive. I assume you'll be willing to keep mum about our conversation?"

Proctor swallowed a mouthful of diet cola. "Don't fret; discretion is my middle name."

"Did you hear about the murder we had a couple of weeks ago?"

The scientist popped a pimiento-stuffed olive into his mouth. "Can't say I did." He chewed the olive, then gulped it down. "Don't read the papers all that often; never watch TV. Who was murdered?"

Parris gave him a thumbnail sketch of the Song homicide, including the cardinal fact that Julio Pacheco's prints were on the Phillips screwdriver. The physicist spread a spoon of green chili on a bagel. "Sounds like you've got it locked up. What brings you to Los Alamos?"

"Need some background information. The victim may have been working on superconductivity. I need to learn a few things."

"Ah, superconductivity. That explains why Protocol asked *me* to chat with you. It's my specialty."

"Tell me," Parris said, "about superconductors. What's so special?"

"There are only a few fundamental things you need to know." Proctor clearly enjoyed his role as teacher. "First, several ordinary electrical conductors, like lead or mercury, are also super-conductors. But only when you cool them to extraordinarily low temperatures. Near absolute zero, the free electrons in the metal organize themselves into pairs. These electron pairs dance through the material without impediment." He closed his eyes and swayed as if waltzing with an invisible partner. "Under these conditions, the material has no electrical resistance."

"And that's important?"

"Important?" Proctor's tone betrayed his astonishment at this question. "Damn right. Remove the resistance from electrical circuits and remarkable things happen. Computer and commu-nications circuits run faster; energy savings are enormous. But that's not all. Magnetic fields can't penetrate a superconductor; my chums call this the Meissner effect. Place a small magnet over a superconductor, the superconductor repels the magnetic field and—guess what?—the magnet floats in midair!"

"And this is useful for . . ."

"In principle at least, for all kinds of stuff. For making super-railroads," Proctor said, "where the train literally floats above the tracks. No noise, no friction, and *whoosh*, the locomotive barrels along at three hundred miles an hour. Problem is, it's awfully expensive to cool the superconductors, so levitating a train costs piles of megabucks." The scientist wiped something off his chin with a napkin. "What does the young lady's super-conductor research have to do with her murder?"

"Probably nothing, but there's a rumor that someone in the RMP Physics Department is about to announce a major break-through in superconductivity."

"RMP has a moderately good physics department for a small university," Proctor said with slightly raised eyebrows, "but I wasn't aware that anyone there was even working on supercon-ductivity."

"As far as we can find out, Priscilla Song was the only person at RMP who ever did any research on superconductivity. Odd coincidence, this rumor, so soon after her death."

"Coincidences," Proctor said, "are nature's way of saying, 'Pay attention!' "

"If someone took advantage of the homicide to pilfer her research, our DA could have a big problem prosecuting the guy whose prints are on the murder weapon. For one thing, we haven't established a motive for Mr. Pacheco. The defense will insist that whoever stole the research results also murdered the student."

Proctor shook his head at this notion. "That's utter nonsense. No sane person would commit murder to steal superconductivity research results . . . unless . . ." He blushed slightly. "No, never mind, that's sheer fantasy."

"What's a fantasy?"

Proctor waved the question away. "Forget I mentioned it."

"Look," Parris said forcefully, "I drove over two hundred miles to pick your brains, so don't hold out on me."

The scientist forgot about his bagel. "There's only one superconductor discovery that would be worth *killing* for. We're talking about a major impact on virtually every application of electricity—a new world. The inventor would become wealthy beyond all dreams of avarice. The nation that controlled the basic patents would be in the driver's seat, both technologically and economically. Whole national economies would be shaken."

"Sounds like science fiction," Parris said doubtfully.

"That's because it *is* science fiction . . . until someone discovers, perhaps stumbles over . . . the Holy Grail."

Parris was leaning over the table. "Precisely what sort of superconductor discovery are we talking about?"

"A material," Proctor said with a faraway look in his eye, "that superconducts at ordinary everyday temperatures. If we didn't need expensive cryogens to make them work, superconductors would be used in practically every electrical circuit in the world. The technological and social implications are absolutely staggering."

"And," Parris said thoughtfully, "a repairman like Pacheco wouldn't understand this sort of breakthrough. But a physicist certainly would."

"Right," Proctor added, "or a chemist, or an electrical engineer, or . . ."

"What are the chances that Priscilla Song or another scientist at RMP has already made a discovery like that?"

Proctor grinned; he made an O with his thumb and finger and peeked through the circle at Parris. "Right at absolute zero," he said.

Parris was far down the road, but Proctor's phrase kept echoing through his mind like a commercial jingle that couldn't be dismissed. "A superconductor discovery . . . worth killing for!" Could Thomson be something worse than a thief? The rational part of his mind, that part that measured and weighed, answered "no." Pacheco's prints were on the screwdriver, so Pacheco was guilty as sin. But what if someone had hired the Mexican to do this messy job?

Claude Potter-Evans winked at the middle-aged woman standing in front of him; she was at the police station to pay a parking ticket. "Ah now, young lassie. Got ourselves crosswise of the law, did we?" He was rewarded with a slight blush, which made his day a success. His flirtation was interrupted when the woman left and Piggy bellowed, "Next!" The fat policeman managed a grimace that passed for an official smile as Potter-Evans moved to the front of the line. "What can I do for you?"

"Potter-Evans calling. I wish to see the chief constable. I have some significant news for your superior."

Piggy Slocum squinted his porcine eyes at the old man. "You talkin' about the boss . . . you mean Chief Parris?"

"Indeed. The very same person. Now will you kindly summon him for me?"

"Sorry buddy, no can do. Main honcho's outta town today. Down in New Mexico. Whatcha want—somethin' I can do?"

Potter-Evans sighed with exasperation. "Afraid not. Tell him I was here. And tell him," he leaned over and fairly snarled, "that he jolly well better be here the next time I call or I will put a curse on him and all his descendants even unto the seventh generation!"

Piggy, missing the intended humor, scowled suspiciously and scooted an inch backward.

"Also inform him I have solved his little riddle; I have unraveled the murder victim's last message and have a name for your chief. I must go now. I have fine wines to taste, supple young women to delight, savory rabbit stew to brew in my iron pot! But not necessarily," he added slyly, "in that order."

Piggy found a pad and a ballpoint. "Gimme a phone number." But the odd visitor had left. Slocum made a note of the time, then scribbled a few barely legible words on his log:

Parris. Old geezer. Pottie-something.
Wants to see chief about rabbit stew, booze, women.

Piggy turned his attention to the tall, extremely thin man waiting for service. "And what can I do for you?"

"Stopped by to pay a parking ticket. Couldn't help but over-hear that fellow who just left. Is he actually helping with the Song homicide investigation?"

"Him and half the county, bub. Bein' a civilian, you'd be surprised how many folks with a screw loose drive us buggy after a major crime." Piggy tapped his finger on his temple. "Some of 'em think they can read tea leaves and tell us who did it. Even Clara's Aunt Daisy is gettin' in on the act. We all know it's that Mexican what did it, so why do they bother us?"

The man appeared to be impressed. "Clara's Aunt Daisy?"

Piggy motioned with his thumb toward Clara's glass-walled enclosure. "Clara Tavishuts, our dispatcher. She's one of them

Utes. Moved off the rez. Now her Aunt Daisy, they say she's some kind of palm reader, came up here with some witch doctor tale for the boss. I hope," he added, "the chief don't believe none of that Injun hocus-pocus."

"No," the thin man said with genuine concern, "I would certainly hope not."

"Well, let's see then," Piggy muttered as he looked at the man's ticket. "You hadda little parkin' violation; fine is thirty-two dollars, unless you want to talk to the judge."

The professor pushed a personal check across the counter.

Piggy squinted at the name printed on the check. "Well, I'll be." He glanced at the visitor with renewed interest. "You any kin to the King?"

"Beg your pardon?"

"Elvis. I hear they saw him up in Aspen last month drivin' a Mayflower van. He was a truck driver, you know, before he got famous. Thought maybe you an' him was cousins or somethin'."

"I doubt it." The man sniffed. "My relatives all have forty-six chromosomes."

"Ain't that somethin'!" Piggy leaned forward and lowered his voice to a raspy whisper. "They say my great-grandaddy Lloyd Slocum had seven toes. On both feet! Extra toes had little webs o' skin between 'em." He splayed his stubby fingers to demonstrate. "How do you figger things like that happen?"

"Your ancestors," the man said icily, "probably shared a rather familial gene pool."

"Oh, I don't know," Piggy said doubtfully, "my incesters was mainly farmers and ranchers and such. Don't think they had much time for swimmin'."

21

The announcement of the news conference had electrified the small university. Science reporters from major newspapers had begun arriving during the morning. By noon, three television networks had lights and cameras set up in the Hatfield Memorial Auditorium. The dean felt short of breath as he gauged his audience through a slit in the stage curtains. They were a surly-looking lot, these reporters, cynical from many disappointments. The administrator assured himself that they would not be disappointed today. He turned to appraise the physicist who stood at his side, the man whose name would be a household word before the day was over.

The scientist, between sips of ice water, was also peeking through a slight part in the stage curtain to watch the audience. At first, he barely noticed the woman who entered at the rear of the auditorium. She wore a wide-brimmed hat that partially concealed her features. As she made her way up the aisle, advancing through the mass of technicians, Anne Foster looked, it seemed, directly at him. The water glass slipped from his fingers and bounced on the hardwood flooring. The dean retrieved the glass. "Looks like a good turnout. They smell a big story."

The physicist's voice was barely audible. "I'm not going out there."

The dean cocked his head and raised one eyebrow. "What's that?"

"I'm sorry, Francis. I don't feel well."

"Got a touch of the butterflies? Never mind. They'll love you. Really."

He turned away to avoid eye contact with the dean. "I can't . . . won't go out there. You can show them the sample, but don't mention my name or our deal is off. I'm leaving." With that, he turned and left the stage.

The dean had developed a habit of talking to himself when under stress. He pulled himself up to his full height and threw his head back with a defiance derived from unshakable self-confidence. "Francis Butterworth," he muttered, "it's all starting to fall apart, and you're on your own. But you can handle this; that's why you're the dean of this university. Now let's go out there and *lie like a champ!*"

The dean marched onto the stage. He tapped on the microphone; there was a squeal of feedback while a technician hurried to adjust the amplifier gain. "We wish to express our appreciation to all of you," he said with evident good humor, "for traveling to our isolated mountain village for this announcement." He paused while the din of conversation from the audience diminished. "One of our senior professors has asked me to make an announcement for the press that is, if I may say so, unprecedented."

The seasoned reporters wondered why the scientist wasn't making his own announcement. Someone called out the obvious question: "Where is this professor?"

Francis Butterworth was ready for the challenge. It was time to manipulate these vermin. He produced a plastic smile. "We've developed a minor hitch; seems there are a few final legal questions to be dealt with, patent questions and the like; you know how troublesome lawyers can be about inventions." He hoped that it would sound plausible. Much better than telling them the scientist was having a nervous breakdown. "Our inventor is eager to discuss every aspect of his work with the members of the press. When he heard about the legal issues that would prevent him from providing you with a full disclosure of his research, he refused to be present at this gathering. I argued against this decision, but his mind is made up. It's basically an issue of ethics; he will meet with you only when it is possible to be completely forthright."

This revelation that the star was not available brought a chorus of groans from the assembled press. "Who is this guy?" someone yelled.

"I'm sorry. He's concerned about his privacy, doesn't want to have a group of media people surrounding his home before he can answer their questions. Therefore, I am not authorized to reveal his identity at this time." Butterworth's collar felt tight around his throat.

"Are you," the man from CNN asked, "the only person who knows the identity of this mystery scientist?" Mystery scientist! Headline stuff! Three score and four journalists scribbled the phrase into their notebooks.

The dean tugged at his collar. "No, certainly not. The inventor's identity is known to a select group of individuals, including the university counsel, and the chairman of the Physics Department." That, he thought, would keep them chasing their tales.

"Could you give us their names, or is that also a state secret?"

"Paul McConnell is RMP's attorney. Professor Arnold Dexter is chairman of the Physics Department. But I hope you won't bother these gentlemen; I'm sure that within a few days—"

"Then we may safely assume that the inventor is a member of the physics staff?"

"I would not presume to limit your assumptions in any way." This brought appreciative laughter.

"If everything is a big secret, what, exactly, are we here for?" asked the woman from *Time*.

"I will," the dean announced, "reveal the nature of the discovery."

The crowd was now completely silent. Scientific breakthrough or an episode of self-delusion, either way it would be hot stuff on the evening news.

"In 1911"—the dean adopted the pedantic tone of a teacher—"a scientist in Holland discovered the phenomena of superconductivity. This conduction of electricity without loss garnered a Nobel Prize for the discoverer, Professor Onnes, and more Nobels were awarded to others for subsequent discoveries in this field."

A murmur propagated through the audience. At the very least, the anonymous scientist was sniffing after a Nobel.

The dean continued. "Nevertheless, the applications of superconductivity have remained limited because it has been necessary to cool the known superconductors to fantastically low temperatures before they exhibit zero resistance. I know," the dean continued with an air of complete self-assurance, "that those of you who report on science and technology are quite aware of the breakthroughs made in superconductivity only a few years ago. This work by researchers in Zurich also won a Nobel Prize in Physics for the discoverers. The operating temperature of superconductors was eventually increased by about a factor of five and has remained there for the past several years. Even with those breakthroughs, which I certainly do not diminish, it is still necessary to use cryogens, like liquid nitrogen, to cool superconductors. This means that applications are still limited and relatively expensive. What scientists have always yearned for is a superconductor that would operate at ordinary temperatures. Scientists refer to this long-sought material as a 'room temperature' superconductor. One of our scientists," the dean paused for dramatic effect, "has discovered a formulation that produces a room-temperature superconductor."

Pandemonium. Reporters elbowed and pushed to get close to the stage. Flash cameras popped like firecrackers. The dean beamed. "You may be interested to know that the new material has a strong superconducting transition at sixty-one degrees Celsius."

A young man from the *Albuquerque Journal* shouted, "What's that in Fahrenheit?"

The dean pulled the microphone toward his lips. The sound of his voice boomed off the walls. "That's about one hundred and forty-one degrees on the Fahrenheit scale, ladies and gentlemen." Those few reporters who understood the significance of this figure were temporarily struck dumb.

Anne Foster raised her hand and got the dean's friendly nod. He thought it politic to give the local press a chance. No one in the press corps knew her, and this piqued their interest. She identified herself as a correspondent for the *Granite Creek Adviser*. The CNN crew turned one of its spotlights on the woman's slim figure. She removed the hat, spilling a fountain of scarlet hair over her shoulders.

"My paper would like to know more about the history of the invention. I assume this research was sponsored by the university?"

"Well," the dean responded, ". . . actually, no. That is, the research was performed at home, in the inventor's basement laboratory."

The journalists were imagining the sensational story: MYSTERY SCIENTIST . . . BIG DISCOVERY IN BASEMENT LAB!

"Then," she continued evenly, "we may assume that the anonymous researcher performed this work entirely on his own. When, precisely, did he develop the first successful specimen?"

The dean forced a strained smile as he responded to the lovely redhead. "I'm afraid I can't answer your question about the chronology of the discovery, since it is related to the question of patenting the invention." In fact, the dean had no idea when the professor had first made the superconductor; the physicist was tight-lipped on that issue. "I can assure you, however, that the inventor has kept careful notes; the times of the tests of various samples has been witnessed and attested to by another member of our faculty." The dean prayed that this was entirely correct.

If the patent fell through, so did the sweet deal the university had made with the inventor.

The dean continued, waving away other questions. "Even though the research was not performed on university premises or with RMP equipment, the inventor has graciously informed the administration that he will, when funds from royalties become available, sponsor a new condensed-matter physics center at RMP. An agreement is being drawn up. It will be a world-class facility." The inventor, it was understood, would be the director of this new facility, probably the next president of Rocky Mountain Polytechnic. That is, unless he was stolen away from them by UC-Berkeley or Harvard or any one of a dozen other top-flight universities.

22

Leading laboratories worked around the clock to duplicate the incredible discovery announced at the RMP news conference. There were already rumors that IBM-Zurich had made a break-through with a formula using carbon-60 buckyballs and undisclosed secret ingredients. A young materials scientist in Beijing found evidence for a superconducting transition just under twenty-two degrees Celsius with a formulation based on thallium, arsenic, and copper. Dozens of scientists saw peculiar behavior at high temperatures, but there seemed to be nothing concrete in spite of thousands of faxed copies of preliminary papers. IBM was not talking, and the Chinese scientist canceled her own news conference when the remarkable effect vanished as mysteriously as it had appeared.

Anne's frustration grew in proportion to the excitement about the room-temperature superconductor. Crowds of media types hung around the campus, probing for information. Most of the university staff knew nothing, or at least admitted nothing. The three persons who knew the identity of the "inventor" were unavailable for comment. The dean was hiding somewhere in Boulder, Paul McConnell was rumored to be spinning the wheels in Atlantic City. Of the Enlightened Trio, as they had been dubbed by the press, only Arnold Dexter remained in town, and the chairman was accepting no calls. A member of the Granite Creek Police Department was stationed outside Dexter's home to ward off the more aggressive members of the press corps. And, most suggestive of all, Waldo Thomson had disappeared. Rumor had it that he was sunning himself in the Virgin Islands.

Thomson had become an obsession. Anne went to sleep plotting strategies to find hard proof of his misdeeds; she woke up wondering when he would identify himself as the discoverer of the room-temperature superconductor. During a breakfast of cornflakes and sliced peaches, she was writing Thomson's name on her pad when a shiver propagated wavelike up her spine and terminated in a tingling sensation to the back of her neck. The mysterious "word" found on Priscilla's computer file was written on the same page of her notebook. Anne drew vertical lines between the repeated characters. She sat, staring at the printed characters. Had she been blind? Had Scott Parris noticed this simple relationship?

Her first impulse was to rush to a telephone and call Parris. But how would the chief of police respond? She imagined his answer: "Interesting, sweetheart, but circumstantial. Nothing the DA can take to court. Priscilla could have typed his name for any one of a hundred innocent reasons. Unless Thomson makes a wrong move, there's nothing I can do."

But why would Priscilla Song use her last minute of life to leave Thomson's name on her computer? Why indeed. The possibilities were frightening. But what to do?

"Well," she said aloud, "I'll slip a burr under his saddle. Then we'll see if he stays on his horse." Dexter was the key. In fact, Dexter was the only game in town. There was no point in barging into the Physics Department and demanding to see the chairman. That would require climbing over at least a dozen reporters camped outside the entrance, and it probably wouldn't work, anyway. Anne dialed the number five times and heard a busy signal each time. On the sixth try, the telephone rang and was immediately picked up by Kristin Waters.

"Oh, Anne, I'm so pleased to hear your sweet voice. Those people have been driving me insane, using every ruse you can imagine to learn the identity of the "mystery scientist." They've been inviting me to lunch, pleading to interview me on television . . . you just can't imagine."

"It must be awful. Are you holding up all right?"

"I've no alternative. But how can I help you, dear?"

"I absolutely must see the chairman."

Kristin sighed. "You might as well ask to see the Pope. Professor Dexter is a rather sensitive man, and he simply can't deal with all the commotion we've had around here. Even if you could see him, he won't discuss the superconductor thing with anybody. Just between you and me, I'm not certain he knows all that much."

"Do this. Tell Dexter I already know the identity of the mystery scientist."

"Do you really know, Annie?"

Anne felt her pulse racing. "I know that and a lot more. Tell your boss it's in his interest to see me before I publish what I know about what's been going on in the Physics Department." There. That should do it. Arnold Dexter was a little slow, but any hint that there might be trouble for his precious department would surely interest the chairman.

Kristin was breathless. "I'll tell him. Stay by the phone."

In less than three minutes, Anne's telephone rang. She recognized the flat voice of Arnold Dexter. He agreed to meet with her.

When Anne parked her car in the gravel lot by the North Park tennis courts, Arnold Dexter was waiting. He wore a gray overcoat and a black wool cap pulled down over his ears. The chairman of the Physics Department looked old, forlorn, and lonely. Anne felt a twinge of remorse for what she planned to do, then forced herself to dismiss any regret for manipulating Dexter. It was her only chance to get to Thomson. She got out of her car and greeted the chairman. "Thanks for seeing me. I know you're busy these days."

This got little more than a nod and a grunt. She sensed that he was irritated, even angry. It was not surprising; he must be under enormous pressure. She walked beside Dexter as they headed toward a thick grove of pines that straddled the boundary between the city park and the national forest land on the mountain slope.

"Why was it so important that you see me, Miss Foster?"

She had to choose each word with great care. Just enough to unnerve him. "I assume you got the message from Kristin? The entire message?"

"I did," he said. "You claim to know the identity of the inventor of the room-temperature superconductor. Why must you talk to me?"

"Because we have something in common. We both know the identity of the so-called mystery scientist."

Dexter stopped in his tracks and seemed to fix his attention on the crumpled remnants of last summer's grass. His lower lip trembled ever so slightly; in spite of the frigid air, perspiration was beaded under his nostrils. "I'm rather exhausted. Make your point."

She decided to push her luck. A chairman, even a quiet man like Dexter, had to know everything that happened in his department. Surely he had his own suspicions about Thomson's "discovery." That would account for his dark mood. Anne drew a deep breath. "We both know," she said, "that the so-called mystery scientist is a fraud."

He raised his head and looked directly at her for the first time.

His expression was a mixture of puzzlement and alarm. "A fraud? But why on earth would you say . . ."

"Priscilla Song discovered the new superconductor. I've known for some time."

"That's absolutely the most absurd . . ." Dexter shoved his hands deep into his overcoat pockets. He stopped walking and looked up at the heavy clouds seemingly spilling over the summit of Salt Mountain. He wished he could be somewhere else. A quiet valley. Somewhere far, far away. "I don't understand your purpose. Why are you telling me this?"

"Simple matter of communication. If someone claims credit for the dead girl's discovery, I'm ready to blow him out of the water. I'm sure we understand each other."

Dexter, openmouthed and pale, now turned and faced her. "What . . . what do you expect of me?"

"You're a bright fellow. I'll leave it to your imagination."

He appeared to be genuinely puzzled. "But I don't understand—"

"Let's put it this way," Anne interrupted, "once Professor Thomson decides to tell the truth, it's all over." She was amazed at her audacity. It was apparent from Dexter's taut expression that she had gotten the message across loud and clear. He would be certain to warn Thomson, and the scoundrel would surely panic. If Thomson was sufficiently frightened, he might even withdraw his claim to the room-temperature superconductor. Anne was pleased with her performance.

Dexter studied the clouds; they seemed to be boiling in slow motion as they spilled down the slope. The physicist turned his attention to the pine grove, as if he yearned for the protection of its deep shadows. A muscle in his jaw twitched; he opened his mouth, then clamped it shut. A pair of joggers, oblivious to Anne and the chairman, passed within a few yards. She turned to leave. "I'm sorry," she said, "but I'm going to publish what I know." Anne hurried away, terrified that this forlorn figure might burst into tears.

23

Parris was musing about Daisy's "vision," when the connection bubbled up from his subconscious. He practically ran to his squad car, and was banging on Walter Simpson's door within ten minutes.

Simpson, somewhat bleary-eyed, opened the door. The medical examiner muttered something about "never a moment's rest" under his breath; he waved Parris in without a word of welcome and pointed to an overstuffed green chair. Parris ignored the chair. "What's the matter, Doc? I interrupt your afternoon nap?"

"What's the matter," the old man replied gruffly, "is that I'm getting old. And tired. What misfortune brings you to my door?"

"I want to talk. About the corpse."

Simpson waved his hand impatiently. "I got four bodies in cold storage downstairs. Which one interests you?"

"You know very well which one." Parris couldn't bring himself to speak her name; Priscilla's shade already cast its shadow over his sleep. "About some of your findings . . ."

"The student?" The medical examiner sat down heavily in an antique rocking chair. Parris was surprised that the old furniture didn't break. "Which findings?"

The policeman hovered over him. "You found traces of adhesive between her breasts. Like something might have been taped to her skin."

"That's right. On the dermis over the sternal angle."

"You said you found odd marks in the roof of her mouth."

Simpson was gradually waking up and taking an interest. "Small abrasions on the *palatum mole*. The soft palate."

"Then there were the senseless mutilations. They may not have been senseless after all."

The old physician cocked his head and squinted one eye. "Go on."

"Look at it like this. The girl was murdered by someone who wanted something she had taped to her chest. It could have been a small container, maybe holding three samples of a superconductor."

The hint of a suspicious grin crinkled the edges of Simpson's lips. "Why three?"

"I have an informer." He wouldn't mention Daisy's dream; Simpson would laugh him out of town. "Anyway, she was determined that her killer wouldn't have them."

"So," Simpson interjected, "she upped and swallowed the stuff?"

"You got it. She tried to swallow them all. We know she was strangled. Let's assume she coughs up two of the samples, but her killer knows, or at least suspects, she didn't spit them all up."

Doc was rocking as he gazed thoughtfully at the Tiffany lamp on the table by his chair. "So he cuts her open to find what might have been swallowed."

"I think that's what happened."

"You don't just think. You know something you're not telling your favorite medical examiner."

"You'd laugh your fool head off. I'll tell you later. Sometime when we're fishing and I'm in a mood to take some of your abuse."

"Fair enough. But I should remind you I already examined the stomach contents. There wasn't anything there you wouldn't expect to find."

Simpson watched Scott's face drop. "Then there was nothing . . ."

"Oh, I didn't exactly say there was nothing. Just nothing in her stomach or large intestine. It's standard procedure to examine stomach contents. Tells your trusty medical examiner lots of important stuff you cops want to know, like when the victim had her last meal, what she ate, maybe even where she ate."

"Then where . . ."

"It's a long way from your mouth to your stomach. The trip goes by way of the *Pars oralis pharyngis,* then the—"

"Try speaking English."

The medical examiner assumed a hurt expression. "If you insist, but it spoils the mystique. Let's say that whatever she swallowed, if she swallowed anything, might have lodged in her throat or esophagus."

"And her killer didn't look there?"

"Murderers, much like your average police administrators, have little knowledge of anatomy. Much like children, actually."

"But you'll take a look? You do still have the body."

Simpson pushed himself up from the rocking chair. "No one has made funeral arrangements. She's still in the icebox. I'll do it right now. Want to come along?"

"Thanks. I'd rather sit here and stare at the wallpaper. Wonderful pattern. All those little yellow flowers."

Parris watched the minute hand on the massive grandfather clock. It was almost a half hour before Simpson returned, wiping his hands on a green towel.

"So. Did you find anything?"

Simpson had a twinkle in his eye. "Oh, nothing much. Except this." He flipped the disk like a coin, and Scott Parris caught it. It was a dead ringer for the picture of the mystery scientist's superconductor sample in *Time* magazine. Simpson was watching his guest with great interest. "Now why would the Mexican disembowel his victim to get something like that?"

Parris was mesmerized by the small black disk in his hand. "Why indeed?"

Eddie "Rocks" Knox had a hunch. It was enough to send him far off his assigned patrol onto a rough national forest fire road east of town. The road was also the access to a few cabins inhabited during the season by hunters of elk and deer. The road made little sense as an escape route for the Mexican, since it dead-ended halfway around the mountain. It made sense that Pacheco, who knew his way around these parts, wouldn't box himself in. But Knox had a feeling. It tickled his gut; it pumped adrenaline, it disturbed his sleep. It was an itch he had to scratch. He stopped at every dirt lane that led to a cabin and got out of the squad car and onto his knees to inspect the dry, hard-packed lanes for signs that someone had driven over them in the past few days. His lower back was complaining and his knees were sore when he found faint traces on the lane to a new log cabin that was hidden from view behind a heavy stand of blue spruce. At first, he noticed a single lump of gravel that had been over-turned. The earth where the stone had been was unmistakably fresh. Knox walked slowly along the lane until he found a dusty spot. Tread marks! The policeman felt his pulse rising, throb-bing in his neck. It was same all-weather radial tread used on all the patrol cars in the Granite Creek PD. The Mexican had not yet dumped the stolen squad car. As he approached the cabin, the policeman's nostrils picked up an unmistakable hint of wood smoke. Sergeant Knox made a wide circle around the structure, taking care not to expose himself to a view from any of the three windows. He was so careful to keep his eyes on the cabin that he almost stumbled into the squad car, hidden in a shallow ravine. It was partially covered with boughs of spruce. He thought about disabling the stolen squad car, then hesitated. Another plan was forming in his mind, a plan that was sweeping in its implications.

The Mexican had holed up in the cabin, and that called for specific actions. The specter of standard operating procedure momentarily visited Knox's consciousness. The appropriate thing to do would be to call in his findings, request backup, then wait quietly on the main road. The city would call in the state troopers to augment the Granite Creek PD. Within an hour, they would have a ring formed around the cabin; the Mexican would have no way out. Knox dismissed the thought. That, he reasoned, would take all the fun out of it. There was a better way. Eddie "Rocks" returned to his squad car, opened the door quietly, and pressed the button on his microphone. "Car Seven. You read me okay?"

"You're coming in ten-two," Clara said. "You breaking for lunch?"

"No. I'm near the end of Twelve-Mile Road. May have had a break-in at that new log cabin, the one near the old silver mine. Goin' to have a look-see."

"I'll send backup. Leggett is available."

"Don't bother. Looks like whoever broke in is long gone. Routine stuff. I'll call back in a half hour or so."

There was a slight hesitation before she signed off.

Knox withdrew an envelope from his inside coat pocket, removed the official report for the tenth time, and read it carefully. No, there was no mistake. But they were wrong, all of them. There *was* a remedy. He removed the twelve-gauge shotgun from the trunk and pumped five slug loads into the magazine. He hadn't felt so happy, so absolutely *alive* since his doctor had given him the grim report.

The policeman inspected the cartridges in his automatic. He removed the regulation nine-millimeter loads and replaced them with illegal hollow-points from a stash in his inside jacket pocket. He would be careful to give the Mexican a chance, but he didn't intend to take the escapee back alive. A simple surrender would be anticlimactic, a waste of a golden opportunity. The man in the cabin was armed with Piggy's .357 Magnum. This was going to be an encounter to remember. For one of them. Knox was moved with a mystic sense of ecstasy; tears rolled down his cheeks as he silently thanked God for this wonderful opportunity. No one at the station knew about this facet of his character: Eddie Knox was an incurable romantic.

24

Clara stared intently at the microphone as if she could see Eddie Knox, alone in a dark mountain forest of spruce and pine. Eddie had inspected the cabins only last Friday. The cabin check was on the schedule for once every month. Eddie's story smelled . . . well, funny. She turned to Leggett. "You hear that conversation with Knox?"

Leggett didn't look up from his paperwork. "Uh-huh. Sounded routine enough."

"You better go check on him. Eddie's got something treed."

It was not a suggestion. Lieutenant Leggett, who considerably outranked the dispatcher, considered her worried expression thoughtfully. He put on his hat and jacket and left without a word.

Julio Pacheco was eating a breakfast of canned bean soup with moldy saltine crackers when he heard the voice. "Hello in the cabin!" Pacheco dropped the spoon and pulled the revolver from his belt.

"I know you're in there, Messican. Now you lissen close, 'cause I won't repeat myself. I called my position in, but I didn't tell 'em you was holed up here. Station thinks it's a simple break-in investigation, but if I don't report back in, say, thirty or forty minutes, they'll start callin' on the radio. When I don't answer, they'll send someone up to check on me. Then your ass'll be in a sling sure enough. I figure you got an hour to get out of here, maybe a few minutes more."

Pacheco's finger played over the trigger; he looked through the curtain to see the man who challenged him. He couldn't see the man, but the voice was familiar. It was the strange man the other cops called "Rocks."

The disembodied voice boomed out again. "Now here is the way it is, wetback. You got yourself three choices. First, you can wait inside until the troops arrive. You surrender, we'll take you back to jail. Number two, you can slip out the back way. If I don't spot you and blow your little ass off, we'll put the dogs on you. With the bloodhounds, I'd guess we'll pick you up before it gets good dark."

Pacheco imagined the dogs . . . long yellow teeth in gaping mouths. He felt cold and suppressed a shudder.

"Then, you got your third choice." There was a slight pause. "This here third one, it's my favorite. You walk out the front door, you and me go head-to-head. If you're man enough to take me out, you drive away before they get suspicious down at headquarters. If I was you, I'd take number three." Another pause. "Course, you ain't nothin' like me, you little cockroach!"

Pacheco smiled ruefully. This man was worthy of his reputation for absolute fearlessness. Stupid, maybe, but a man you had to respect. He cupped his hand beside his mouth. "Hey, you dumb-assed gringo. I hear you ain't had no sex since your little sister ran away from home!"

Eddie "Rocks" released the safety on his pump shotgun and laughed out loud. "Come on out, you little donkey fart," he yelled, "and I'll get you ready for the undertaker!" With this, Knox left his cover behind a sandstone boulder and moved directly into view. He stood, legs planted firmly apart, in the middle of the lane. Pacheco licked his lips. Somewhere over fifty yards. Not a hard shot, but not a sure thing by any measure. He had no doubt that the crazy policeman was telling the truth. Knox was by himself. If the other cops were along, they would never let him expose himself like this. It was to be an honest contest. An encounter between two men who were willing to face death for the privilege of playing the game. Pacheco sensed that this man was, in some mystic way, his brother.

Julio opened the cabin door and stepped onto the rough-hewn plank floor of the porch. Eddie Knox raised the shotgun barrel to waist level. Pacheco held the revolver at arm's length and squinted one eye as he drew a bead on the policeman. "You're dumber than a stump, man. You can't kill me with a shotgun at this range."

"Loaded with slugs" was the calm reply.

Pacheco felt his stomach lurch. Those slugs could tear a hole through your gut big enough to drop a fence post through. "Still a long shot," Pacheco called out, struggling to match Knox's confident tone.

"Hell, Messican, life's a long shot. But tell you what; since I figure you couldn't hit a number ten tub with a ball bat, I'll give you first shot if you don't get too much closer. Then I'll put one through your liver and you can go join your worthless ancestors. Now if that ain't a sportin' proposition, you can file a grievance on me."

Pacheco stepped off the porch, plotting, calculating. "How much closer can I get for my first shot, Mr. Rocks?"

"Keep on a-comin', you silly sumbitch. You take one step too close, I'll let you know." Knox chuckled. "Now go on . . . admit it! Ain't this more fun than ridin' that big rolley coaster up in Denver?"

"I'm having myself a fine time." Pacheco took a half dozen deliberate steps toward his adversary; he thought he saw the muscles in Eddie's face tighten. Pacheco fell forward to a prone position and got off one shot as he hit the ground—a wide miss. The crazy policeman was smiling, but he didn't budge from his position in the middle of the lane as he pulled the trigger. There was a booming report; the slug kicked dust into Pacheco's face. Pacheco squeezed the trigger on the revolver. He saw Knox spin and tumble as the Magnum slug crashed through the policeman's leg.

Knox was on the ground. His right leg felt like a heavy hitter had swung a Louisville Slugger into his thigh. There was considerable pain, but it was manageable. He watched the arterial blood squirting a scarlet arc halfway across the dusty lane. Artery severed. Time was short. Maybe a few minutes at the outside before his blood pressure would drop to a level where the brain would slip into half-life, then forever into darkness. He couldn't see the shotgun, then realized it was underneath his body. From his peripheral vision, he saw Julio Pacheco approaching. The officer withdrew his mostly plastic Glock nine-millimeter automatic from its holster and rolled away. Another .44 Magnum slug blew a trench in the road, inches from his face. He squinted to focus on his target, but the Mexican was a blur. Then there were three Mexicans. Sergeant Knox aimed at the middle Mexican and pulled the trigger three times. Then he drifted off into a dark, silent void. He was thinking that if he had his life to live over again, he would give up chewing tobacco. Maybe take up snuff.

Parris looked up and saw Clara Tavishuts standing in the doorway. He had never seen such pain on the Ute woman's face. "Leggett just called in from Twelve-Mile Road. Knox is down."

He met Leggett at the emergency entrance to Presbyterian Community Hospital. The young officer was shaken. He wouldn't look at Parris as he turned his hat in his hands. "Eddie . . . he's lost a lot of blood. Barely found a pulse. He'll lose his leg for sure."

"Damn, damn," Parris muttered.

Leggett stuck his hand out. "Look at what I found in his pocket."

Parris read the report from Granite Creek Pathology, Ltd. It was a long moment before their eyes met. Parris cleared his throat. "Says here Knox had something called melanoma."

Leggett wiped at his eyes. "Eddie must have flipped out when he found out he had cancer. That's why he didn't call for some help. Wanted to die up there on the mountain."

This was too much to digest in one sitting. First things first. Parris clamped a hand on Leggett's shoulder. "Any notion who shot him?"

"It was Pacheco, probably with the sidearm he took from Piggy. He abandoned Car Three when he ran out of gas a couple of miles from the site of the shooting, but we'll get him for sure."

The chief was surprised at this; Leggett was usually cautious in his predictions. "How can you be so certain?"

The lieutenant's face was like stone. "Rocks got off some shots; at least one connected. We found blood where Pacheco left the car. He's wounded; can't get far in that country."

Parris shook his head doubtfully. "Julio Pacheco is resourceful. We can't take any chances that he flies the coop this time, not with an officer shot. Call up that old guy in Pagosa who owns the bloodhounds and rent the whole bunch of them, the ones that sniff and the bad ones that like to chew on what they catch. We'll turn the damned dogs loose on him."

At that very instant, somewhere deep in a mountain ravine, Julio Pacheco stopped, examined the wound where Knox's slug had penetrated his abdomen, and glanced back over his shoulder. For the first time since he was a child, and for reasons he could not comprehend, Julio shuddered in cold animal fear.

Parris pressed the telephone receiver against his ear so hard, it hurt. "You did get the sample from the victim's esophagus? The courier swore he'd have it in your hands by ten this morning." He waited for Otto Proctor's reply.

"Yeah, it got here okay. I'm sorry. There's no sign of superconductivity at room temperature. Not even at zero Celcius. I can check it out at cryogenic temperatures, but that'll take some time. The magnetic susceptometer is scheduled by some guys from P Division, and I don't have much pull with them."

Parris wanted to grind his teeth. "Are you absolutely certain? I mean it looks exactly like the stuff the university is hyping."

Proctor seemed to be taking the results with his usual upbeat attitude. "Maybe the university's stuff is junk, too. Or maybe . . ."

"Maybe what?"

"New superconductors," Proctor said, "are like delicate new blossoms. They're fragile, easily bruised. That's because we don't yet know the best way to put them together. Get them wet, expose them to a bit of acid, like the fluids in the esophagus, and whammo, they're dead. But there's still hope."

"Tell me about it before I fall into a deep depression."

"I tested the entire sample, as a bulk unit. What I didn't do was break it open, find an internal grain that may not have been exposed to gastric juices. When I do, who knows what I'll find?"

Parris was unconsciously twisting the telephone cord around his fingers. "I'm not sure I can authorize you to break the thing. It's evidence and . . ."

Proctor ignored this negative comment. "And maybe the best part of all, even if the disk is completely dead, we can still analyze its chemistry, find out what the ingredients were for the Song girl's recipe. Give me a few days, I'll know exactly what it's made of."

"It's not only a matter of evidence. The thing belongs to Priscilla's estate, and she left everything to the Thorpe kid."

"Relax, I promise to take good care of it."

Clara Tavishuts dropped a note on his desk. "Hold on, Proctor, I've got another call." He pressed the HOLD, then the 7 button. "Parris here. That you, Thorpe?"

"It's me. Been trying to get in touch with you since breakfast. I heard about the news conference at RMP. Who is this guy . . . the one who won't go public about his superconductor discovery?"

"I can't help you on that one."

"It's got to be Priscilla's adviser," Buster said, "it's that guy Thomson."

"Whoever it is, I expect he'll make an announcement when it suits his purposes. Could happen any day now."

"Remember the ring Pris sent for my birthday?"

"I remember. Real nice. Turquoise, wasn't it?"

"I think it may be important."

Without warning, something stirred deep in Parris's subconscious. A ring? A dream. Priscilla Song, wearing a yellow dress. Also wearing a ring too big for her small finger, a ring on her thumb. A man's ring? "So," Parris urged, "what about this ring? Why do you think it's important?"

"Well, when I saw a picture of the superconductor–thingamajig in a news magazine, I thought it looked kinda familiar. Then I remembered. The ring Pris sent has the turquoise set in some kind of black rock."

"A black rock?" Parris could feel his pulse racing.

"It's a funny-looking stone, sort of dark gray, with lots of little holes like Swiss cheese. I thought it was some kind of lava stone. Wondered why Pris would have the jeweler use something in the ring that was . . . well, kind of ugly. Wasn't like her. Thing is, it's a dead ringer for that superconductor rock in the magazine picture."

"How soon can you get the ring to my office?"

"See you in the morning, if the creek don't rise."

"Ford the damn creek—just bring it here," Parris said. He got Proctor back on the line. "This," he said, "you won't believe."

The cowboy eased his muddy pickup into a No Parking zone directly in front of the Granite Creek Police Station and glared darkly at the motorcycle cop, who started to say something and thought better of it. Buster Thorpe was in no mood for nonsense; the policeman sensed this and roared away in search of less belligerent prey.

Thorpe was ushered into Parris's office, where he greeted Anne Foster shyly and was introduced to Otto Proctor. "I brought something else," Buster said. "Came in the mail after I talked to you yesterday. It's postmarked the day she died." Parris accepted the package and unwrapped a bound notebook. "Why did it take so long to get to you?"

Buster grinned. "Pris was careful with money. She sent it book rate."

Proctor wrenched the book from Parris and began examining the last few pages. "This is the icing on the cake," he said. "It's her lab notebook. *Everything* is here."

Buster produced the ring from his jacket pocket and offered it to Proctor, who grabbed it as if he was after the gold ring off the carousel. The scientist twisted a magnifier into his eye socket and squinted at the dark stone under the turquoise. "Somebody have a pocketknife?"

Buster produced a wicked-looking stock knife from his pocket. Without asking anyone's permission, Proctor pried the turquoise from its setting and dropped it unceremoniously on Parris's desk. Compared to what he was interested in, turquoise might as well be gravel.

Proctor looked up at Anne. "I brought along a magnet, just in case, but your main squeeze here"—he gestured toward Parris—"insisted you should have the honors. You got the dog?"

This brought a puzzled expression from the cowboy. Anne removed a small black plastic Scottie from her purse and gave it to the scientist. It was mounted on a magnet. "I hope there's a big story here," she said. "I've had that puppy since I was a little girl."

"That," Proctor said with a sly wink, "could not have been so long ago. He used Buster's pocketknife to cut the plastic dog from the inch-long bar magnet. "Give me the pliers."

Parris handed the scientist a pair of heavy long-nose pliers. Proctor deftly snapped a small segment off the magnet, then crushed this into tiny fragments. He pushed the ring onto his finger. It was loose. Proctor rotated the ornament so the dark stone was on the palm side of his finger. It was a miniature tabletop of pockmarked ceramic.

He grasped a tiny fragment of the broken magnet with a pair of eyebrow tweezers and smiled as he observed his rapt audience. "Well, this is the acid test. Everybody ready? Don't get your hopes up."

His answer was a tense silence. Anne had her hands clasped prayerfully. Parris put his arm around her waist. Buster Thorpe pulled nervously at his mustache.

Proctor moved the tweezers to a location that positioned the tiny Inconel fragment directly over the setting in the ring. When it was dead center, he released the miniature magnet. It fell, wobbled, then floated over the dark ceramic as if suspended by an invisible thread. Parris remembered Daisy Perika's vision. One of the black disks had floated over the water.

Otto Proctor breathed deeply. A tear rolled down his cheek. He waited until the tightness in his throat relaxed, until he was able to speak. "Behold," he said reverently, "the Holy Grail."

25

Again, Julio trembled, but now he knew why. Though they were still far away, he could hear their voices. There was a low, mournful baying as the floppy-eared demons surged through the underbrush, following the scent of his blood. Julio counted the bullets he had left; it was not enough to face the dogs. He knew what must be done. The Mexican limped down a spruce-covered slope to the edge of a rocky cliff, then skirted its edge until he found precisely the right spot. Pacheco knelt, held one palm over his bleeding wound, and whispered his final prayers to God and to the saints. He offered his thanks for a life that had been good, a man's life. He offered no apologies to the saints for his multitudinous sins, but he did mention his genuine appreciation that his life would not end in a *Yanquí* jail, or, even worse, as his body was torn apart by a pack of hounds. He removed his meager possessions from his pockets and placed them on the pine needles under the giant ponderosa that hung over the edge of the precipice. The dogs were now drawing close, and the excited pitch of their call revealed that they knew this.

Julio gathered his last reserve of strength. He stepped to the edge of the overhang, spread his arms, and hurled himself into space. As he lost all sense of gravity, he heard a terrified shriek. It was his own voice.

* * *

Leggett and a state police sergeant had followed the tireless man who owned the bloodhounds. Now they sat under a huge pine that spread its branches over the precipice and considered the neatly stacked assortment of artifacts of Julio Pacheco's life: Slocum's revolver, three .357 Magnum slugs, a red bandanna, a half-used package of mentholated cigarettes, and a wrinkled photograph of an aged woman they assumed was Pacheco's mother. The animals were confused; the Mexican's scent ended somewhere in the spruce thicket along the edge of the cliff over Badger Creek. The bloodhound man gathered his animals, fed them chunks of rank-smelling horse meat, and shook his frizzled gray head with wonder. "Damned if'n I can tell you what happened, fellers. I expect we've been over every inch of the terrain from here to yonder an' back agin. A bleedin' man can't hide his smell from my dogs, and he ain't nowheres over that cliff. Looks like that Mexican bird just flapped his wings and flew away from here."

Fifteen hundred miles away in Tuxtepec, Prudencia Pacheco abruptly raised her face; the prayer book slipped from her fingers and fell to the floor. The woman was wiping tears away when she spoke to her husband. "It is Julio. I have just seen our son."

"So you have seen him," her husband answered acidly. "How is my prodigal son? Is he in trouble again? In jail?"

Prudencia's hands trembled as she kissed her rosary. "He is in a tree. My little Julio hangs in the branches of a great tree."

She had tried to call Parris, but he was not in and her calls were not returned. Anne couldn't wait to publish. The information from her contacts on campus was compelling. First, Thomson had not been seen for days. Moreover, her contact in Public Relations confirmed the report that the announcement of the identity of the mystery scientist was being put off indefinitely. A news release was being prepared for the media, and the essence of this missive was read over the telephone in a whisper:

Unexpected complications regarding the contract between Rocky Mountain Polytechnic and the inventor of the new superconductor have placed the university in a position where absolutely no public statements will be made until further notice. We regret this course of action, but are compelled by legal necessity . . .

Anne's antennae were up. The other journalists were not idiots. Some of them had been snooping around for weeks, asking embarrassing questions. Who knew what they, with their considerable resources, might have already uncovered on Thomson? If she didn't file a story within hours, she could be scooped by the out-of-town crowd. Her once-in-a-lifetime chance would be gone. She called her editor, and he concurred. Only one guideline, he insisted—name no names. The *Adviser* was a small daily with insurance that would poop out if a judgment was over 2 million bucks; one successful slander lawsuit could put them out of business permanently. It would make the story more difficult, but she had no alternative. She could walk the tightrope. Anne would refer to Thomson as "an RMP professor acquainted with the murdered girl."

The special edition of the *Granite Creek Adviser* appeared late on a Saturday afternoon. It was a sensation. The wire services picked up the story an hour before the paper would hit the streets. CBS News executives preempted three minutes of Charles Kuralt's show "Sunday Morning," squeezing the segment on a young jazz pianist from St. Louis. Kuralt protested this meddling until he read a synopsis on the piece from Granite Creek.

The physicist was using a friend's cabin in the mountains. Following a light breakfast of toast and coffee, he switched on the television at precisely eight o'clock. "Sunday Morning" began in the usual fashion, with announcements of a string of interesting feature stories to follow the news. Charles Kuralt then announced, somewhat somberly, the physicist thought, that there would be a special presentation about a late-breaking story related to the "reported discovery of a room-temperature superconductor in Colorado." But first the news.

The physicist drummed his fingers on the table while he watched the five-minute litany of new outrages in the Gaza Strip, continuing starvation in the Sudan, and the assassination of a Ukrainian parliamentarian. None of this was of the least interest to him.

Immediately after the postnews commercials, Kuralt was perched on a wooden stool in front of a large visual that asked: "Who is the Real Inventor?" The affable commentator turned to a thin, pale colleague. "Fred, what's this we hear about a potential scandal in the unfolding story about the discovery of a room-temperature superconductor?"

The pale man looked as if he had been up all night. "Well, Charles, that's exactly what seems to be happening. The story broke late yesterday evening, with a report on the wires from a newspaper journalist in Granite Creek, Colorado. You'll remember that's the picturesque village in the Rocky Mountains where the mystery scientist had been proclaimed to be the sole discoverer of a room-temperature superconductor that will revolutionize the way we live. The reporter who filed this startling story, Anne Foster, is standing by at our affiliate in Denver."

The CBS journalists turned to view an oversized television screen that projected an image of Anne Foster. Kuralt smiled congenially. "Good morning, Ms. Foster, and thank you for getting up so early to appear on 'Sunday Morning.' "

ANNE: "You're quite welcome, Charles. I'm pleased to be here."

KURALT: "Your report, which will appear in today's newspapers, is quite a sensation. Could you tell us, briefly, what the facts are behind the story you filed?"

Anne was nervously twisting the rose-quartz pendant. "Certainly. Only a few weeks ago, Priscilla Song, a graduate student at Rocky Mountain Polytechnic, was brutally murdered. There is evidence that her scientific research may have been stolen following the murder."

Anne's face was briefly replaced by a black-and-white image of Priscilla.

KURALT: "And the subject of her research was . . . ?"

ANNE: "Superconductivity."

KURALT: "And was she successful in this research?"

ANNE: "She developed a room-temperature superconductor."

KURALT: "That is . . . astounding. Are you certain?"

ANNE: "I've seen the samples myself. They have been tested and verified by an expert from the Los Alamos National Laboratory."

KURALT: "This graduate student . . . tell us . . . what was her connection with the anonymous scientist, the person who the university represents as the sole discoverer of this remarkable new superconductor?"

ANNE: "This so-called mystery scientist was a close associate of Priscilla Song."

Kuralt smiled at Anne's image. "I believe you know the identity of this shy academic. Why don't you share that information with us?"

Anne laughed and flashed her dazzling smile. "I'd love to, but not just yet. When the time is right, you'll be the first to know."

The physicist felt that he was barely connected to his body. As he watched the talking heads, he felt oddly distant, a mere observer of a catastrophe.

PALE MAN: "We understand that the mystery scientist has evidently applied for a patent."

ANNE: "That patent application will undoubtedly be the subject of vigorous litigation."

KURALT: "Apparently, a dispute will develop about who actually invented the superconductor, but it's for the courts rather than journalists to decide on that issue. We're interested in a more immediate question. The wire reports on your story suggest that the student's death may have been related to her research. Will you comment on that?"

ANNE: "Understand that I'm making no charges of any kind, just reporting verifiable facts. Priscilla Song left two samples of the room-temperature superconductor behind. She swallowed one; it was recently recovered from her body by the county medical examiner. The chief of police believes that the victim swallowed the sample to keep it from her murderer." This brought raised eyebrows from Kuralt. "The second sample was sent to a close friend for safekeeping and has now been recovered."

KURALT: "We'll certainly be following this fast-breaking story. Thank you for being with us this morning."

Kuralt turned on his stool to observe the pale man with a quizzical look. "What do you think, Fred? A tempest in a teapot, or is something serious brewing here?"

Fred smelled a great story. "Anne Foster isn't that well known, but she has a reputation for being a solid, reliable journalist. CBS has used her reports before; she was instrumental in uncovering that big real estate scandal near Colorado Springs last summer. The newspaper that employs this reporter stands behind her story. I think we'll hear a lot more about this before it's finished."

The scene broke to a commercial describing laptop computers.

Parris stopped at the Corner Drug Store and bought a copy of the *Denver Post*. He groaned audibly as he saw the headline:

RMP MYSTERY SCIENTIST
IMPLICATED IN COED SLAYING?

It was Anne's story. Several phrases jumped out:

. . . student gave boyfriend sample of superconductor . . .
swallowed another sample during death-struggle . .
. . . Los Alamos scientist verifies sample superconducts at room
temperature . . .
. . . DA has no immediate comment . . .
. . . Ute woman assisted local police in investigation . . .

He had expected a conservative report, one that dealt with the issue of who had invented the room-temperature superconductor. He had not dreamed that Anne would reveal virtually everything she knew, or thought she knew, about Priscilla's murder. He was grateful for one blessing. Anne had not mentioned Waldo Thomson's name.

Parris drove to Anne's home; he found a note taped to the front door:

Sorry, Scott. It's 4:00 A.M., didn't want to wake you. Called into Denver for CBS interview. If you see this in time, catch me chatting with Charles Kuralt at 8:00 A.M.! Don't worry about missing the show; I've set the VCR to tape it.
Miss you,
Anne

The policeman ripped the note off the door and stuffed it into his shirt pocket. Suddenly, he didn't feel so great. He had gotten used to the notion of Anne, lovely Anne, being there for him. Now, there would be plenty of travel for her. Endless television interviews for the reporter who exposed the "Coed Murderer." Probably, a book contract. There would be job offers from big-name newspapers. Maybe television. She certainly had the looks and personality. And then, she'd be gone. Gone. He detested that word. Helen was gone. Priscilla was gone. Now, Anne would be gone. At least Helen had departed without his assistance; he had helped Anne along the way toward her inevitable departure. If he had kept Anne at arm's length during the investigation, she might still be writing columns on sewer bonds and animal-rights issues. The policeman buttoned his raincoat and wished he had worn a sweater under it. Parris felt cold. And middle-aged. And alone.

The madman vomited into the toilet. He tried to vomit once more. His chest heaved, but his stomach was empty. He pushed himself to his feet and flushed the toilet. He pressed a wet washcloth to his forehead and leaned against the wall while he waited for the nausea to depart, for his strength to return.

The Voice had returned, and there was something more: the odor of rotting flesh. The physicist held the washcloth over his nose, hoping the presence would not be offended. The Voice spoke to him about those who had ruined his plans. He gradually became furious as he considered the injustice of their meddling. "I despise them," he said, "but what can I do?"

The Voice told him.

Parris pressed the buzzer and waited. The heavyset woman who opened the door frowned at the sight of the chief of police on her front porch. "Is anything wrong?"

He tipped his felt hat. "No . . . sorry to show up unannounced. Just took the chance you'd be here. Can we talk?"

Kristin Waters opened the door and pointed at a fiber mat, where Parris dutifully wiped his wet boots. She took his raincoat and draped it over the back of a chair, then instructed him to sit. He did, with his back straight, his hands folded in his lap. She raised her eyebrows to signal that he could begin.

He opened his pocket-sized notebook. "Just a few questions. Tying up loose ends, that sort of thing. You understand."

"Yes. Of course I do. I understand that you must ask questions, then write the answers in your little book." She looked at the heavy man's watch on her wrist, a hint that she didn't have a lot of time to spare.

"On the day of the murder, Julio Pacheco was in the laboratory with Priscilla Song."

She leaned forward and spoke softly, as if someone might overhear. "Mr. Pacheco was called in to look for a gas leak. Gas can be very dangerous, you know."

"Yeah. Did Pacheco find the leak?"

Her blank expression was impossible to read. "Don't know. Didn't see him after he made his checks. You want me to be sure before I answer, don't you?"

"Of course. I understand you summoned Pacheco."

"Most certainly. Asked him to drop everything and get right over. If I could have smelled it myself, I'd have ordered an evacuation of the building."

"Then you didn't smell the gas? Who asked you to call Pacheco?" Parris was sure he knew what the answer would be.

She told him.

26

Claude Potter-Evans had spent the morning gathering dead wood and dry pinecones from the deep forest. He had dumped a basket of cones, which he would use as fire starters and Christmas decorations, into a rough wooden box by the stone fireplace. The old man had a light lunch of dark bread, a boiled egg, and canned peaches. He decided to forgo his after-lunch nap and get right into the pleasurable task of sawing the wood into twenty-six-inch lengths to fit the fireplace. The Englishman was deeply involved in this work when he heard the vehicle approach. He was pleased to hear the sound. It would be the woman who delivered the mail. Most of the stuff, which was junk or bills, she left at his handmade mailbox, down where the gravel road petered off into a weed-choked dirt lane. When there was something special, like his Social Security check or a package from one of the mail-order houses, she drove her four-wheel-drive pickup all the way to his cabin. She was somewhat thin for his taste, but nevertheless an attractive woman whose innocent smile and lithe figure hinted of rare delights. There were, truth to be told, few women young or old whose innocent smiles and figures (lithe or otherwise) did not suggest such fantasies to Potter-Evans. Like the aged Moses, his "vital forces had not departed." For months, the old recluse had connived various means to delay the postal maiden's departure; he greatly coveted the pleasure of even the briefest of visits from this fair lass. Like others of her tireless profession, she usually did not tarry long. Nevertheless, he was the soul of patience, and an incurable optimist about his appeal to the fairer sex. She liked his stories, and would occasionally clasp her pale hand over her lips and giggle at his obscure jokes. Today, he decided, he would tell her about the time he had hunted buffalo in Uganda.

He was rehearsing his performance, entertaining fantasies about how she might accept an invitation to tea, when he saw the pickup. The color was wrong, and this truck was quite new compared to the postal maiden's wheezing vehicle. His brow furrowed in puzzlement. Had she purchased a new pickup? Potter-Evans's mind, normally as agile as the young prong-horn's limbs, was momentarily fastened onto one of the female objects of his passion. The truck was within yards, close enough for him to recognize the driver, when he realized that he had been careless. Unforgivably careless. His mind instantly discarded the young woman who delivered the mail. Where was the shotgun? Leaning against the woodpile. Too far away? Yes. Run? The only chance.

He was backing into the brush when he saw the hand with the pistol extended from the open window of the pickup. He simultaneously saw the flash, heard the explosion, and felt a searing pain in his abdomen. He had no sense of falling; it was as if the damp earth had reared up to whack the breath from his lungs. He looked up and was partially blinded by the sun.

Now the intruder with the pistol was speaking to him. "You're only the first."

The bleeding man heard every word, but his thoughts were not concerned with his assailant, who now seemed quite irrelevant. Potter-Evans's mind bounced from one favorite subject to another. Madeline, the librarian; her soft red lips, the pungent kerosene aroma of her cheap perfume. His mind jumped again. He could see Winnie clearly; the prime minister was dabbing a small brush at an oil painting of a red brick wall in the garden of his country home; long vines of yellow roses adorned the edifice.

The grand old statesman turned and motioned for Potter-Evans to approach. He could not; he was back on the ground in America; he closed his eyes to block out the sun. Then again, back to England. Nineteen and forty-three? He was standing by the gate to his father's farm in Yorkshire. Potter-Evans could see the old house, constructed of rough-hewn gray stones; he was certain that he could smell the aroma of fresh bread and steaming black tea. Then, back again, on the Colorado earth, staring into the sun. The visitor kept talking, shrieking like a spoiled child about the others who would die for their meddling. Then the assailant fired another shot, this one directly into his chest. Potter-Evans felt the slug slam into his ribs, but there was not as much pain as had accompanied his first wound. He reasoned that he must be drifting away, loosing the ability to feel pain. He heard the pickup door slam. The sound of the engine slowly receded into the distance. Cold blackness surrounded him, blocking the pain. The darkness was welcome. He felt himself, like the sound of the vehicle, gradually receding into the distance . . . leaving his body shell behind.

Parris hoped Potter-Evans had sorted out Priscilla's mysterious message. Piggy, as usual, had provided a fuzzy report. The old hermit had, according to Slocum, said something about women and booze, and a curse on the chief's grandchildren! Parris, who was childless, was unconcerned.

Anne was sitting close to him, her head resting lightly against his shoulder, her delicate fingers on his right arm. It made shifting gears inconvenient, but Parris had no complaint. He should have been watching the turns in the gravel road, but he preferred to turn his head and sniff the fragrance of her red hair. Honeysuckle? Was the scent artificial, or did she produce this wondrous perfume from her pores? He was acting the fool over this most remarkable woman. He knew this and did not care.

She had gradually drifted down from her high. He had no intention of offering any negative comment about her article.

Never mind that her target could be a calculating killer who might make an attempt (or his second attempt?) on Anne's life. Thomson would be far away now. Anne, on the other hand, was here. Close to him. She hadn't said a word about another job, and he had no intention of broaching that subject. Even if she did move to another state, perhaps he would follow her. If she would let him. It shouldn't be all that hard to find another job on another small-town police force.

"How," Anne asked, "is Sergeant Knox doing?"

"Wound was pretty bad; they had to take his leg off," Parris said. "Looks like he'll pull through."

"I heard he had some kind of cancer."

"Yeah," Parris said, "it was on his leg."

"You don't mean . . ."

"That's right"—Parris grinned—"the one they amputated. Expect he'll come hobbling in on a wooden peg in a few months, demanding to go out on patrol."

"What about Julio Pacheco?"

Parris didn't answer immediately. "Vanished. We're still watching the area where the hounds lost his trail, but haven't turned up a trace. It's like he sprouted wings and flew away."

The pickup truck appeared as he turned a narrow curve; Parris jerked the steering wheel to avoid a head-on collision. The sun was in his face; he barely caught a glimpse of the driver who was in such a hurry. "Crazy road hog! Ought to turn around, pull him over."

"Don't always play the policeman," Anne said. "It wasn't on purpose."

When they left the gravel section, the lane became bumpy. Anne lifted her head from his shoulder and blinked her long lashes apprehensively at the shadows gathered under the pines. It was a dark forest with mossy boulders, the sort of place where Grimms' monsters fed on innocent children. "Are we there yet?"

This sometimes cynical woman, now at the top of her professional career, had an almost childlike quality. He leaned over to kiss her ear and received a happy smile in return. "Almost. He'll have a fire on a cold day like this; we should see the smoke from his chimney when we top this ridge."

"Do you think he's already seen the papers?" she asked. "I'd like to have the pleasure of showing him the front-page spread myself."

"Doubt it. He only walks into town about once a week. Then, he reads the paper at the library. He has a sweetheart there."

"I heard. Madeline. I think that's kind of icky, don't you? An old man like that. She's young enough to be his daughter."

Parris reminded himself that he lived in a small town. There were no secrets. At least not for long. He wondered what the gossips were saying about the chief of police and the lovely journalist who appeared destined for the big time.

There was only a hint of gray smoke drifting lazily from the chimney, as if the fire was almost out. Parris had an uneasy feeling as he set the emergency brake. He noticed the handsaw on the woodpile, then spotted the shotgun. The old man might be absentminded, but he would never leave his treasured shotgun outside. Was Potter-Evans ill?

There were tire tracks in the lane. He remembered the pickup that had almost forced him off the road. He heard the sound, something between a whimper and a groan.

Parris followed the direction of the sound, then he heard a weak cough. The old man was flat on his back. His threadbare checkered shirt was splattered with blood, still wet near his wounds, but dry and flaky at the edges. As he bent over Potter-Evans, the policeman heard Anne getting out of the squad car. Instinctively, he pressed one finger lightly on the old man's neck. The carotid artery was pulsing weakly; he estimated the rate at no more than forty-five beats a minute. Blood pressure must be low; in spite of the sunlight in his face, Potter-Evans's pupils were dilated.

Anne appeared at his side. "Get his shirt off," she snapped.

= 196 =

"I'll make some bandages. She stepped out of her half-slip and ripped it into long, narrow strips, then leaned against a tree and pulled off her panty hose. Parris unbuttoned the old man's shirt. There were two wounds. The small hole in the abdomen was bleeding slowly; the chest wound pulsated a mottled mixture of scarlet blood and transparent serum as Potter-Evans drew short, intermittent breaths. Anne pressed folded strips of her slip against the wounds; Parris lifted the man's shoulders so she could apply a makeshift panty-hose bandage to hold the compression pads in place.

This brought a gasp from the old Englishman. "Don't move me, you silly twit! Can't you see I'm . . ." He blinked at his visitors. "She looks like an angel, but who the hell are you?"

"Scott Parris. You remember me. Now who did this, old fellow?"

The wounded man glared through bleary eyes. "Parris. Oh yes, the constable. I've been abroad, you know. Had a session with the prime minister. He was in top form. We reminisced about the Great War; he painted a beautiful picture, roses and bricks, grass and sky. I painted a picture of Winnie." He paused and reflected. "Didn't realize I could paint, you know. Rather strange, wouldn't you say?"

Parris eased him back to his former position on the ground. Potter-Evans wheezed as blood dribbled from the corner of his mouth. The chief spoke softly. "Now think carefully and tell me. . . . It's very important. . . . Who did this?"

Potter-Evans glanced at the makeshift bandages covering his wounds and then at Anne. He attempted to smile but grimaced with pain. "You're the reporter, what?"

She smiled gently and touched his forehead. This small gesture seemed to give him strength. "The bloody . . . drove the lorry right up, right on my own property, and then the nasty blighter shot me." He strained to focus his eyes on Parris. "A man's home is his castle, old stick. Isn't that right, even here in the Colonies? Isn't that the law? Oh I *say*, I think you should transport me to hospital."

Parris was patient. Mustn't make any suggestions; a dying man's testimony was heavy evidence in a court of law, but not if he was delirious and merely responding to an overture from a zealous lawman. "Please, you old cuss. Give me a name."

Potter-Evans stared blankly. "Name? Never could remember a name . . . had a fine time with Winston. Only real prime minister in this century worth mentioning. Dear old Margaret kicked the Argies asses out of the Falklands, and Majors was a decent chap, but . . ."

Anne bent over and whispered in his ear. "The person who shot you . . . was it someone you know?"

He grinned. "My but you're a pretty thing. Kiss an old man and I'll tell you *anything*."

"You," she responded, "are a naughty boy." She kissed him lightly on the cheek.

"It's true," he said. "You are an angel, it's certain. The Angel of Death. And I am in Paradise!"

She smiled and wiped his forehead with her handkerchief. "Remember your promise?"

His eyes were wild. "The Allied invasion . . . that's what you want, isn't it? Holland, that's where to look. Tell that little house-painting, Jew-hating pervert it'll come across the dikes." Potter-Evans appeared smug at this pronouncement.

Parris gripped his shoulder and the old man winced at the pressure. "Tell us who shot you . . . loud enough for Anne to hear you."

Potter-Evans was slipping into a mild delirium. "Major Claude Potter-Evans, serial number four-seven . . . can't remember." The old man coughed up a spittle of scarlet fluid. "One more thing," he offered more lucidly, "I'm merely the *first* one. That's right. Yes. I'm only the first."

Parris felt the Dread flexing its dark limbs in the pit of his stomach. "What do you mean?"

Potter-Evans gripped Parris's wrist with surprising strength. The old man closed his eyes as if in concentration. "Let me remember . . . exactly. Yes. Yes. 'Now, I'll kill the old Indian witch. . . .' " Potter-Evans sighed and his voice became a harsh whisper. "Must rest a bit. Been rather a rum day, you know." The old man's eyes rolled upward.

Anne's face was a study in horror. She turned to fix a wide-eyed stare on Parris. "Oh my God. My article . . . I mentioned the Ute woman. Thomson must have read it . . . and . . ." She clasped a hand over her eyes.

"Put it out of your mind. There's just no time for—keep an eye on him." He left them together, isolated in their pain.

Parris switched on the radio in the Explorer, adjusted the squelch, and pressed the transmit button on the microphone. Piggy answered his summons and Parris moaned with disappointment. He had hoped to get Clara Tavishuts, but it was evidently Slocum's shift.

"Slocum, this is Chief Parris. Now listen carefully." He spoke slowly, enunciating each word, as if to a child who barely understood anything but the simplest phrases. "Get a notepad. We have an emergency. Write down *exactly* what I tell you."

"Ten-four, Chief. I'm ready." Piggy switched the transmission from his headphones to the loudspeaker and found a pad. He couldn't locate a pencil. Never mind, he thought, I'll remember whatever big shot Dick Tracy has to say. It's not like I'm stupid!

"We have a citizen with two gunshot wounds. Lost lots of blood. Send an ambulance to the Potter-Evans cabin, about five miles off the pavement on Slingshot Road. Do that first, while I wait, then get back on the horn."

"Got it, Chief."

Parris waited impatiently. Please, God. Just let Slocum get it right. Just this once.

Piggy barked over the radio. "Paramedics on the way, Chief. They know where his place is."

Parris was flooded with relief. "Good work, Slocum. Now

listen carefully. Call the Southern Ute Tribal Police at Ignacio, then contact the FBI. Tell them that a Ute woman, Daisy Perika, is in considerable danger. Someone is planning to kill her. Male Caucasian. May be in a late-model half-ton pickup, light blue or green: Didn't make the plates. Mrs. Perika doesn't have a telephone, but the tribal police will know where she lives. Do you have that written down?"

Corporal Slocum pointed at his temple. "Got it all right here, Chief. I'll get right on this." Piggy was enjoying this assignment. Real big-time police work! He had found a ballpoint, but it wasn't working all that well. No problem. He could remember everything!

Parris continued. "I'll stay here with the victim until the paramedics arrive, then I'll head for the Ute reservation and check on Mrs. Perika."

"Roger, Chief. Anything else?"

"No. Just make those calls. On the double."

Parris hung the microphone on its chrome hook. When the pressure was on, maybe Piggy would get his act together.

Piggy squinted at the blue scribbles on the yellow pad, then searched his memory. Pickup truck. Indians. Someone going to be killed. Hot damn! This was the real thing. What, exactly, had the chief said? Oh yes, call the Ute Tribal Police. Piggy dialed Information and nervously banged his ballpoint on the desk while he waited.

A young woman's voice responded. "City please?"

"Ain't no city. Gimmee the number for the Ute Injun reservation po-leece."

"Which reservation, sir?"

"The damned *Ute* reservation. Let's get a move on now, girl. This here is a freakin' po-leece *emergency*."

"Which reservation do you want, sir? There are the Ute Mountain Utes and—"

Piggy interrupted. "That's it. Just gimmee the number, sweetheart, and make it snappy." The next voice he heard originated from the bowels of a computer. Piggy dialed the number and thumped his fingertips on the desk while the telephone rang in Towaoc.

"Hello there, this is Officer Slocum, Granite Creek PD. Wanted to give you a warnin'. One of your wimmen is in big trouble. Yeah. Somebody's on the way down there to kill her, I guess. Sure I do. Her name is . . ." He squinted his little porcine eyes at the faint ink markings on the yellow paper. "Name is Daisy Paprika. And you better get your asses in gear, 'cause this particular bad actor already shot up a white man here in our neck o' the woods."

Less than thirty minutes passed before the Granite Creek Rescue Squad's all-terrain ambulance arrived; it had seemed like hours. Claude Potter-Evans had not spoken; the intervals between the old man's rasping breaths were growing longer; his lips had turned a pale blue. He was slipping away. The paramedics who took charge of the bleeding man were businesslike and efficient; they had an IV feeding plasma into a vein in his arm even before they lifted him onto a stainless-steel gurney.

Parris didn't like the ominous tone of their comments as they pushed the gurney into the rear of the ambulance and fitted a transparent oxygen mask over the old man's drawn face, which was now of grayish hue. "Pulse thirty-two and weak," the freckle-faced girl announced curtly to her colleague. "Pressure eighty-five over forty and falling," the curly-haired young man replied as he released the pressure on the cuff and removed a heavy pair of shears from his black bag. "We'll get his volume up with the saline; let's get those rags off and stop the bleeding."

Parris put his hands on Anne's shoulders. "I've got to get down to the reservation, find the Perika woman's home. I'll drop you off in town. You should go home, try to get some rest, and—"

Her eyes flashed. "Forget it. I'm coming with you."

He adopted a firm tone. "You're in no condition, and besides, this is strictly police business now. If I run into this nut, there could be—"

She was not to be dissuaded. "Your people have already alerted the tribal police by now. I heard you call it in. If Thomson is on the reservation, they'll have him locked up by the time we show up. I want a chance to talk to Daisy Perika, to apologize for publishing her name." Left unspoken was the fact that Anne was now a part of her own story. Thomson couldn't last much longer, and she wanted to be there when he was run to ground. It was no longer merely a matter of journalistic interest; this delicate woman with the pale skin wanted to smell the blood.

Parris had felt her shoulders stiffen under his hands. He could drop her off in Granite Creek, but he knew it wouldn't do any good. This stubborn journalist would simply follow him to the Southern Ute reservation. He considered the implications of this situation and made a decision; it would be better to keep her close to him. He was feeling very protective, but having her nearby was important for other, more elemental reasons. And she was right. The Southern Ute Tribal Police would drop everything to protect one of their women against a crazed outsider.

He pulled her close. "You win. Let's get on down the road, then."

Once they were on paved road, Parris pushed the four-wheel-drive Explorer to the margins; the speedometer needle danced against the eighty-five mark on straightaways. The tires complained with a high-pitched squeal as the vehicle careened around the mountain curves. He remembered the city manager's refusal to pay for new tires until the tread depth was down to one-eighth of an inch, and prayed that the rubber wouldn't peel off.

27

Daisy Perika had felt the Presence since her small lunch of posole and fried corn bread. She had tried to abolish the feeling by watching the television, but even the interview of a San Diego couple who had just returned from their voyage to the hidden planet 'Terra II' (it was in the same orbit as the Earth, but always on the opposite side of the sun from Terra I!) was not enough to hold her interest. She switched off the set, opened the trailer home's door, and stepped out on the small wooden porch. When she saw it, she gasped and clasped her hand over her throat.

An angry dark cloud bank, a billowing, rolling, "masculine" vapor, was slipping over the rim of Three Sisters Mesa. The old woman pulled her knitted shawl more tightly over her shoulders and watched the shadowy haze eject misty fingers toward the mesa walls, as if to anchor itself onto the towers that were the Three Sisters' stony forms. This was a sinister omen. It was not the actual Presence, but it was a precursor of the Darkness to come.

She heard his light step, then saw his gray eyes, his panting muzzle. The creature, which she knew was no animal, at least not in the usual sense, was waiting expectantly at the edge of the clearing. This was not a coyote; this was Coyote! The shaman closed her eyes and relaxed, waiting to see the vision that would surely come. There was a half-darkness for a brief moment, and then the phantasms danced in front of her closed eyes. Red and green, fire and feathers. The message from the dwarf was clear and unmistakable. Darkness approached and an old woman, even a Dreamer who conversed with the *pitukupf*, could not delay its coming.

At Capote Lake, Parris hit the brakes and turned the squad car off Route 160 onto State Road 151. Chimney Rock loomed over the western horizon, a gray-brown sentinel of stone penetrating the misty clouds. He fumbled in his wallet until he found the scrap of paper with Daisy's directions. Route 160 was the top of a *T*, Route 151 was the vertical bar. Halfway down the vertical section was an exit that pointed to the west. Daisy had scribbled "Spirit Canyon"; an *X* marked the location of her home. He slammed the breaks, making a skidding right turn on a gravel road and over a wooden bridge that crossed the splashing Piedra. Once across the river, the road forked to the west and north. He took the west fork and rattled along a road that had been made worse by the corrugated tracks of a road grader. The turn off the gravel road took him down a rutted dirt lane that meandered through a sparse stand of juniper and piñon. The ruts were wet from the rain that had preceded the snow; Parris shifted into four-wheel drive and low gear to spare Anne the bone-jarring effect as the Explorer bounced along the lane. They saw the lights from the old woman's trailer before it was possible to see the home itself. When he turned the last bend in the lane, the silhouette of the mobile home was stark against the remnants of pale yellow light glowing in the western sky. He had expected to see a Southern Ute Tribal Police car, but the yard that surrounded the forlorn-looking domicile was as empty as the twilight sky. An aluminum door over a small wooden porch was swinging in harmony with the gusting wind. Parris switched on the spotlight mounted on the roof of the Explorer; he swept the beam over the yard but saw nothing.

He tried to sound hopeful. "I'd guess the tribal police have taken Mrs. Perika to a safe place. Probably already picked our man up . . . if he even showed."

Anne shivered. "Why would she leave her lights on . . . and the door open!"

"Folks leave their lights on to discourage burglars. Maybe she pushed the door shut and it didn't latch." Would Anne buy this explanation?

Parris thumbed the selector on the radio transceiver until he had the frequency for the Colorado State Police. The state cops could relay a message to Piggy, find out whether Slocum had gotten through to the Southern Ute Tribal Police. It would be nice to know why Daisy's trailer appeared to have been abandoned in a hurry, why the Ute police weren't here to meet him. He pressed his mike button, reset the squelch, and made several attempts to raise someone. There was heavy static, a few garbled words, but no clear answer.

Parris unclipped the Remington pump shotgun from its mount on the rear of the front seat. He unlocked the glove compartment and found a flashlight, an unopened box of twelve-gauge 00 buckshot and a half-full box of one-ounce slug loads. He was able to push five of the three-inch buckshot shells into the magazine. He dropped a half dozen slug loads into his jacket pocket.

He removed the snub-nosed Smith & Wesson from his shoulder holster, checked the cartridges, and offered it to Anne. "Get under the wheel. I've got to check this place out. If you see anyone except Mrs. Perika, burn rubber out of here. If anyone threatens you, just point and pull the trigger." She accepted the .38 between finger and thumb, as if it were a viper that would bite, and dropped it into her purse. He left the keys in the ignition and the motor running.

He pumped a load of buckshot into the twelve-gauge chamber and approached the mobile home in a crouched run. He circled the trailer, taking a quick look into each window. Finally, his heart racing, he mounted the creaking steps to the wooden porch. Silence. All he could hear, aside from his thumping heart-beat, was the occasional gust of wind through the junipers and the creak of the metal hinges as the door swung with each breath of wind. The trailer was surely empty. He waited for the wind to open it, then slid through the swinging door. Methodically, he searched the kitchen, the living room, finally the bedroom. He pushed the bathroom door open with the shotgun barrel and peered into the darkness. Nothing stirred. The small home was clean and orderly. No evidence of a struggle, no sign that anyone except the owner had been inside. It must have been just as he suggested to Anne; the tribal police had taken Daisy to another location, safe from her tormentor. Since the Ute cops weren't here waiting for his arrival, the suspect must have been picked up. Either Daisy would be staying with a friend tonight or the tribal police would bring her back after she signed a complaint against the intruder. He paused, relaxing, willing his throbbing pulse to slow. He left the trailer, closing the flimsy door behind him.

He leaned on the Explorer. "Nobody home. Looks like she didn't quite get the door closed. I'll do a quick walk-around, then we'll leave."

"All right." Anne touched his sleeve. "Just be careful and don't stay too long."

Parris set the safety on the shotgun; no sense in taking a chance of some damn fool accident. He headed through the juniper thicket to the south. Inside the thicket, he found faint tracks, prints that might belong to Daisy Perika. There was a pale blue light on the horizon, but darkness was spilling over the slopes of the San Juans. He followed the footprints along a winding deer path and then into a shallow arroyo. As he moved along the arroyo, it gradually became deeper, until he could not see over the sides. The footprints led him up the bank of the arroyo and onto the talus slope of the south face of the big mesa with three stone towers. The tracks were more difficult to follow on the rocky terrain, but he was still able to find a partial print every few steps. He climbed for a few steps and then paused. There were no more footprints.

He studied the base of the mesa, where the tracks had seemed to be leading. There was a conical hollow in the cliff, cast in a deep shadow. His nose caught a hint of wood smoke. Parris cradled the shotgun in his arms and climbed the talus slope. The aroma grew stronger and more pleasant as he approached the conical depression in the cliff wall. He switched off the safety on the shotgun, held the flashlight off to his left in straight-arm fashion, and flicked the switch.

A small brush hut was nestled in the shelter of the depression. Wisps of blue-gray smoke curled from gaps between the twigs. He placed the flashlight on the ground and nudged at it with his boot until the beam played upon the small opening into the shelter. He moved a yard to his left. If someone fired toward the flashlight, he intended to be well away.

"Police," he called with an air of authority. "Who's in the shelter?" He had no jurisdiction here, but it would take a while for anyone to figure that out. There was a slight delay before he heard a response.

"Chief of the *matukach* police? Is that you?"

He recognized the voice of Daisy Perika. "Yeah. It's me. You okay in there?"

He saw the burlap cloth that covered the entrance being pulled aside. Her round face appeared, her eyes squinting into the flashlight. Parris picked up the flashlight and turned it off.

"Come inside," she said. "I've got me a fire."

He set the safety on the pump shotgun and crawled inside the crude shelter. Daisy was huddled over a small fire. The flames were intermittent and small, but the red embers of the dried piñon wood cast a scarlet glow on her brown face.

"I'm glad to see you, Mrs. Perika, but what are you doing up here in this . . . this . . ."

Daisy placed a few twigs on the embers and watched him with

black eyes that reflected glints from the fire. "I will be safe here until the companion of Darkness leaves."

So, the old woman was on the ball. She must have spotted the intruder and headed for this hiding spot. "Then you've seen him? My man called the tribal police. I imagine they've already picked him up."

"I can't see my home from this place, but I can see the road coming in and I can see all the way up into Cañon del Espiritu. Every few minutes, I go out and look. Then I come back inside and get warm. I am an old woman, and I get cold quickly. I haven't seen nobody."

"You haven't seen the tribal police? They should have been here an hour ago. . . ."

"No police come, except you. How did you know where to find me?"

"Blind luck, I guess. Followed some tracks but lost them at the foot of the mesa. Then I smelled your smoke." The Southern Ute Tribal Police had not arrived, and they should have showed up hours ago. Had Piggy screwed up again? And the suspect. Where was the killer? Had he already come and gone? Maybe he hadn't come at all. Maybe he wouldn't. The thought was comforting.

"Why did you come up here? You say you didn't see anyone . . ."

She waved her hand in front of her face as if to dispel a fog. "It was the dwarf; the one we call *pitukupf*. He warned me that Man-Who-Walks-with-Death would come tonight. He also told me you would come, so I am not surprised."

Parris suppressed a smile. The "prophets" were all alike. They only predicted what had already happened. "Is this dwarf expecting any other visitors?"

"One more. The woman with *tuwisi* hair."

"Two what?"

"*Tuwisi*. Strawberries. Pretty red hair. The *pitukupf* told me this woman would come, that she would meet the evil man. When *muatagochi* is ten circles high—"

"When what . . ."

"The moon. When it rises ten circles high"—she made a circle with thumb and finger and held her hand over her head to demonstrate—"Man-Who-Walks-with-Death will come out of the darkness and strike this woman." Daisy noticed the hollow expression spreading over the policeman's face. "The woman with strawberry hair . . . is she with you?"

Parris nodded; he felt his stomach churn. The old woman could not possibly have seen Anne's red hair from this distance. Not in this light, not even if she had a binoculars stashed somewhere. He crawled out of the hut and stared at the moon, its edge barely peeking over the sharp profile of Summit Peak. How long until it was ten disks high? How long had he left Anne huddled in the squad car? He glanced back at Daisy's anxious face protruding from the hut.

"I've got to get back."

"I know. Hurry, now. Don't worry about me."

He stumbled down the talus slope, praying he wouldn't fall or twist an ankle. His life now had a single, focused purpose: to get back to Anne, to protect her from Man-Who-Walks-with-Death. Nothing else mattered. Nothing.

His hiding space was small, damp, and dark. As a child, he had feared the darkness, but everything was different now. Darkness offered protection, concealment. The man sat, huddled in a fetuslike position, fingers locked around his knees. He yearned for a cigarette, just a puff, but that would not be prudent. And he was the soul of prudence. The policeman had come close. Very close. He could hear the pretty woman moving about. His nostrils caught the scent of her perfume. His senses had sharpened as the inevitable triumph approached. This would, he promised himself, be a pleasure.

28

Parris ran; the cold air pierced his lungs with a thousand icy needles. As he approached the small clearing in the juniper stand, the lights from Daisy's trailer filtered fuzzily through the snow flurry. He slowed to a brisk walk, his only comfort the cold metal of the pump shotgun, whose seven-plus pounds now pulled at his arm like twenty. Had he pumped a round into the chamber? Yes, he remembered this distinctly. Don't panic now. Concentrate on the problem at hand.

The lights on the squad car were out; the engine was not running. Anne was no longer inside the car. That could mean many things; he pushed the worst pictures from his mind. After making almost a complete circle, he stepped into the clearing in the darkest spot available. He moved with his back against the trailer, then stopped to look into the bedroom window. A dim light from the kitchen end of the trailer illuminated the bedroom, but he could see no one. Parris slipped as quietly as possible to the next window. It was the bathroom, black as pitch, so the door must be closed. The living room was empty. He peeked through the lower corner of a kitchen window. Anne, who appeared to be singing, was busy brewing coffee on Daisy Perika's gas stove.

"Anne, Anne," he whispered, "why can't you, at least once, do what I ask!" Parris was woefully aware that no one, not even his subordinates on the police force, did precisely as he instructed. Not the independent Clara Tavishuts, certainly not Piggy. Well, perhaps Leggett. In a world where few people could be counted on, there was always Leggett.

He glanced at the moon. It was much higher. His mind was a jumble. The rational part wanted to ignore the old woman's prediction. Superstition, that's what it was! A deeper part of his consciousness, the part that invented dreams and gave sinister shapes to every shadow, dreaded to see the moon ten disks high. Parris climbed the porch steps; they groaned and creaked under his weight. He remembered his revolver in Anne's purse. If she had heard the steps squeak, maybe the .38 was already in her small hand. A delicate finger might be pressing the trigger. That would be the final irony, shot to death with his own revolver! "It's me," he shouted. "Don't get trigger-happy!"

He heard her slide the bolt on the aluminum door, then saw the knob turn. He hurried inside, closed the door, and was rewarded with a tender kiss. His annoyance at Anne's recklessness evaporated in the presence of her warm embrace. "Why, he protested weakly, "didn't you stay put in the car?"

Anne kissed him on the neck and unbuttoned his coat. "Thought I'd be safer in here; I felt positively naked out there." He held her closer. She pushed him away, but gently. "This," she said, "is hardly the place. What if the Indian woman comes home? Whatever would she think?"

"You're right," he replied grimly. "She catches you taking over her kitchen, it's curtains for both of us." He grinned oafishly. "I don't expect she'll be back for a while. I found her up there"—he pointed with the shotgun—"in a little shack made out of sticks."

Anne's eyes expressed concern. "Is she all right? I mean . . ."

"She's fine as frog hair . . . made herself a little fire." He wanted to gather Anne in his arms again but resisted the impulse. Mustn't push. Parris sat down and checked the safety on the pump shotgun, then placed that instrument of his profession on the kitchen table. Anne poured him a steaming cup of black coffee.

"Did the tribal police warn her? Why didn't she go with them?"

Parris sipped the coffee. It was bitter. "Tribal cops never showed. Ten to one, Slocum has struck out again. First order of business, I'm gonna fire that incompetent meatball." They both knew he wouldn't.

Anne couldn't put this together. "Then why is she hiding out there?"

Parris mixed a spoonful of sugar into the coffee. "Well, you know she has these . . . visions or something. Says some midget told her to hole up until the bad guy was gone. When I'm around her for a few minutes, I almost start believing that stuff myself." He held his arms wide. "Why don't you sit down, right here?"

She slipped onto his lap and draped her arms lightly over his shoulders. He held her around the waist and nuzzled against her neck. She was so warm! Anne kissed his forehead. "You," she whispered, "are incorrigible. You'll have to excuse me for a sec." She left for the bathroom.

Memories of the past few weeks flashed through the madman's consciousness in intermittent fashion: his futile attempt to reason with Priscilla; her stubborn refusal to share the results of the superconductivity research. Why hadn't she understood? It was his natural right. If a student published a significant paper, wasn't it traditional to include the professor on the list of authors? The teaching staff didn't actually have to participate in the research . . . but didn't they control the grants, the research facilities, select the fortunate students who would benefit from their favors? After all, it wasn't as if the university was there for the *students!* But she had laughed at him. Even his threats to block her Ph.D. had no effect.

Then there had been his lie about smelling gas, Kristin's emergency call to University Maintenance, the theft of Julio Pacheco's screwdriver. The long wait until Priscilla returned to the lab that night. The telephone call to Pacheco . . . the fabricated report about a broken water pipe in the solid-state lab. His relief when the surly repairman agreed to come fix the problem. The quick switch from his street clothes into coveralls and rubber gloves. The startled expression on Priscilla's face . . . her hands trembling on the computer keyboard. Then she swallowed something . . . something he wanted! He vaguely recalled choking her. The blow to her face, the crunching sound as her jaw broke, the screwdriver shaft driven deep into her brain. Blood. Tearing off her clothing . . . ripping her abdomen with the butcher knife . . . blood everywhere . . . even in his eyes. Slipping out of the coveralls and gloves . . . trying to wash off all the sticky blood . . . Pacheco's headlights at the curb . . . running naked down the hall to his office . . . stuffing the bloody clothing into a desk drawer . . . hurriedly dressing . . . Pacheco's hysterical screams when he discovered the corpse. Then, of course, the call to the police. The Mexican's flight had been an unexpected blessing.

Initially, his recruitment of Waldo Thomson had turned out rather well. When he had fallen ill with the stomach flu just before the NAPS meeting, Waldo had agreed to leave for Washington immediately to arrange for the analysis of the superconductor sample and to file the patent application. Far more important than these services, Waldo had inked his signature into the forged patent notebook, providing testimony that his "research" on superconductivity had begun more than a year ago. All in exchange for 10 percent of the expected royalties from the superconductor invention. Not a bad deal.

Things had begun to go wrong after Waldo had told him about Anne Foster's appearance in Washington, her blatant meddling. He had calmed Waldo and, following instructions from the Voice, had taken care of things. At least it seemed so, until the journalist showed up at the news conference. He had been certain she was dead . . . how had she survived? After the journalist had the gall to arrange a meeting and reveal her suspicions about the theft of Priscilla's research results, he had still believed there was a chance. The woman was bluffing. She had no proof. But Waldo, despite his minor adventures in the South American drug trade, his verbal exhibitions of machismo, had his limits. After the Foster woman made her threats, Waldo had panicked. Then there was the department gossip about the eccentric Englishman's dramatic appearance at the local police station, Potter-Evans's boasts that he had discovered a name in Priscilla's encoded message. That did it. Signing the logbook was one thing, Waldo whined, but things were getting way too dicey now. Waldo knew everything, and Waldo was no longer dependable. There had been no alternative; he remembered the odd popping sound the stone had made when he crushed his colleague's skull.

No need for anything so crude again. Now he had Waldo's little pistol. He was not familiar with guns, but he understood the physics of a rapidly expanding gas accelerating a small mass of lead to velocities of hundreds of feet per second. Point the thing, pull the trigger, ignition. That was all there was to it. Three bullets expended, three bodies. So much cleaner than ripping out intestines to find precious superconductor samples!

He was eager to have this thing finished, but his mother had always told him that patience was a virtue. Odd, though . . . try as he might, he couldn't remember his mother's face. But it hardly mattered. The Voice was now his mother and his father. The Voice whispered a promise in his ear; his patience would soon be rewarded.

The Ute woman's home was incredibly quiet. Parris heard Anne turn the knob on the bathroom door; his ears picked up the slight squeak of the hinges as the door moved, then a snapping sound as the bolt closed. There was a distinct click as she flipped the light switch. The silence was interrupted by a sudden gust of wind that rattled the mobile home.

The policeman got to his feet and stretched. He had a plan now. They would stay inside the trailer, with the shotgun at the ready and the doors locked. Daisy would be in her small hut until dawn or until he returned to bring her back. There was no hurry; the old Ute woman was tough as a boot and her stick house was surprisingly good shelter. He would be here, where it was warm, with Anne. Warm indeed. With Anne. Parris could feel the excitement build, his pulse thumping in his temple. He tapped lightly on the bathroom door. "Don't take all night. It's getting lonesome out here."

She didn't answer. He returned to the kitchen and added coffee to warm his half-full cup. He heard the bathroom door open, the soft padding sound of footsteps. So, she had taken her shoes off. He wondered what else she might have taken off. Funny, though, something about the footsteps didn't sound quite . . . The blow caught him on the back of his neck. Stunned, he tried to stand up, reaching instinctively for the shotgun. A second blow caught him squarely in the temple; this was followed by an impulse of nausea and a gray half consciousness. He wasn't aware of falling, but he felt the cold linoleum under his face. He tried to move, but his limbs were enormous and heavy. He heard someone laugh, as if this was the punch line of a terribly funny joke. Then he slipped away into darkness.

Daisy Perika sat huddled before the small fire. She dropped another small piñon branch on the embers and watched the yellow flames lick hungrily at their new food. Outside the hut, *pitukupf* paced. Back and forth across the mouth of the cave shelter, he paced. She could not see him, but Daisy could hear the rhythmic sound of his badger-skin moccasins on the sandy floor of the cavern.

Abruptly, the dwarf stopped his restless pacing and waddled into the shelter. He squatted on the opposite side of the fire, where the chief of the *matukach* police had sat only minutes before. A visitor would have seen no one in the shelter with the

Ute woman, but the old shaman perceived much that was invisible. The *pitukupf* appreciated the warmth of the small fire and did not mind the piñon-wood smoke that drifted into his hairy nostrils.

"Are you hungry?" Daisy opened a dilapidated cigar box and produced a six-inch section of beef jerky sealed in transparent plastic. He took little notice until she tore the wrapper and he picked up the scent of the dried meat. Daisy warmed the delicacy over the embers and then offered it to her guest. The *pitukupf* snatched the morsel, popped it into his mouth, and proceeded to chew. After he swallowed the jerky, he held up two fingers and pursed his lips. The shaman understood; she reached into the cigar box and found a half pack of Lucky Strikes. She placed one of the cigarettes between her lips and lit it with a piñon splinter from the fire. She drew a deep breath, so that the tip of the tobacco turned cherry red, then offered the cigarette to her guest. *Pitukupf* accepted the offering and settled before the fire to puff with contentment.

"They say those things aren't good for you, old man. Might take a thousand years off your life." Her frame shook with laughter. The dwarf, who laughed only rarely, and then only at his own jokes, ignored the insufferable woman.

She watched him smoke, and considered her words carefully. "Those people came here to protect me from Man-Who-Walks-with-Death; now he plans to take his revenge on them. I think you should do something."

Pitukupf watched her face as he blinked his smoky eyes. He made no sound, but she knew the answer as if it had been written in the sky with fire. It was not her place to instruct the dwarf. Traditions were important, but this was a special circumstance.

"I hope," she remarked offhandedly, "that Man-Who-Walks-with-Death does not harm anyone in my trailer. If someone dies in my home, it will be cursed. I will not be able to sleep there again."

Pitukupf flicked the butt into the fire; he obviously had no interest in this problem.

Daisy played her hole card. "If I cannot sleep in my home, I will have to move away. I could live with my second cousin up at Altonah on the Uintah reservation. She has three grandchildren who live in her house, all of them spoiled, so I would not be pleased to go there. And I would miss you, *pitukupf*. I would worry about you." She glanced slyly at the elfin figure. "No other Ute knows you. Who will bring gifts to your home under the earth? Will someone else dream dreams? Will another woman bring you cigarettes?" They both knew the answer.

The *pitukupf* curled his upper lip. His teeth were streaked with yellow, his eyes dark as midnight. Daisy unconsciously shrunk back under his flinty gaze. Had she gone too far?

Parris could feel the nothingness fading away. There was a persistent buzzing in his ears, the harsh taste of vomit in his mouth. Dim orange light penetrated his eyelids. A dull pain throbbed inside his head, rising and then falling like waves on a windswept beach.

He tried to remember where he was. Yes. The Ute woman's home. What had happened? He remembered the blows, the nausea. His feet were cold, but his hands were tingling as the sensation returned. He could feel the cold linoleum on his cheek. Should he open his eyes? No, not just yet. He listened but could hear nothing except the hum of Daisy's refrigerator. His right arm was twisted under him; his right hand rested near his buttocks. He tried to move his fingers ever so slightly. Good. They moved. He wiggled his toes inside the cold boots. Wonderful. He was not paralyzed. Where was the man who had clubbed him? Did he believe his victim was dead? Had he left? Please, God . . . let Anne be alive. And unhurt.

Parris cracked his eyelids. The images he saw were fuzzy; he waited for the scene to come into focus. There were a pair of feet in expensive, mud-splattered dress shoes. He had no doubt who the feet belonged to and was not surprised to hear the professor's voice.

"Feeling better, are we? I'm so relieved; wouldn't want you to expire just yet."

Parris gathered what strength he could and tried to push himself up on his right elbow. It was then that he felt the handcuff on his left wrist. He looked up, his vision gradually focusing on the man's face. Professor Arnold Dexter, his eyes bloodshot and moist from lack of sleep, was smiling benignly at his victim. "Had to cuff you to a good solid anchor." He flipped the handcuff key onto the table and sat down heavily on one of the chairs. "Gracious, I'm tired. Had a big day, you know, accomplished a lot. But it's true—there's no rest for the wicked!" The physicist rubbed his fingers over a two-day stubble of beard and giggled. Dexter had a small revolver in his hand. Parris focused on the muzzle, the copper-plated lead slugs in the cylinder. Twenty-two-caliber? Not heavy artillery, but sufficient to get the job done.

Parris managed a sitting position and examined his predicament. His left hand was cuffed to a leg of Daisy's gas stove. His right hand was free and Dexter's leg was barely within reach. He blinked and examined the man more carefully. Why hadn't Dexter already used the pistol? It was as if the physicist could read his thoughts.

"Prefer not to shoot you just yet. That old Indian witch is out there somewhere, hiding, plotting against me. If she hears a gunshot, she'll stay out there all night. I'll have to kill both of you before I leave, of course."

"Both of you?" Did he mean Anne, or did he refer to Daisy? Parris licked his lips. His mouth was dusty dry. He tried to speak and croaked like a frog. "Anne . . . is she . . . ?"

Dexter waved the revolver in Parris's face. "The meddling bitch was lucky last time, but her good fortune ran out tonight."

Parris wanted to swing a hard right into the man's groin, but his limbs were still heavy. Wait for the circulation to return with a life-giving supply of fresh oxygen to the muscles. Not enough strength. Not yet.

Dexter dropped the revolver into his trousers pocket; he lifted the pump shotgun off the table and fondled it curiously. Parris closed his eyes and concentrated all of his effort on formulating a sensible plan. If he moved too early, did something that had no chance of success, it would all be finished. If Dexter felt obliged to shoot him, Anne's life, if she was still alive, would be snuffed out moments later. The sound of two gunshots wouldn't alert Daisy more than one.

Dexter turned and left the kitchen. Parris watched the man enter the bathroom, then pull Anne out by her heels. Her red hair trailed out behind as he dragged her along the floor toward the bedroom. Anne's purse was on the kitchen table. If Dexter hadn't searched it, the Smith & Wesson revolver would still be tucked away inside. The physicist disappeared into the bathroom. There was a splashing noise as he urinated into the toilet. Parris scooted backward on his buttocks and managed to get both hands under the edge of the gas stove. The metal was sharp and rusty. He pulled upward, gently at first and then applied more force. The rusty metal cut into his fingers. There was a popping sound as the leg parted from the linoleum. He strained; just a little more and he could pull the cuff from under the leg. Parris heard the toilet flush; he released the stove when Dexter appeared in the hallway.

The physicist, zipping his trousers, returned with the pump shotgun. He straddled a dinette chair, then leveled the shotgun muzzle at Parris's face. His finger caressed the trigger. "A moderate pressure," he murmured, "and off with your head!" Dexter smiled lopsidedly, with half his mouth drooping as if from an injection of novocaine.

"You could cut a much better deal if you unlock these cuffs. The FBI and tribal police are on their way," Parris said, "probably show up any minute now."

Dexter's eyes narrowed; his pinched face turned pale. "If

that's true, perhaps I should pull the trigger now, have done with it. The old Indian witch won't be able to hide forever. . . . I'll come back and find her another day. I have, you understand . . . supernatural assistance." He pushed the shotgun muzzle into Parris's face. "If you wish to beg for your life, I might change my mind."

Parris knew what the buckshot would do to his face. He clenched his hands into fists to keep them from trembling.

Dexter waited; there was no response. "So you won't beg. Laudable. Any last words at all, then? A pithy phrase I can remember when—"

"Yeah," Parris rasped, "kiss my ass!"

The madman's finger tightened on the shotgun trigger; Parris ground his teeth and waited for the explosion. His mind screamed as he anticipated the discharge, a blinding flash of pain, then dark oblivion.

It did not come. Dexter studied the shotgun with an expression of bewilderment. Parris realized why he remained among the living. A mere detail: The safety was on.

Parris licked his dry lips. "Well, don't that beat all," he offered lamely. "I forgot to load it."

Dexter grunted impatiently and pitched the shotgun onto the table. As it landed, the policeman noticed a pronounced wobble of the table leg nearest his right hand. The leg was loose. Very loose.

Dexter pulled the small revolver from his pocket. He raised it to aim carefully at a point between Parris's eyes. His movements were deliberate; this was a moment to be relished. He thumbed the hammer back. Something, perhaps a raccoon, clattered across the roof of the trailer. It was just enough to distract the physicist, who glanced toward the ceiling.

Parris swung his right arm in a long arc, ripping the leg from the rickety wooden table. Time shifted into slow motion. He followed through until the heavy cylinder of wood connected solidly with Dexter's shin. The madman's howl was punctuated by the deafening crack of the revolver as the slug passed through the oven door half an inch from Parris's left ear. As Dexter fell, the table also toppled, spilling the shotgun onto the floor. Parris flung the table leg, missing Dexter's head by a whisker, then grabbed the shotgun by the stock. He pressed the safety button just as Dexter saw the barrel of the twelve-gauge swinging in his direction. The physicist lunged for the door as Parris pulled the trigger. The policeman's aim was high, but he saw the fabric of Dexter's trousers rip as a round of buckshot penetrated his buttocks. The man's scream was barely louder than Parris's angry roar. The policeman swung the shotgun barrel close to his cuffed left hand and pumped another shell into the chamber.

He raised the barrel to get off another shot. Too late. Dexter had been swallowed up by darkness. The wind caught the door, swinging it back and forth like a great pendulum, banging it against the metal door frame. Would he have another chance? Dexter might enter the trailer by the bedroom door, use Anne as a hostage. Parris strained to consider the possibilities. Every second was an eternity while he considered his options: He dare not take his finger off the shotgun trigger, but it was essential to lift the stove leg off the handcuff. Every time the door swung open, Dexter had a chance to fire the pistol from the darkness. Parris made his decision. The first order of business was to get loose from the stove leg. Then the odds would be in his favor. He dropped the shotgun into his lap, got a firm grip on the stove, and gathered his energy to lift it.

Parris was interrupted by a presence . . . a sudden palpable stillness . . . a deadly quiet. He thought he saw a shadow flicker across the porch. Was someone on the steps? No, there was no creaking sound from the wooden steps. It had to be his imagination. He gritted his teeth and pulled on the stove until he thought his finger joints would dislocate. There were creaking sounds as sheet metal bent; he had the stove almost high enough to free himself, but the handcuff was caught under the tip of the metal leg. He released his left hand from the stove, hoping to snatch the cuff from under the leg, but a single arm was not strong enough to do the job.

There, as the door was swinging open, was the shadow again. It was very real, this shadow of . . . a man? There was no more time to get free.

The stove came crashing down, the handcuff still secured by the leg. "Son of a bitch," he muttered in desperation. He would not be shot like a fish in a barrel. Parris grabbed the shotgun with his right hand, set the butt against the floor, and aimed at the plastic light fixture on the ceiling. He yanked the trigger. There was an explosion as the buckshot shattered the light fixture and opened a ragged hole in the ceiling. He heard a startled grunt and a dull thud as someone fell off the porch. Shards of razor-sharp glass from the sixty-watt light bulbs stung Parris's face, but now he was protected by the darkness. He pumped another load of buckshot into the twelve-gauge chamber. As his eyes adjusted to the dim light, he could see the snow-sprinkled landscape outside the trailer each time the wind whipped the door open. The open door that had been an invitation for Dexter when the light was on would now be a portal of darkness.

Now . . . let him come. This was no longer police business. This was personal. In his growing fury, Parris fervently hoped Dexter had recently had a full meal; he would gut-shoot the miserable bastard.

29

Parris leveled the pump shotgun at the door. "Come on in, you sorry son of a bitch," he muttered to himself, "and I'll cut you in half."

There was a slight pause before a deep voice answered. "Well thanks for the invite, pardner, but I s'pose I'd just as soon stay out here if you intend to shoot me."

He released the pressure against the trigger. "Who the hell is that?"

"Sergeant Charlie Moon, Southern Ute Tribal Police. Are you Parris? The cop from Granite Creek?"

He lowered the gun barrel. "Yeah. You better get inside; there's an armed lunatic out there somewhere."

This time, the steps groaned as the policeman climbed to the small porch. As the Ute policeman's flashlight beam illuminated the kitchen, Parris laid the shotgun aside and used both hands to tug on the stove. Sergeant Moon closed the door and whistled as he swept the beam over the debris on the floor and then to the wrecked remains of the ceiling light. "Aunt Daisy's sure gonna be pissed off when she sees this mess. Her table's broke and you shot a big hole clean through the roof. If I was you, I'd make myself plenty scarce before she gets back. I'm not foolin'; she'll likely kick your butt up between your shoulders."

Parris pulled the handcuff from under the metal support as Charlie Moon lifted the gas stove with one hand. "My man must've called hours ago; what took you so long?"

Moon's tone was good-humored. "Well, I just couldn't get away. Us redskins were having this big dance to make us some rain and . . ."

Parris smiled sheepishly. "Sorry. I've had a bad day. I expected to meet you when I got here, find out you had this thing all wrapped up. Instead, I had a set-to with this citizen who intended to stop my clock."

Moon accepted the apology. "Took us a while to get things sorted out. Your man called the wrong Ute reservation."

Parris rubbed his legs to coax some circulation into his numb muscles. "Slocum strikes out again."

"The Ute Mountain cops called our dispatcher; we finally put it all together after we called Granite Creek PD and had a talk with your guy. We figured you must be on your way to see Aunt Daisy." Moon attempted to prop the table up with the disconnected leg. "What's the situation here? Aunt Daisy all right?"

"Mrs. Perika's hiding in a shelter on the mesa; I expect she's safe enough if she keeps still." Parris found his keys and unlocked the cuff dangling from his left wrist. "Arnold Dexter is outside. White male, about five ten, one seventy. He's packing a twenty-two revolver and some buckshot in his ass, so I expect he'd like to shoot somebody."

"Seems like everybody around here is trigger-happy," Moon said. "I almost wet my britches when you fired that scattergun through the roof."

"Sorry about that, Sergeant." The Ute knew he wasn't. "A friend of mine is in the bedroom." He felt the lump in his throat. "We better go have a look at her." Parris reluctantly followed the Ute to the bedroom. Anne was vainly attempting to get to her feet. Moon lifted her onto the bed and gently pressed a wiener-sized finger under her jaw. "Pulse kinda jumpy, but strong." He ran his hand over her skull and she winced with pain. "Good-sized lump, could have a concussion. No bleeding, though."

Anne pushed herself up on one elbow. "I think," she said weakly, "my head is going to fall off."

Parris, overcome with relief, leaned over and touched her hand. It was moments before he found his voice. "It was Dexter. We'll need to get you looked at." He turned to Moon. "Can you take her to a safe spot?"

The Ute helped Anne to her feet. "There's a nurse lives a couple of miles from here."

Anne leaned on Moon's arm, gradually assimilating her thoughts. "Professor Dexter? But what . . ."

"Dexter was behind everything." Parris remembered pumping the shotgun, but he checked to be certain. The chamber was loaded. He addressed his next comment to the Ute policeman. "That fruitcake's still out there somewhere. We'd best be real careful."

"We'll turn all the lights off," Moon replied. "You give me some cover with that scattergun while I get her to the squad car. Once I'm on the road, I'll radio in for some help. In an hour or so, we'll have us a posse here."

"Dexter must have a vehicle hidden close by," Parris said, "if he hasn't already left in it. I'll see if I can find—"

Moon's tone, reflecting the fact that Parris was in his jurisdiction, was authoritative. "You stay put. If this hombre shows himself, I'd appreciate it if you didn't blow him away just for the sport of it. You shoot him, I'll be filling out paperwork for weeks."

"Don't fret, Sergeant. I'm a sworn officer of the law. I want this guy alive." Like hell I do, he thought.

"Like hell you do," the Ute observed dryly, "but if you do shoot him, I'd better find the suspect dead as a stump and with a gun in his hand . . . any damn gun." Moon disappeared into the night with Anne, apparently unconcerned that Dexter might take a potshot at his large frame. Parris followed closely, sweeping the twelve-gauge barrel in a wide arc, ready to fire at anything that might move in the shadows.

After the sound of the Ute patrol car had faded into the night, Parris circled the trailer. Nothing was moving in the darkness, but Dexter was out there. He could feel the madman's presence. Was the professor hunting for the shaman? It was time to check on Daisy.

The juniper thicket cast stark inky shadows on the thin blanket of moonlit snow. A slight depression in the frosty whiteness caught his eye. Parris dropped to one knee to have a close look. A fresh set of footprints was visible in the snow. These had to be Dexter's prints, and the lunatic was heading directly toward the foot of the mesa, where Daisy was hidden. The killer, of course, could be waiting in ambush. He followed the trail through the thicket, expecting to hear the sharp report of Dexter's .22 at any moment. Parris's finger rested lightly on the shotgun trigger.

Now there was another set of prints beside Dexter's. They were very small. A child's footprints? But that made no sense at all. And who was following whom? He squatted to examine the trail. It was a roundish print, three or four inches long and not so sharply defined as Dexter's shoe print. Moccasins? There was no question about who was doing the following. One small footprint had partially obliterated the crisp imprint of Dexter's heel. Dexter was being followed. Or stalked? The policeman moved slowly along the trail in the snow, pausing at intervals to listen. The deep silence was unnerving.

Parris slid down the bank of a small arroyo and followed the prints until the ravine opened onto a sloping meadow. Now there were dark marks on the snow; Parris squatted and picked up one of the splotches. He rolled it between his fingers. Congealed blood. That, he observed with satisfaction, would be from the buckshot in Dexter's buttocks. He sprinted across the open meadow and was less than thirty yards into a sparse stand of juniper when he saw the Ute woman. Daisy was standing over something . . . a body. He trotted toward the woman. It was Dexter, facedown in the crystalline snow. Was the old woman praying or singing? Perhaps the two acts were one and the same for a Ute schooled in the old traditions. She fell silent as he approached.

Parris dropped to one knee, using the pump shotgun as a support. He had not entirely conquered the weakness. His head seemed to spin as he tried to study the body. The physicist's hands were stretched outward as if he had tried to break the fall. The seat of Dexter's trousers was wet with blood. A couple of the buckshot had found their target. His face was suspended slightly above the snow-packed earth. There was a dark pool of something under Dexter's face . . . blood congealed in the frosty snow. How could that be? The buckshot couldn't possibly have hit the fleeing man in the face. No . . . the professor had fallen onto a broken juniper snag. A short broken branch had penetrated his left eye, was apparently embedded in his twisted brain. It was complete now, justice as understood in ancient Zion. Dexter's eye for Priscilla's eye. *Ojo por ojo.* There was, evidently, a harsh symmetry in the universe.

Daisy began to sing again. The choppy Ute phrases recalled heroic deeds, tales of past ages . . . lost except to those who could hear the spirits whisper.

Parris tried to move Dexter's head, but it was firmly impaled on the dead branch. He felt the nausea returning. Why had he touched the corpse? To verify that the man was dead? That was hardly necessary. He sat down in the snow and held his head in his hands until the weakness passed. "Don't touch the body, Mrs. Perika. The Ute cops and the Bureau boys will be all over this one; the fresher the crime scene, the better." Daisy, a Ute to her core, had no intention of touching the corpse.

He used the shotgun again, pushing himself to his feet. He backed away from the body and surveyed it in a professional manner. The crusty old sergeant from the South Side of Chicago had explained it to all of the rookies in those days when Parris was still moist behind the ears: "Never let on that you're the least bit unsure of yourself, no matter what happens; you gotta

act like you know what you're doing or the civilians will panic."
He turned his attention to the Ute woman, whose face was
without expression. No worry that this particular civilian would
panic. "Looks like we finally had a break," he said. "After all of
this, he trips and falls. Now is that the luck of the Irish or what?"

Daisy squatted by Dexter's body, taking care that her skirt did
not brush against the corpse. She pointed. "Look right there.
See that?"

Parris focused his flashlight on Dexter's feet and felt a chill
ripple along his spine. A vine was wrapped tightly around the
man's ankles. Several times. He hoped she could take a hint. "He
must have tripped over the vine. You understand? It was an
accident!"

Daisy, misunderstanding his intentions, was incredulous at
this white man's apparent lack of understanding. Clara Tavishuts had told her aunt that the new man from Chicago was a
clever policeman. "Look closer," Daisy said patiently, "then tell
me if you think it was an accident."

Silently praying that she wouldn't confess to this killing, Parris dropped to his knees and ran his fingertips along Dexter's
ankles. The cord, wrapped around the man's ankles, was braided
from several strands of a pliable green vine. He felt something
hard and smooth . . . a flat pebble the size of a hockey puck. He
lifted Dexter's feet and directed his flashlight beam onto a black
stone. The vine passed through a hole in the pebble; it was held
in place by a heavy knot on one side. A picture was gradually
forming in his mind. Daisy had come down from her hideout,
heard the shots, watched Dexter flee from the trailer. Somehow,
she had flung the stone-weighted cord around his ankles. But at
just the precise instant for him to fall and impale himself in an
ironic imitation of Priscilla Song's death? But there it was, the
warm corpse of the physicist, his sick brain penetrated by a dead
branch.

The FBI investigated all major crimes on Indian reservations.
When the hotshots from the Bureau found the stone-weighted

cord on the professor's ankles, there would be no end to their searching questions. They would have only one suspect for this killing: the Ute shaman who had been threatened by the crazed scientist. It would surely be a case of justifiable homicide, self-defense, but Daisy could be tied up with the legal system for months, maybe longer. That possibility seemed terribly unjust. There was only one way to salvage some measure of justice. He unwrapped the vine from Dexter's ankles, wound it around the heavy pebble, and offered it to Daisy. "Get rid of this, and forget you ever saw it. A Ute policeman has already shown up, Sergeant Moon. If the Bureau finds out I tampered with evidence, there'll be hell to pay and I'll get the whole bill. Understand?"

"Sure." She patted him on the shoulder and pocketed the evidence. "You're a good man, for a *matukach*. But you don't need to worry about me. Charlie Moon is one of my nephews. I used to change his diaper. Anyway, I can take care of myself."

That's right, he thought. You manage to take care of yourself. Me, I'd be dead if it weren't for a rickety table leg and an amateur criminal who didn't know about the safety on a shotgun. Luck, or something. Deep down, he knew it was more than luck. But what? Did the angels, along with their duties to take care of children and drunks, also watch over careless cops? Was it a touch of grace?

Daisy fixed her gaze on the big dipper, hanging above Three Sisters Mesa. *Akwuch* was indeed pouring out the stars. From some lofty precipice, Coyote yipped, and the sound was like raucous laughter. The dark Presence had been swept away from her homeland! For the first time in weeks, Daisy felt the harmony return. She tilted her head sideways, brushed her coarse dark hair away from one ear, and cocked her head expectantly. "It's started. Can you hear it?"

Scott Parris listened intently; he could hear nothing beyond the occasional whisper of wind in the thick branches of the juniper. Daisy heard something else. Older than the world. Calling to her soul. It was the night song of the spirits. She reached up and touched two fingertips to his temple. Immediately, he heard the rhythmic chanting, the bittersweet call of someone . . . who knew him. Softly, far away at first, then swirling about him like a fresh breeze. He felt as if he had slipped outside himself.

Daisy tugged at his sleeve. "Come back; you're not ready to listen too closely. Let's go home." The music in his head fell to a whisper. She took him firmly by the arm and led him away from Dexter's corpse. Even the memory of his vision was fading, flitting away like a dream after waking.

"When we get home," she said in a motherly tone, "I'll make you some fresh coffee and warm up a bowl of posole."

As he breathed deeply of the crisp air, Parris realized that he was famished. "Now that," he said, "sounds like just the ticket."

"You know," she said solemnly, "as you take on a lot of years, you yearn for the old ways. But I got tired of that brush hut. The snow blew in the cracks in the wall. It'll be nice to get back to my little trailer house, where I got a good roof over my head."

A picture of the jagged hole he had blown in her ceiling flashed into his consciousness. The kitchen table was wrecked; there was a bullet hole in her stove. Daisy felt the muscles in his arm tense. He didn't notice the mischievous smile that flickered over her face.

"Much as I could use a bite to eat," he said with the sober tone of one unselfishly committed to his professional duties, "Sergeant Moon will want a detailed report on Dexter's . . . accident. Maybe I better take a rain check."

"Whatever you think is best," the shaman said.